SWEET SIREN

Fiona was too tired to struggle when Tyrell deftly picked her up and began carrying her away from the beach, apparently following the surgeon to his house. But by the time they reached the boardwalk she felt much better.

Fiona looked up at Lord Wesmont's stern profile as he carried her. "I'm quite capable of walking now."

"I don't doubt it."

"Then, you should set me down." She intentionally didn't remove her arm from around his neck. There was no hurry.

"I can't oblige you on that score."

"Why not? The seawater is ruining your coat."

He shifted her in his arms and, finally, looked at her. "Because, Miss Hawthorn, what little clothing you had on is now torn to shreds and plastered to your lovely body with the very seawater you mentioned. Make no mistake, my dear, your elusive charms no longer elude me. And I have no desire to expose them to this mob you have attracted."

Fiona felt herself turning red.

BOOK YOUR PLACE ON OUR WEBSITE AND MAKE THE READING CONNECTION!

We've created a customized website just for our very special readers, where you can get the inside scoop on everything that's going on with Zebra, Pinnacle and Kensington books.

When you come online, you'll have the exciting opportunity to:

- View covers of upcoming books
- Read sample chapters
- Learn about our future publishing schedule (listed by publication month *and author*)
- Find out when your favorite authors will be visiting a city near you
- Search for and order backlist books from our online catalog
- Check out author bios and background information
- Send e-mail to your favorite authors
- Meet the Kensington staff online
- Join us in weekly chats with authors, readers and other guests
- Get writing guidelines
- AND MUCH MORE!

Visit our website at
http://www.kensingtonbooks.com

LADY
FIASCO

Kathleen Baldwin

ZEBRA BOOKS
KENSINGTON PUBLISHING CORP.
http://www.kensingtonbooks.com

ZEBRA BOOKS are published by

Kensington Publishing Corp.
850 Third Avenue
New York, NY 10022

All Kensington titles, imprints and distributed lines are available at special quantity discounts for bulk purchases for sales
promotion, premiums, fund-raising, educational or institutional
use.

Special book excerpts or customized printings can also be created to fit specific needs. For details, write or phone the office
of the Kensington Special Sales Manager: Kensington Publishing Corp., 850 Third Avenue, New York, NY 10022. Attn.
Special Sales Department. Phone: 1-800-221-2647.

First Printing: September 2004
10 9 8 7 6 5 4 3 2 1

Printed in the United States of America

Note to the Reader

It is sometimes said that members of the Regency era did not indulge in swimming. While this was generally true of the average person living in Town, it cannot be said to be universal, and in particular, was not true of the country gentry.

Fiona Hawthorn, the heroine in this story, is certainly not the average sort. Quite the contrary, she is *Lady Fiasco*, up to all kinds of mischief, including swimming.

Chapter 1
Coming Home

He stood like a smoldering statue, and if she were not his mother he would have strangled her.

"Tyrell, for pity sake, won't you please dance. You're embarrassing me. Surely one of these young ladies . . ."

Not bloody likely.

"Your father would have wanted it this way. He abhorred excessive mourning. You know he did. He would have wanted you to have a proper welcome home. You've been gone so long, it's only right to reintroduce you to the neighborhood. Really, Tyrell, I planned this whole party for your sake."

He knew exactly why she'd thrown this abominable ball and for what purpose.

"It's true." She fanned herself a little harder. "How can you doubt my intentions? I am, after all, your mother. It's my duty to look after you."

Knowing how punishing silence can be, Tyrell said nothing.

"Have you no heart?" She sniffled.

Heart? No. That useless mechanism stopped working in Spain, on the battlefields of Badajoz to be precise.

Music jangled through his ballroom, infuriating him with the sound of frivolous plinking harpsichords and squealing violins. Candles flickered, as dancers stirred up the air, bounding across his floor like a flock of mindless sheep. He would rather be trapped in a bat-ridden cave than here.

To distract himself from his mother's prattle he studied Fiona Hawthorn as she made her way through the guests on the other side of the room. She looked nothing like the sobbing young girl who had run after him when he rode away to war. She'd grown into a woman, shapely and undeniably striking. And now, his idiotic neighbors stepped out of her path as if she had the plague. The women backed away, clutching their skirts like frightened children in the wake of a specter. Superstitious morons.

His mother whispered a plea that lashed across his thoughts. "How can you treat me so ill? All I ask for is one small grandson, so I'm not thrown out in the cold should anything happen to you."

He remained as immovable as a wax general at Madame Tussauds. The dower cottage would serve her adequately.

"I simply can't bear to think of my home entailed to some distant-uncle's-cousin-or-other, who won't care two figs for what happens to me." She clutched at his arm. "A baby boy I can dandle on my knee, that's all I'm asking for, an heir. Is that so much?"

Yes, too much, much more than he could give. Sons required fathers, preferably with the aforementioned heart intact.

He continued to watch Fiona as she moved to the rear of the ballroom, away from the dancers and the gabbing, giggling circles of young women. She sat on a chair swathed in shadow behind a column. *Hiding.* Tyrell clamped his jaw tighter.

"Must you seethe like some sort of caged tiger? Truly, it can't be good for you. You'll rupture your spleen."

What would she have him do? Upturn the tables? Shove all of her unwanted guests down the stairs and out of his house? Smash that musician's squeaky fiddle over his white-wigged head?

"Our friends came here with the perfectly reasonable expectation that you would honor at least one of their daughters. You simply must dance with one of these young women or I shan't be able to show my face in society again. We have our name to consider. At the very least you could—"

"Very well. One." He marched straight across the ballroom, heedless of the dancers, who moved quickly out of his way while trying to maintain their places in the set. The heels of his shoes reported loudly against the wood floor, but he didn't slow his pace until he stopped squarely in front of Fiona's chair behind the column.

She sat in a dreamlike pose, swaying to the rhythm of the country dance. He cleared his throat and waited for her to open her eyes and focus. He continued to wait as her gaze slowly climbed up to his face. She blanched.

"Oh dear," she murmured and rose abruptly, upsetting her chair. In a tangled string of movements she reached back, caught the chair before it clattered to the floor, curtsied, and then seemed to lose her breath before she could speak.

He forestalled her. "Good evening, Elf."

He folded his arms across his chest and leaned against the column, watching, as she glanced furtively over her shoulder toward the other guests and grimaced when she realized she had, after all, been noticed. Then she sighed with unflattering resignation. "Good evening, Tyrell—I mean Lord Wesmont."

He straightened. "Enjoying the evening, are you?" Obviously, she could not be doing any such thing.

"Yes, my lord, excessively." She annoyed him by staring at the floor.

"Oh yes? Well then, perhaps you would explain to me why you are hiding behind this pillar?"

Her hands fluttered at her sides, grasping for a nonexistent railing to hold on to. "I merely wished for a nice quiet place where I might sit and enjoy the music."

"The music? Surely you jest? These musicians sound more like a gaggle of squabbling geese than—"

"Oh no, they're quite wonderful." She looked up and fixed him with an expression of pure delight. "I assure you. I was just thinking that I like music nearly as much as water." She winced, and color flushed her cheeks.

"Water?" He arched a questioning eyebrow.

"What I mean is, music is nearly as beautiful as a lake. That's what I meant to say."

"Indeed." Tyrell scrutinized her odd, dark eyes and wondered if the lovely Fiona had perhaps taken a tragic fall from her horse and damaged her brain box while he was away on the Continent. "Tell me, do you still ride your horse like you were shot from a cannon?"

"Oh. You remember that, do you? Yes, well, I suppose it might be said that I do." She smiled with unmistakable chagrin and played the toe of her slipper against the polished oak floor. Then she faced him boldly.

"My esteemed father must bear some of the blame. You see, while he's away fighting Bonaparte he allowed our steward to buy me a splendid new mare. She's more temptation than I can bear. If he had not provided me with such a magnificent animal, well then, I would not be able to go tearing about the countryside, would I?" She beamed up at him innocently. "A nice retiring nag, that is what I would give a daughter like me, if I were the father."

Tyrell very nearly smiled. A sensation he had not experienced for some time, but it was short-lived. The musicians screeched to a halt. He spotted his venerable parent whispering into the ear of the violinist. A moment later, the trio began tuning for a waltz *sans* the promenade.

"Mother—" He hissed a futile warning under his breath and then turned back to Fiona. "Quite daring, is she not, to risk the censure of our neighbors by playing a waltz at a country ball?"

His mother was orchestrating the situation like a field marshal at a battlefront. Her determination to push him into the arms of a female far outstripped his ability to remain composed. He would simply have to strangle her. He inhaled deeply and struggled to keep from grinding his teeth.

Apparently, Fiona perceived his mother's strategy as clearly as he did. She smiled sympathetically, which made Tyrell feel all the more annoyed.

Her fingers touched his sleeve gently and then fell away. "Perhaps, my lord, it is not so very exceptional. Some of the most distinguished balls in London last Season boasted of a waltz. Your mother is simply setting the style for our neighborhood."

"I doubt it." He fixed his face into an inscrutable mask and held out his arm. "Will you do me the honor?"

Fiona shook her head and backed away. "Oh no, I'm sorry. I mustn't—I couldn't."

Tyrell stepped back, temporarily nonplussed. He puzzled it out for a moment and then leaned down next to Fiona's ear. "Is it because you have not yet been approved for the waltz? I assure you, none of Almack's patronesses will ever hear of this absurd country party. I hardly think—"

She pulled away and looked up at him, her features brimming with anxiety. "No, it isn't that. The truth is, you see . . . well . . . I'm rather *dangerous* on the ballroom floor. There've been several incidents. Surely, you've heard the stories?"

When he simply frowned at her, she opened her hands in petition. "My last dance partner slipped and collided with a servant carrying a punch bowl. The bowl crashed down onto poor Lieutenant Withycomb and broke his collarbone. The pain must have been dreadful."

She shook her head mournfully. "He was such a sturdy fellow. It was dreadful to hear him yelp like a whipped dog as they carried him away. Poor man, he had to stay home from the war for nearly six months. Naturally, everyone thought it was my fault. I heard them talking. They said the army should send *me* to the Continent and Napoleon would surrender within the week. So you see, it's much too risky to dance with me."

The muscles in Tyrell's cheeks forgot their vow of austerity and twitched into a half grin. "A most entertaining account."

Fiona's cheeks turned a vivid shade of pink. "I assure you, my lord, it is all true. Every word."

"Come." He grasped her hand and pulled her to him. "Waltz with me. We'll show them all."

Tyrell swooped her out into the company of dancers.

"But you don't understand. I fear for your safety."

"Only look!" he ordered her. "Here we are dancing and I am not yet killed." He glanced down at her, feeling more at ease than he had in a long time. "You forget, I have danced with you before. We were children—I believe it was a Yule party. I survived then and I shall certainly survive now."

"One can only hope," she muttered.

"You greatly overrate your threat to my person, Miss Hawthorn. I've faced far worse danger than dancing with a beautiful young lady."

She blinked, and then her dark exotic brows angled down into an intriguing frown. "You mustn't flatter me, Lord Wesmont. I know full well that I'm not beautiful, merely passable. My hair, you see, refuses to stay where it is put. We have tried pomades, sugar water, and potato starch, to no avail. It merely sticks out looking wilder than ever. So now, we just pin it up and expect that it will remain horribly disobedient."

Tyrell felt an odd thumping sensation in his breast as he looked down at the delicate tendrils of dark hair drifting around her face. She was no hothouse rose with perfectly coifed curls and a pinched-up little mouth. No, she was an unpretentious wildflower. "I like your hair. It suits you perfectly—lovely and unstarchy."

"Kind of you to say, my lord, but, I fear it is just more flattery. The unfortunate truth is, I have changed since you saw me last. I grew up to be something of a menace. Most of the villagers even think I am jinxed."

His momentary delight evaporated. He contemplated her coolly. "In the first place, Miss Hawthorn, it is not my habit to practice flattery, quite the contrary. Secondly, how is it you cannot accept a simple compliment from me, and yet you seem more than willing to believe the malicious gossip of our superstitious neighbors?"

"So, you have heard the rumors."

He lifted his chin and turned his attention to a bland study of the portraits and landscapes hanging on the walls as he whirled around the ballroom.

"Please don't be annoyed with me, my lord. It isn't merely the opinion of our neighbors. My own family and a number of our London acquaintances are of the same mind."

He exhaled loudly. "Jinx, indeed. Only a fool believes in such nonsense." He glanced covertly down at her.

She had lowered her head and was staring blankly at the medals on his coat. He immediately regretted chastising her and was on the brink of apologizing when her feet tangled up. She tripped in the middle of a turn and plummeted into his chest.

Tyrell congratulated himself on deftly handling the awkward moment. He recovered his balance, held on to the damsel in distress, and accomplished the turn without so much as an audible curse word. And yet, she still clung to his chest, her eyes wide with fright.

"Miss Hawthorn, we are safe. You may recover yourself now, with ease."

"No, my lord," her voice rose up to his ears, a high-pitched whisper. "I'm stuck!"

Tyrell glanced down at the maiden on his chest. The bosom of her dress was caught on his Merit Cross. He looked up at the ceiling, incredulous.

"Well, pull it off." He locked his jaw in the imperial position he'd always found useful as a commanding officer.

"No!" she whispered desperately. "I can't. Not without serious repercussions."

He murmured an epitaph of doubtful quality. Espying a possible solution in the form of the balcony with open doors, he maneuvered her, still pressed against him, outside. They escaped into blessed darkness, away from the doors and windows, and the prying eyes of his mother's guests.

"Now," he said coolly, "we have some privacy in which you may extract yourself from my coat."

She sniffed at him and began wrestling with her bodice and his confounded medal. "It's so dark out here, I can hardly see. I think it's snagged on this big gold star with all the sharp points."

"Cross, it's a deuced Merit . . . oh never mind. Just unsnag it, will you. Immediately." He tapped his foot, waited, and then slapped at his thigh. "It's certain we were observed. This is ridiculous. How difficult a task can it be?"

Her head snapped up and her eyes flashed at him. "Do stop railing at me."

"Get on with it then."

She bent back to the task.

"And hurry."

She huffed back at him. "Now see. You've made me so nervous my fingers won't do as they're told."

Exasperated, he pushed her hands away. "Here, let me see to it. Perhaps, if I open the clasp it will be easier to remove it from your gown."

There wasn't enough light to sort out the problem. Tyrell nudged Fiona toward a window, which had the desired effect of casting more light on their tangle. It also cast light across the neckline of her gown, which was stretched further from her person than the cut of the dress intended. It revealed far too much of the smooth round breasts against which Tyrell struggled to extricate himself.

He drew in a steadying breath and tried to concentrate on unpinning his troublesome badge. Her perfume wafted up and the sweet smell of rosewater teased his nose.

He exhaled and continued his task with determination. The summer breeze taunted him by lifting errant strands of her hair up to tickle his cheek. He endeavored to unlatch the medal without touching her. It was impossible. His fingers brushed against her soft skin and frustration of another kind bolted through him.

His breathing changed tenor without permission. Next, his hands betrayed him. Hands that could be relied upon to load a musket during a skirmish in blackest night failed him. They trembled. He ordered himself to stop shaking. Her wicked hair caressed his cheek again. Her fragrance filled his nostrils. Her enticing breasts lifted as she drew in a breath.

Tyrell growled like a bear caught in a trap and threw up his hands. "Blast it, woman!" He glared down at her. "I can't do this."

"I'm sorry," she murmured. "I did warn you not to dance with me."

He rolled his eyes heavenward. "Pray, do not start prattling on about that again." He took hold of her shoulders and glared at her as sternly as he could in the dim light. "Listen to me, Fiona Hawthorn. This has nothing to do with curses, or jinxes. I don't believe in any of that rubbish. Now, I'm ordering you to unhook us—"

She stared back at him far too evenly. Why the devil wasn't the girl properly frightened? His brain turned to mush—a senseless puddle of drivel. He had the most inane urge to kiss this troublesome female. He must be going mad. But then, he didn't have far to go did he.

She spoke amiably, just as if she were inquiring about the weather, instead of staring into the face of a madman. "Perhaps, Lord Wesmont, if you will remove your coat . . ."

It took him a moment to realize she had a plan. He let go of her shoulders and tried to regain his senses. "Yes, yes, of course. Keep the deuced thing. And the medals. I never want to see them again anyway. I only wore it at the insistence of my mother."

"I hardly think that will be necessary."

He twisted and shrugged out of the coat, grimacing when he heard a slight tearing sound as the weight of his coat dropped below Fiona's bosom. However, they'd achieved their aim, the medal had indeed disengaged from her dress.

"There! We are free." She announced triumphantly and handed him his coat.

"Yes," he said, eyeing the front of her gown. She looked deliciously wanton with her torn dress and her hair falling out of place. Staring at her as he dressed back into his coat and dusted off the sleeves, he said, "You, however, require some assistance. The front of your gown is torn. I'll send Lady Hawthorn to you."

"No!" she blurted. Fiona looked down at the ripped fabric of her bodice and clasped her hand over it. "Please. I promised her I wouldn't create a scene tonight. I'll think of something. Truly, I will. Oh, if only you had left me behind that comfortable column."

"Don't be difficult, Fiona. Your dress is torn. You need assistance. Your stepmother is the logical choice, but if you prefer, I'll send a maid."

"No. You mustn't. The servants will gossip. How would it look? Think of your reputation, my lord, and mine." She shook her head insistently. "No. Please, just go back to your guests. I'll think of a way out of this."

Circumstances looked bad. He had waltzed her out onto the balcony in front of a ballroom full of witnesses. Now, she had a torn gown, and her hair was tumbling down. Perhaps she planned to trap him by saying he'd compromised her. He studied her face. The eyes pleading with him were clear and dark like the night sky—and completely guileless.

"I'm not a coward, Miss Hawthorn. I refuse to leave you unattended in this predicament."

"Please, go," she implored. "Every moment you stay makes the situation worse for me. Someone might come and then—"

"Then, you think they would assume I had compromised you," he finished. "Ridiculous. Aside from that, do you think I care for their opinion? Let them think what they choose."

She took a deep breath and in a calm voice, as if explaining to a recalcitrant child, answered him. "I, on the other hand, care a great deal. And as I must spend the rest of my life in this neighborhood, I think it callous of you to have so little regard for my reputation."

Callous? Naturally, and why not, he was callous. Why then, did he feel as if she had just slapped him?

So be it. He bowed. "As you wish. I will not trouble you further with my offers of assistance." Turning crisply, he shut the balcony doors behind him and returned to the ballroom with his chin fixed squarely at a ninety-degree angle.

He approached a cluster of fluttering young misses and in scarcely civil tones he asked Miss Belinda Compton for the next country set. During the ensuing half hour his eyes may have wandered toward the balcony doors, but he had no interest. What was the welfare of one obstinate country miss to him? Nothing. Nothing at all.

The set ran on interminably. When the dance finally ended, it was mere curiosity that beckoned him back to the balcony, or perhaps it was an aggravating sense of duty.

But when he stepped through the doors, his aggravation turned to astonishment. The balcony was empty! He checked in the shadowy corners for Fiona and found them vacant. He admitted to himself that he had covertly watched the doors during the entire set. Fiona had not reentered the ballroom. Of that, he was certain. What then? Where was she?

A grizzly solution entered his mind. He clutched at the balustrade in panic. Surely, she hadn't jumped? The situation was not that dire. Dear God, he shouldn't have left the foolish chit alone.

He castigated himself while searching the ground two stories below, squinting to see through the darkness, praying fervently that he would not see her body lying crumpled on the grass below. He did not need another gut-twisting nightmare added to his repertoire. He couldn't bear it. Frantically, he pushed aside the leaves and branches of the huge old Sycamore blocking his view.

He stopped midpanic—staring at the bough in his hand. The

impish face of Fiona Hawthorn as a child flashed before him. He remembered her scampering perilously high in just such a tree. He mentally traced a route across the limbs hanging over the balcony down the tree to the ground.

"Infernal little minx!" He shook his head and laughed in relief. "In a ball gown. Now that's a feat I would like to have seen."

Tyrell returned to the ballroom, knowing from experience that when he smiled this way, he bore an uncanny resemblance to Satan himself. He didn't care. He looked forward to tomorrow's duty calls with sardonic pleasure. He would make her squirm for her part in this stunt.

Chapter 2
Escaping Thorncourt

Early the next morning Fiona walked down a rutted country lane into Timtree Corners. She strode up the cobbled streets, which were lined with tall narrow Elizabethan buildings huddled together like ponderous old women. The second and third stories of the aged, half-timbered wattle-and-daub structures jutted out over the street. Bedding hung airing out over the upper window sills as women set about their morning work.

Fiona dashed out of the way as the contents of a chamber pot splashed to the ground. Then she heard a woman screech. "It's her!" She winced and tried not to look up, as shutters slammed shut above her head.

She lengthened her already vigorous stride and crossed the street. But it was too late. Villagers stepped back inside their shadowed doorways. Worry lines creased their brows. The boot maker hung out his CLOSED placard as she approached. Doors shut. The hum and rattle of morning activities tapered off into an eerie silence.

Fiona passed by Mrs. Twillhammer's open window. Nearly deaf, the old woman's voice carried like a foghorn through the hushed streets. "Such a pity it is. No matter where she goes, folks do stumble an' fall. Tables and chairs break to pieces. An', I suspect, the milk turns sour. The dear girl is well and truly cursed."

"Yes, a pity, her being such a pretty girl an' all." Mrs. Twill-hammer's elderly sister agreed, loud enough for the deafened woman to hear. Fiona hesitated, slowing her steps, knowing she shouldn't listen, but unable to stop herself.

"Why only last month, Squire Thurgood's wife told me about her expensive new soup tureen—shaped exactly like a gigantic cabbage—an' didn't it just slip straight out of the footman's fingers on the very day—the *very day,* mind you, that Miss Fiona Hawthorn and her sister came calling."

Mrs. Twillhammer gasped. "No!"

"Oh yes, terrible, it was simply terrible. That lovely bowl smashed into a thousand pieces. Fish soup splattered every-where. Oooh, an' the smell, well, just you imagine the smell . . ."

"Never mind." Fiona whispered to herself and picked up her pace, striding briskly past the milliner's, the wheelwright, and the baker's. She fancied she could hear people exhale in relief as she passed them by, and the clank and clatter of life began again in her wake.

She carried a book tucked under one arm and headed in a straight line toward Mr. Quentin—Bookseller. A red-haired young lad stuck his head out from a narrow passageway be-tween two buildings. His eyes opened wide and he darted off like a rabbit. Fiona shook her head. They were so fright-ened of her, perhaps she ought not venture into the village anymore.

Finally, she stood in front of the bookseller's open door. Mr. Quentin, a small, plump man, balanced precariously at the top of a ladder. Fiona watched from the doorway, reluc-tant to enter the shop while he was perched in such a hazardous position. He slowly, cautiously, reached out to place a leather-bound volume onto the top shelf of his floor-to-ceiling bookcases. At that perilous instant, the red-haired boy flung open the rear door and burst into the shop. The door banged into the ladder unbalancing it. Mr. Quentin flapped wildly at the air for balance.

"Granfer!" shouted his young grandson. "She's comin' here. That Miss Hawthorn, what has a curse is comin' here!" He spun around, just in time to see his grandfather frantically waving a book in one hand and gripping the falling ladder with the other. The old man crashed down onto a table of books. Leather-bound tomes shot out in every direction.

"Oh, Granfer!" cried the boy, dodging a flying book.

Fiona dashed into the room to help. The boy saw her and turned white as a sheet. "You killed 'im."

"Nonsense," she snapped.

But Mr. Quentin lay motionless in a contorted heap on the book table. She ran to him and leaned close to listen for sounds of life. His chest quivered with a huge spasmodic gasp as he sucked in a breath. Struggling back to consciousness, his eyelids fluttered, and he blinked up at Fiona, who hovered above him.

"'Pon my word!" he exclaimed. "I've gone to heaven."

She smiled. "Oh no, Mr. Quentin, you are still quite on the earth." Fiona found his broken spectacles amongst the books and set them on his nose. He peered back at her through the thick lenses, one cracked.

"Why bless me, 'tis Miss Hawthorn! I thought you were a beautiful angel, come to take me to the heavenly throne."

"No, Mr. Quentin. I'm sorry to disappoint you. It's only me, come to bring you a book. Tell me, sir, are you injured? Shall I send your grandson to fetch the doctor?"

He shook his head and slid his stocky figure to the floor. Fiona sighed with relief and helped him straighten his demolished book table. She purchased a few more books than she had originally planned to do.

Poor Mr. Quentin, Fiona reflected as she walked along the pathway back to Thorncourt, yet another casualty on the long list of those wounded by "Miss Hawthorn's curse." At least he hadn't broken any bones, which was more than some of her other victims could boast.

She stopped walking, and threw her head back, calling out

to the maker of the brilliant blue sky, "Why must these things happen?"

Placid sunlight radiated onto her upturned face. Its warmth comforted her, but provided no answers. The smell of ripening grain on the breeze made her sigh and smile with pleasure. The bluffs rising east of the road enticed her.

Still morning, she thought, plenty of time. She spun around, checking behind her to make certain the lane was empty. It was.

With uncivilized glee she grasped the bottom of her skirt, dropped her books into it, and held it like a bag. Then, in what she knew was a shocking display of unladylike behavior, she sprinted up the hillside, and did not stop running until she reached the top.

Breathing hard, she stood on the crest, taking in the unobstructed view of the lands below. White cotton balls of sheep dotted the upper pastures. Other fields, thick with yellow grain, stretched toward Thorncourt. She waved to one of the grooms exercising her father's favorite hunter on the road below.

Turning, Fiona darted in and out of the trees. She ran toward the lake, which fed the pastures and fields below. Poplar and ash trees shimmered in the sunlight, sending golden dots flashing across the ground as she ran. Finally, she came to a small thatch boathouse. Inside, she plopped her books on a table in the corner and began removing her clothing.

She emerged later on a short pier that extended from the rear of the boathouse, wearing a dark blue bathing dress. The morning sun was only partway to its apex, which meant she had nearly a whole day ahead of her. In a performance that would have appalled the entire neighborhood, Fiona ran to the end of the wooden dock and dove headfirst into the lake. Plunging down into the crystalline water where she no longer felt human, but like a bird soaring through the freedom of the skies. The cool liquid of the lake surrounded her like a nurturing womb. She spent the remainder of the morning exploring its depths, chasing fish and practicing the strokes her father had taught her as a child. How fortunate she was to have a father with such vigor and love of life. He had rejected the constraints of society and granted her the same freedoms he would have given a son. They spent many happy afternoons here at the lake. Now that he was so far away, her world kept shrinking until this was the only place she felt completely at ease.

Fiona knew her solitary disappearances did not worry her stepmamma. On the contrary, she was probably quite relieved not to have Fiona underfoot (or painfully *over*foot as the case might more often be). Certainly Lady Hawthorn could never have approved of a young lady from Thorncourt bolting headlong across the countryside for the pure joy of it and plunging facefirst into a lake.

Under that same brilliant sun, Lord Wesmont rode toward Thorncourt on Perseus, his temperamental white thoroughbred. As Tyrell posted up the long gravel drive, he calculated how best to make Fiona pay for those moments of panic she'd caused him. Naturally, his presence alone ought to be enough to disturb her.

She'll wonder if I'm going to mention, in front of Lady Hawthorn, her torn dress, or her extraordinary mode of escape from the balcony. And well she should be afraid—the wretched elf—giving him a start the way she did. Although he planned to do nothing except make her nervous, a smile curled at one side of his mouth as he anticipated her discomfiture.

His momentary amusement vanished as he looked up at Baron Hawthorn's manor. He pictured Fiona's father still garrisoned in Spain and swore softly under his breath. Suddenly his whole errand seemed frivolous and wrong. How could he make social calls while other men, good men, like Hawthorn, men to whom he owed his life, were perhaps facing death at this very moment? The sound of crunching gravel under his horse's hooves awakened Tyrell from his dark visions of the Spanish battlefront.

Perseus snorted, tossed his head and danced sideways while Tyrell stared up at the three-story limestone house. A curtain moved in the upstairs window. No doubt he'd been observed. He swore softly, and contemplated turning around and going home. He ought not be here—not for a mere moment's sport.

A stable lad came running up to take his mount, and the die was cast. "I'll see to 'im, sir."

Tyrell sighed and swung down. "Keep him close, I won't be long."

He trudged up the front steps and handed his card to the butler awaiting him at the door. The foyer reverberated with the sound of hammering pianoforte strings, as someone upstairs, most likely Fiona, with scant regard for meter, plunked out a sonata.

The butler returned, and led him up to Lady Hawthorn's sitting room, announcing Tyrell with a grand flourish. The pounding of piano keys stopped abruptly, for which he silently thanked God. But as Tyrell stepped into the room, his mouth fell open, and he could only gape in disbelief.

He could not comprehend a room so riotously cluttered with mismatched decorations. For a moment, he stood as rigid as a post, just staring, trying to make sense of it all. But it could not be done. Order and reason had no part in the creation of this room. Maroon Chinese vases clashed with the blue Georgian side chairs. Egyptian artifacts looked crude atop the Baroque gold-encrusted credenza. Over the mantel hung a Georgian-style painting of a young woman, whose birdlike features closely resembled Lady Hawthorn's. It was a pastoral scene, except that surely the lady had donned every jewel she owned for the portrait, and was outfitted to meet the Queen rather than entertain sheep. The entire room consisted of such a garish jumble of paraphernalia that it all seemed to march toward him like an army of lunatics.

He glanced back, over his shoulder, down the stairs, wishing he'd turned around and rode away while he had had the chance. But Lady Hawthorn came forward and extended her hand. He took it and inclined his head, noting that Lady Hawthorn smiled with her lips, but the rest of her face neglected to come along.

He recouped his equilibrium, remembered the purpose for his visit, and turned his gaze toward the pianoforte—toward his intended quarry. His newly regained composure relapsed into confusion again as he realized the pianist was not Fiona.

In her place sat a chit whose blond hair was arranged into a platoon of ringlets, hanging in stiff attention around the perimeter of her head, so that it looked as if she were wearing a wreath of straw. He quickly schooled his expression as Lady Hawthorn introduced her daughter, Emeline, a daughter from her previous marriage.

". . . A good man, but dead lo these last eight years. May God rest his soul." Lady Hawthorn bowed her head in a brief mournful homage, and then looked up as shrewdly as if she'd just found a shiny new gold piece in her stocking. "Surely you remember Emeline. Your mother introduced her to you last night at the ball."

He muttered an incoherent response. *Of course, he didn't remember her. He'd stared straight ahead in a blind angry cloud as the reception line had passed by. He'd merely shaken the hands offered him and grunted, while his mother prattled on about every eligible chit in the district.*

Next, Lady Hawthorn presented a freckle-faced girl of about thirteen years, her youngest daughter. Sylvia stood up beside a large embroidery hoop and curtsied prettily.

He glanced around the room in search of Fiona. It was possible she sat crowded behind one of the voluminous floral arrangements. Or she might be hidden behind the imposing bronze statue of Neptune riding ocean waves on the back of a sea serpent, lightning bolt clasped in one hand and a trio of mermaids clutching at his hips. But no, Fiona was not to be found in the crowded room.

Lady Hawthorn directed him to a yellow silk Egyptian sofa, which promised little or no comfort, and clashed mightily with the red roses painted on the blue-striped wallpaper. Tyrell inhaled, and tried not to curse aloud as he sat down.

Emeline scurried over to take up the position on the other end of the sofa. He winced. Garbed in a frothy ruffled concoction with dozens of bows, her pink dress set against the yellow couch bruised his eyesight. He would need something stronger than the tea Lady Hawthorn was ringing for to get through ten more minutes in this room.

Sylvia bent her head laboriously over her embroidery frame and tried valiantly not to cry out as she stuck her finger with the needle. He silently wished himself anywhere but here, South America, back on the Peninsula where he belonged, darkest Africa—anywhere.

Refreshments arrived. Tyrell took a bite of the biscuit offered him. It crumbled like dry, sugary sand in his mouth, which behooved him to drink down his dish of tea with some haste. Lady Hawthorn poured another cup for him, as she gossiped about their neighbors. He nodded politely and tried to change the subject by mentioning his encounter with Baron Hawthorn in Spain at the ill-fated battle of Salamanca. When she frowned, he assured her of her husband's good health.

Emeline used her mother's brief silence to seize the conversation and ply him with questions about his adventures on the Continent. Unfortunately, she began to ask too closely about actual battles he had fought. Lady Hawthorn's left eyebrow shot up. "Emeline, my dear, we do not discuss such indelicate matters."

"No, Mama. I didn't mean to offend." She clasped her hands together and directed a pleading look at Tyrell. "Lord Wesmont, you must forgive me. Oh, say you will."

It was an overdone performance, he thought. Even the tiny

upended portion of her nose turned pink, as if it were under her complete control. She really should go on the stage.

"I assure you, no offense was taken." He left the subject and expressed his disappointment at not having found Miss Hawthorn at home. "Is she feeling poorly?" he pried.

Sylvia answered his question while pulling needle and thread up from the frame. It sounded like one of those remarks a young person makes in imitation of the adults she has overheard. "Oh"—she sighed with adultlike weariness—"you know how it is on a sunny day. Fiona is, no doubt, tearing up the fields on her horse, or drowning herself in her precious lake."

This mimicked speech was rewarded with a subtle but swift kick from her sister. Sylvia yelped and looked up from her needlework in surprise. Her sister's expression gave nothing away, but Tyrell felt certain that Sylvia's quick glimpse at her mother's face had apprised her of the fact that she had committed some sort of faux pas.

He took mercy on the freckle-faced understudy and smiled. "With such a glorious day beckoning, who could blame Miss Hawthorn for not remaining indoors. I'm certain, she has forgotten all about our dance the other night."

Emeline mewed like a disconcerted kitten. "I could never forget dancing with you." She cast him a quick adoring look and then fussed with her big fluffy skirt, contriving to look properly embarrassed, as if she had divulged too much of her affection for him.

Poor Sylvia, who had opened the door for this theatrical scene, stared in amazement at her sister, and then bent over her embroidery with renewed interest in the less complicated intricacies of tying a French knot.

Tyrell consulted the clock on the mantel, wishing he were the one out tearing up the fields on his horse, rather than Fiona. *And what the devil did Sylvia mean when she said, "drowning herself in her precious lake"?*

His ten minutes were up. Tyrell stood abruptly, made a

quick bow, and left Lady Hawthorn's chaotic drawing room with as much haste as he could apply without running. Downstairs, he seized his hat from the butler, and as soon as the door shut behind him he dashed down the front stairs, fleeing like a fox from a pack of hounds.

Free of the house, he took a deep breath and exhaled, assuming a more leisurely pace. He pulled out a coin and flipped it up into the air. Sunlight glinted off of it as it spun up and then down into his waiting palm. The stable lad, holding his horse, smiled, probably guessing the flashing silver was meant for him.

Tyrell patted Perseus's nose. The groom was about fourteen and had intelligent brown eyes, which he lowered as he pulled at his forelock in obeisance, but he couldn't hold back his praise for Perseus. "A prime 'un he is, sir. I mean, yer lordship, sir."

"Thank you." Tyrell flipped the coin and caught it again. "Give you any trouble, did he?"

"No, m'lord."

"Unusual," said Tyrell. "Perseus is high-spirited. Won't let just anybody handle him."

The boy's countenance rose. "He din'na give me no trouble."

"Excellent." Lord Wesmont took the leads from him. Then, as if it were an afterthought, he turned back to the groom. "Perhaps, you know which direction Miss Fiona rode to?"

The boy looked at him, obviously puzzled. "Miss Fiona din'na ride out today, yer lordship. 'Er mare is still in 'er stall."

"My mistake." Tyrell stared absently into the distance and flipped the coin once more. "I was given to believe she was not at home."

"Oh, well tha's true 'nuff. She ain't home." The boy offered enthusiastically and then caught himself.

"No?" asked Tyrell. "Then she must have gone for a walk?"

"I dunno it were a walk 'xactly."

He flipped the coin and bore down on the lad. "What then, exactly?"

The young groom stepped back and eyed him and the silver coin warily. "Miss Fiona is a kind 'un. An' I won't say nuffin' to get 'er in trouble, now will I?"

Intrigued, Tyrell played his hand carefully. "Come, lad. I've known Miss Hawthorn since she was in leading strings. We're old friends. Do I seem like the sort who would cause her any trouble?"

"No, m'lord, exceptin' "—he scratched at the back of his head and grimaced as he tried to figure out what he ought to say. Then a flash of anger played across his face, and words came flying out. "Well, sir, it ain't fair. Miss Fiona lands in the briars more'n what's right. Things at the house ain't ex-actly right, if anybody was to ask me. Master 'as been gone too long. It's shameful, them servants laying all them acci-dents at her door. Shameful, that's what it is. If'n the upstairs maid drops a vase, there ain't no call pinning it on Miss Fiona, but that's the way of it. And, the master's new wife has taken to payin' the servin' staff danger pay. Fah!" he spit and looked up, obviously calculating whether Tyrell was going to scold him for criticizing his employers or not.

"Danger pay?"

"Yes sir, a quarter-day bonus, so as they won't leave her employ and go to houses where it ain't so dangerous. Ha! Small chance o' that, when they make more workin' here than they could anywheres else. An' if that ain't enough, then they goes an' complains to other folks about all the risks o' workin' here."

"Ah," Tyrell said almost to himself.

"Aye, but me an' the steward, we know what's what. Maybe Miss Fiona does have more ginger than a yearling. Still, it ain't her fault if the butler falls over 'is own feet. And what if she do run like a boy from time to time. Ain't no crime in it, is there? The master never minded it, she's a spirited lass, says he. O' course, Lady Hawthorn, she wunna like it none, now would she?"

Tyrell tried to sort through the boy's ramblings and wondered if he'd understood him correctly. "Surely, you're jesting with me? Ladies do not go running about."

"Amn't jestin' you! No, sir. I seen 'er m'self. 'Tis a sight, it is. She jus' hitches up 'er skirts an goes like the wind, she do. Looks summat like a duck 'bout to lift from the pond, if'n yer ken me."

Tyrell chuckled at the boy's imagery. "Well, if that don't beat all hollow." He tossed the coin to him, and the lad clasped it with glee. "And exactly where does Miss Fiona run to today?"

"More'n likely she's gone up to 'er lake."

"Which lake do you mean?"

"The high meadow lake, yer lordship."

"But that's two miles or more, surely she doesn't run all the way."

"Oh yes, m'lord, she do. Now, don't *that* beat all hollow?" The boy grinned, obviously pleased with himself for correctly using the same expression Tyrell had.

"That it does, boy." Tyrell laughed and swung up into the saddle. "That it does."

Chapter 3
The Lady of the Lake

Tyrell rode up to the lake and found the old boathouse. He tied Perseus to a tree and took a well-worn path around the little house. Planted with garden flowers and a small strawberry patch, clearly, this was no ordinary boathouse. He opened the door and found books stacked on a crude table. Pinned to the thatch were several watercolor studies of the lake, painted in various aspects of light. He walked over to take a closer look. Fiona's love of the lake came through superbly. He carefully pressed down a curling corner of one particularly lovely painting of the lake swathed in early morning light.

He noticed her clothing hanging on a hook at the back of the room. What was she wearing, he wondered, for both under and outer garments hung there. The answer seemed obvious. She'd done what he, and other lads throughout time had done. She must be swimming unclad. An image of her formed in his mind. He shook his head and left the boathouse.

"Utter folly for a female to be up here unchaperoned, unaccompanied," he muttered, as he mounted Perseus and prepared to ride home. *Alone,* his mind whispered. *Naked,* some deeper oracle spoke. *Go home,* his conscience instructed. He couldn't help looking toward the lake and feeling disappointed that there was no sign of her.

While enduring the conflicting counsel in his mind, Tyrell guided his horse along the edge of the lake. It was his duty to see that the young woman was unharmed. She was, after all, a childhood friend, and he owed at least that much to her father, or so he argued.

He might have missed finding her at all, given the noisy society in his head, except sparkles of sunlight on splashing water caught his attention. She was twenty yards out, heading toward shore with a slow, even stroke. It was as if little white stars shot from her fingertips as water and light mingled. He slowed Perseus and held his breath in anticipation, as he watched Fiona's rhythmic movement through the water.

It seemed to take an achingly long time before she got to the shore. At last, she rose out of the lake, like a mermaid emerging from the sea, but to his great disappointment she wore a dark blue bathing dress. She climbed up onto a large rock and sat there squeezing the water out of her hair, letting it drip onto the ground. He nudged Perseus and ambled toward her.

She started at the sound of his approach and turned around. He touched the brim of his hat in mock salute. "A pleasure to see you again, Miss Hawthorn."

She stared up at him, disbelief plainly written on her elfin face. "Lord Wesmont, what a surprise."

He swung down from the saddle and knotted the reins around the trunk of a nearby sapling. "You didn't expect me?" he teased. "Our waltz last night was quite memorable. Surely, a duty call would be expected?"

"No." She bit her bottom lip. "Well, that is to say, I expected you would simply send your regards. How did you find me here?"

"Chance." He lied, although it was partly true. "And I must say, I cannot countenance you being alone in such a secluded place. What if some other man should chance upon you, someone without scruples."

"My lord, I'm long out of the schoolroom. I assure you, I don't need a chaperone for every activity. Besides, I've been coming here alone for years and no ill has ever befallen me.

Quite the contrary." She tossed a small pebble into the water. "This is the one place in all the world where I am free from trouble."

He leaned against a nearby tree trunk and considered her for a moment. Droplets of water glittered on her skin and the wet garment clung enticingly to her figure. "You underestimate the dangers of this world, ma'am."

"You, sir, are forgetting that I am one of the *worst* of those dangers." She smiled wryly. "Why, most men would quake with fear, just to stand as close to me as you are now."

"What errant nonsense you speak."

"Oh? Begging your pardon, my lord." She made a pretense of haughtiness, "Perhaps you haven't heard the many titles I bear. Let me see, there is Lady Fiasco, the Duchess of Doom, Countess of Calamity and, I suppose, a dozen more I haven't had the good fortune to overhear."

He frowned, imagining the embarrassment it caused her to overhear such prattle, and shook his head. "It's all rubbish to me. What if a man, unaware of your *dangerous* reputation, happened through these woods? What then, young lady?"

"Unfortunately, my reputation is rather broadly known," she said softly, staring out across the placid waters.

"That's ridiculous. You grossly overrate the extent of your fame." He picked up a small flat stone and skipped it across the water. "You're taking a grave risk to be here alone and unchaperoned."

Fiona chuckled. "Grave risk? I think not. But, let us suppose, for the sake of argument, an unsuspecting marauder should appear at my quiet lake. I would simply jump in the water and swim away. There isn't a man alive who can outswim me." She beamed up at him like a child who has just presented her tutor with all of her sums correctly tallied.

In spite of the fact that she didn't appear to be boasting, Tyrell felt she had thrown down a gauntlet. He stepped forward and straightened his silk waistcoat, which was becoming unbearably hot. "Brave words, my girl. But that is all they are—words. You might swim faster than one or two country lads who've never learned how properly. But, you are still a *female*. And any man worth his salt could catch up to you in a trice." He snapped his fingers in her face. "A trice."

She stared back at him, as if he were a creature she'd never seen before. Slowly, a mischievous smile spread across her face, mocking him, challenging him.

"You can't seriously think—"

She laughed, as if he were a foolish boy.

Her cocked brow, her smug little grin, these felt like a glove slapping him soundly across the cheek. There was no option for Tyrell, none at all. "We shall see then, won't we?"

Without another word, he removed his coat, waistcoat, cravat, and hung them over a tree branch. He began unbuttoning his shirt and for a moment thought better of it. But one more look at her mocking expression and there was no turning back.

She was convulsing with suppressed amusement. He snorted, feeling hot and annoyed—like a bull ready to charge. She tossed back her head, and a delightful laugh bubbled out. The quality of her laughter was so infectious he nearly grinned back at her. But the imp was laughing at him—and that was unforgivable.

He yanked off his shirt and several buttons flew off into the underbrush. Fiona instantly sobered, her mouth dropped open and her eyes widened. He tossed his shirt over a tree limb and turned squarely toward her. Now, it was his turn to taunt her.

"Not so brave now, eh, Fiona?"

Her face reddened, and she quickly turned away.

He sensed he'd just gained the upper hand. "Oh, I see. I wager you've never seen a half-naked man before."

She turned back to him with her jaw set. He noted she kept her eyes fixed on his face. "You are ridiculing me, sir, shamefully. I'll have you know, I'm not as naive as you think. I—I've seen paintings of—" she stammered. "And—I've seen the Greek statues in the London museum." She folded her arms across her breasts. "You do not look any different than they do."

The corner of his mouth twitched. "Thank you for the compliment." He bowed his head.

She jumped down from the rock. "That was not a compliment! Nothing of the kind. I meant—I simply meant, you look like—or rather, that I have seen other—Ohhh, you are a wicked man!"

He chuckled and bent to remove his boots, a task that proved to be difficult without a chair. While he struggled, she quietly slid into the lake. He cursed under his breath, still tussling with his boots while she stood waist deep a few yards out flicking playfully at the water.

At last, he threw down his boot and charged into the lake after her. The cold water caused him to inhale sharply. This foolishness would cost him the ruin of a good pair of breeches. He'd be lucky if they didn't shrink so tight he'd have to be sliced out of them. In a huff, he sloshed out toward her. He intended to put an end to this contest in short order.

She giggled, turned, and like a dolphin, dove in and swam away. The race was on. He plowed through the water in pursuit. Thrashing his hardest, he tried to gain on her, but the distance between them remained constant. Tyrell felt the lake increase in depth, the water grew colder and the bottom was no longer within his reach. A quick glance and he saw they were some distance from the shoreline. He pursued her with more determination.

By George, he'd been tossed into the canals at Eaton and had learned to swim with the best of them. No twit of a girl was going to beat him. No, sir.

After another quarter hour, his faltering breath told him there was actually a chance he might lose. He resolved to kick and pull at the water even harder.

Just as defeat seemed eminent and his breath threatened to give out, the gap between them closed. Swimming just ahead of him, Fiona rolled onto her back and seemed to lie effortlessly in the water. Her foot kicked up in front of his face and flicked water into his eyes. He fought to catch his breath. Over the throbbing in his ears, he heard her giggle. The vixen was laughing. Laughing! While he neared collapse. He watched her in amazement; she rolled over in the water and cast him a backward teasing smile.

Like a viper striking, his hand shot out and caught her ankle. He had her. She cried out. Although, it did not sound like a cry of alarm—more like an excited scream of delight. Tyrell held fast to her foot but, to his surprise, she dragged him under water.

In the misty view under the lake, she glided in front of him like a mermaid, pulling him effortlessly along behind her. His lungs began to ache. A flurry of bubbles escaped from his mouth. Desperate for air, he let go of her ankle and fought his way up to the surface.

He burst up through the water, gasping and coughing in fits. Fiona's head bobbed up a few feet away from him.

She grinned, looking exhilarated, and not in the least breathless. "Do you cry craven?" she taunted him.

Wicked, teasing female, he thought. Worse yet, the little baggage had defeated him. Tyrell would rather die than cry craven. He gulped air. She still beamed triumphantly, as he sank under her lake.

Fiona did not comprehend at first what was happening, but soon she realized he had been under too long. "Lord Wesmont!" She screamed for him. "Tyrell!"

He didn't come up. Fiona dove under the water and saw him sinking, eyes closed, bubbles trickling out of his mouth. She swam down and grabbed his hair. Turning, she kicked violently up to the surface dragging him behind her. She held his head up out of the water and tried to swim using only her legs. His weight pulled them both down. Soon, she was fighting just to catch her own breath.

They were not making fast enough progress toward the shore. She had to find another way. Fiona tucked his head under one arm. It might strangle him, she thought, but she had to get him to shore. So, with her arm around his neck she contrived to swim on her side. They moved faster. Fiona side-kicked with all her might. Tyrell gasped and flailed at the water.

"Try not to struggle! I'll save you!" she shouted, but he only sputtered and went limp in answer.

As she swam, she fought to keep down the rising panic in her heart. He was dying. She refused to allow herself to yield to the tears that tried to fill her eyes. *Swim, just swim,* she told herself.

Finally, she made the last kick that grounded them on the beach. Her jaw locked in determination, she stumbled up and hoisted him onto the bank. She stumbled under his weight and he flopped facedown in the sand and didn't move. Fiona moaned softly, and knelt beside his motionless body.

"Please, not this! Not him!" She covered her face with her hands, and pled with the Almighty. "Oh God, please, don't let him die. What should I do?"

Then it came to her that she must discover whether or not he was still breathing. She rolled him over, onto his back. His lifeless arm thumped to the ground, and his eyes remained closed as if in final sleep.

"No. No! Please, let him be alive." She pressed her ear to his chest to listen for breathing. But before the hairs on his chest could tickle her cheek she felt her shoulders clamped in an iron tight grip. Fiona screamed.

"You are caught!" Tyrell shouted. His eyes were open and flashing with life—and triumph.

Fiona jerked away from him in disbelief.

"You! You're not drowned! Not dead! You weren't—"

"No." He coughed. "Although, dragging me across the lake you nearly did the job."

As quickly as the realization that he was alive brought relief,

it brought anger. She raised her hand, intending to slap his arrogant face into the next province. But before she could, Tyrell
caught her hand and held it tightly.

She balled up her left hand. He grabbed that fist before she
could give him the pummeling he deserved. Writhing and
struggling under his grasp, she made furious noises. She was
so angry she couldn't speak coherently.

Tyrell laughed. "You really are a wild little vixen, aren't
you?"

In answer, her animal-like noises turned into a screech.
Frustration and outrage finally formed actual words, and she
spewed them out. "You despicable, unfeeling— wicked—
You tricked me! I thought you were dead."

He roared with laughter, and made the mistake of loosen-
ing his grip on her. Fiona jerked free and slapped his face as
hard as she could. The crack startled her, and for an instant,
felt as though everything froze.

Like lightning, Tyrell's features hardened into fury. He
roared like a charging animal. Before she understood what
had happened, he had grabbed her, flung her over, and pinned
both of her wrists to the ground.

Time slowed to a crawl. He loomed over her like an enraged bear. Fiona felt his breath hot on her face. She closed
her eyes and waited for him to strike back.

When nothing happened, she peeked at him. His eyes were
dangerously close to hers, but he no longer looked as mad as
before. He stared at her, as if looking at a stranger. Slowly his
features cooled, but he still held her firmly beneath him.

"I'm sorry," he said raggedly, his breathing rapid. "I forgot
for a minute . . . don't know what happened."

She swallowed, relieved. Then chewed her lip for a moment.
"Perhaps, I shouldn't have hit you."

He didn't answer. He still studied her features, as if noticing
them for the first time. She became aware of the weight of his
body, pressing down on hers and felt heat flooding into her
cheeks.

He inhaled deeply, and shook his head as if trying to clear it. "I just reacted—never mind."

He squinted at her as if trying to figure something out. "Did you know . . . you're so—" Droplets of water fell down from his hair, onto her cheeks and nose. "Beautiful. Like a water nymph or something—and I—" He looked confused, shaken. Before she understood what he meant, his mouth came down on hers, and he kissed her lips slowly, carefully, as if tasting her.

He let go of her arms and leaned up. "I—I'm sorry, and I really shouldn't have done that either. Oh hell—" He kissed her again with an intensity that filled her with the most incredible sensation of being wanted.

The smell of lake and wood mingled with the scent of Tyrell's skin. It all swirled together, into a whirlwind of delicious feelings. No other man could possibly smell or taste like he did. With each kiss, he seemed to throw open doors in her heart. Doors she'd feared would always remain dark and hopelessly unopened. Fiona wrapped her arms around his neck and kissed him back with all her heart. Nothing else mattered. She fully intended to go on kissing him forever.

But a strange sound jarred her senses. It wafted across the water, the high-pitched melodic trilling of the shepherd's flute. On one of the nearby hills, a shepherd boy must have begun playing a tune to his sheep.

Tyrell stopped kissing her and stared down at Fiona as she lay completely contented in his arms. He pulled out of her embrace and sat up, raking one hand through his wet hair. Then he swore.

Fiona blinked her eyes open, wishing desperately she could return to the euphoric dream she was just having. *But isn't that the way dreams are, just when they become pleasant, morning arrives.*

"Damnation!" He jerked away from her. "What, in heaven's name, am I doing?" He jumped up and charged into the lake, dousing himself in the cold water. He splashed handfuls of water over his face and chest. Then he stopped and stared out over the lake. Suddenly, he slammed his fist against the ripples sending a spray of water arcing through the sunshine.

Tyrell stomped back out of the lake and pointed his finger at her. "You!" He shouted it as if it were a profanity. "You *are* dangerous, Fiona Hawthorn." He jerked his clothes off the tree branch. "And I'm a fool for coming here!"

Fiona sat there and hugged her knees, trying not to watch him as he marched to the rock, sat down, forcefully plowed a foot into each stocking, and yanked on his boots. He made a lump of the rest of his clothing, tucked it under one arm, and mounted his horse, all the time muttering self-reproaches for putting himself in a position where he might have compromised her.

"Listen to me!" he shouted. "I don't care who you tell about what happened here. I'm not getting leg-shackled to you or anyone else! I can't. I won't. Not now. Not ever."

He kicked his white horse into a gallop. When the sound of hooves crashing through the underbrush finally faded, Fiona shivered. Biting her lip to hold back the tears, she looked up, beseeching the heavens for comfort. The blue sky and the gathering white clouds seemed oblivious to her anguish. In the end, she gave herself over to racking sobs of shame and confusion.

Chapter 4

Notorious Visitor

Fiona walked home to Thorncourt with slow ponderous steps. She idly brushed some stalks of wheat loaded with grain upright, and watched their heavy heads bounce until they bowed back down under their fertile weight. She drew a long, laborious breath. The late afternoon air had turned sultry, heavily laden with pollen and insects.

It would storm, maybe tonight, or maybe in the morning. Fiona confined her thoughts to the weather. Thinking of anything else hurt too much. She hoped the coming rain would not ruin the harvest.

Inside Thorncourt, the butler greeted her with unsettling news. "The Countess Alameda is here. She awaits you in the upstairs parlor. And may I say, Miss Fiona, she has been sitting with Lady Hawthorn for well over two hours."

"Two hours? Aunt Honore and Mama? Oh dear." Fiona lifted out her skirts and surveyed her present state of dishabille. "A moment. Tell her, I'll come to them in a moment."

She rushed wildly up the stairs to her room and stood in front of the mirror. Her eyes were puffy and red, her dress had mud around the hem, and her hair was a mess of wavy tendrils flying in every direction. She moaned. There was no help for it. She quickly braided her wild tresses and wound the braid up into a coil. Without a second glance in the mirror she leapt up and fled to her stepmother's parlor.

The butler opened the door for her. Fiona clasped her trembling hands together and marched into the room to stand in front of her aunt.

The Countess Alameda sat poised regally on the settee. Her hair, which in her youth had been brown, was now an unearthly shade of red, nearly maroon. She wore an extravagant morning dress of bottle green silk and black lace.

Fiona's voice shook. "Lady Alameda, I'm very pleased to see you." She sank into a deep curtsy and started wobbling dangerously close to the tea service perched on a slim table in front of the two ladies. Hopelessly unbalanced, Fiona shot an apologetic look toward her stepmother. Lady Hawthorn rolled her gaze up toward the ceiling. Obviously, she did not wish to witness the tea splashing across her guest, as it undoubtedly would.

But before Fiona could topple into the tea table, Lady Alameda grabbed her arm in a viselike grip. Once Fiona regained her balance, her aunt let go and raised her lorgnette to her eyes. "Stand up, child, and let me have a look at you."

Lady Hawthorn's head snapped back to the scene as if she had been slapped. "How very odd," she muttered and checked the teapot to see if the contents were indeed where they were supposed to be. "Very odd, indeed." She frowned at the silver teapot as if it had erred somehow.

The countess studied Fiona from head to toe, took obvious note of the muddy hem, dropped her peering glass into her lap, and turned on Lady Hawthorn. "I confess, I am unbearably hot. Madam, your parlor is stifling. It needs a cross breeze. I suggest you have another window cut into that wall over there. Do it. You will see that I am right."

"But that wall adjoins the library, not the exterior. I can't very well—"

"And while you're at it, tear down this atrocious wallpaper." Honore waved her hand in an imperial dismissal and rose abruptly, shaking out her skirts and sending tea cake crumbs bouncing across the floor. "Come, Fiona. I wish to see the gardens my sister laid in."

With a rueful glance at her stepmother, Fiona led her aunt out of the parlor. The gardens lay downstairs and to the side of the house out through the breakfast room. However, the out-of-doors offered little respite from the heat, and the humid air teemed with bugs.

"White roses, hmm. Lovely, I suppose." Her aunt scarcely looked at the flowers. "Your mother always had such subdued taste. Quite unlike my own." She walked briskly through the garden and sat down on a bench facing the house.

"I want to make sure we are not interrupted. This will serve. Do come and sit down."

Fiona poised herself on the edge of the bench, remembering to keep her back straight. Her aunt whipped open a fan and flapped it at a bevy of gnats. "I have no desire to mince words with you, my girl. I will tell you plainly, that I have come to take you first to Brighton and then back to London to live with me."

Fiona's mouth fell open.

"I can see by your face you are wondering, why. Why now, after all these years, have I suddenly taken an interest in you? Do close your mouth, dear. The bugs are thick. I can't like to watch you swallowing insects."

Fiona snapped her mouth shut.

"The truth is, my dear, I've no inclination toward children. Never could tolerate 'em. Pesky things—not unlike these dratted mosquitoes." She waved at the air with her fan. "Fortunately, Fiona, you are no longer a child. I've decided you might prove a rather interesting undertaking. Since I've never had any offspring of my own, and your mother was my favorite sister, I'm in a way of feeling parental toward you."

Fiona knew full well that her mother was Honore's only sister. She had several uncles, but there had only been two girls in her mother's family. She also knew, that her aunt was as unpredictable as the weather in the English countryside. Today, Aunt Honore felt like playing the parent. But, tomorrow? Tomorrow, she might very well board a ship bound for

Egypt simply because she decided she wanted to climb a pyramid. Given the woman's history, it certainly wasn't prudent to rely on her as a benefactress. Fiona might find herself abandoned to her own resources.

On the other hand, she felt an overpowering urge to leave the neighborhood. The prospect of staying here and chancing a meeting with Tyrell again, promised only pain and embarrassment. Aunt Honore might just provide her with an escape. Of course, there was also the matter of *the accidents*.

Fiona twisted the cloth of her skirt. "My lady, this is a most generous offer. However, you may not have heard about my disastrous Season. I cannot wish to burden you with the catastrophes that seem to follow me wherever I go."

"Catastrophes? What nonsense is this? I heard nothing untoward about your Season. Whatever can you mean? Indeed, I never could fathom why your family left London so suddenly."

"Because of poor Lieutenant Withycombe. He was dreadfully smashed up while dancing with me, broke his collarbone. Surely you heard? He couldn't return to the Continent to fight Bonaparte. Everyone blamed me. If only I hadn't danced—"

"Folderol! That young nodcock was just trying to avoid his duty." Honore sputtered as a mayfly tried to land on her tongue.

"Oh, I cannot think so. The poor fellow screamed horribly as they carried him away. I seriously doubt he was playing us false."

"Yes, well, he would scream wouldn't he," she muttered.

Fiona sighed. "Sadly, he's not my only victim. And most of our villagers believe I carry a curse."

"Do they, indeed?" Honore lifted her lorgnette and studied Fiona until she fidgeted with discomfort.

"A curse, you say—how very diverting. We leave in the morning." With that, Aunt Honore stood abruptly, slapped at a buzzing insect, and marched into the house.

* * *

True to her word, the next morning Countess Alameda had them ensconced in her carriage as it rolled toward Brighton. Fiona gazed out through the carriage glass as rain splattered against it. With a heavy heart, she watched the home she loved disappear behind her.

And him. She was leaving *him* behind. Why didn't she feel relieved? She would never have to see his scowling face again. But, all too vividly she recalled the sensation of his mouth covering hers, and the feel of his arms holding her. She would never feel that way again either. Tears slid out of her eyes and trickled down her cheeks.

Honore sniffed at the air, as if she smelled something foul. "Come now, Fiona, you cannot miss your home already? We are but a few miles away and here you are weeping. I should think you'd be glad to be shot of that uncomfortable heap of stones, and that insufferable cow your father married."

Fiona wiped away her tears and tried to smile.

"Well, speak up, girl. Are you homesick?"

"No, my lady."

"Humph. Are you often this morose?"

Fiona smiled at her aunt's pouting expression. "I apologize, Aunt. I'm behaving like a fool."

In a flash, Honore's face changed from that of a pouting child into a shrewd ferret. The ferret calculated her prey through thinly slit eyes. "A fool eh? Then, it's a man causing those tears. Ah, that would explain your puffy eyes yesterday."

Fiona's mouth opened and then clamped shut.

"Ha! See there, your face convicts you. You are in love." Honore tapped the side of her cheek with one gloved finger. "And, this man has broken your heart, otherwise you wouldn't have been so willing to come to Brighton with me."

"No!" Fiona nearly choked. She swallowed hard and shook her head vehemently. "Certainly not. In love? No. Impossible.

Not with someone so cruel and heartless and—" She lowered her head under her aunt's scrutiny.

"Come, come, my girl. We'll have no secrets standing between us. I'll not have you suffering like a martyr, whilst I attempt to show you the delights of London. That would make fools of both of us. You will tell me all, so that we can decide together how best to proceed."

"I couldn't. I have been so—" Fiona clenched her teeth and balled her hands into tight fists. "Such a fool."

"You will discover, my dear, as I have, that there is no one as foolhardy as a woman in love. And I might add, that there has never been a bigger fool than I was, when I fell in love with Francisco de Alameda."

With a flourish, Honore recounted to Fiona the story of the handsome Portuguese count stealing her heart away at a masked ball in London. A blush spread on Honore's cheeks, and her eyes softened. "The young devil thought he would trifle with my affections and then go merrily on his way. Ha!" She smacked her hand against the velvet seat cushion and announced triumphantly. "I wouldn't have it! I stowed away, aboard his ship bound for the African coast. Oh, he was angry, of course. But by the time we reached Cape Delgado he could not bear to be parted from me."

Honore closed her eyes for a moment. "I can still remember his strong arms around me. Ah, yes, my dear," she whispered. "Love makes fools of us all."

Her aunt's love for her late husband touched Fiona's heart. In turn, Fiona told Honore of Lord Wesmont's visit to the lake. She remained modestly obscure about the length and depth of his kisses.

Honore chuckled. "I cut my eye teeth some years ago, child. A simple scrutiny of your face speaks volumes where your words do not. He became passionate with you, did he not?"

Fiona nodded and exhaled slowly, some of the hidden anguish and humiliation flowed out as she did.

"And then?"

"And then his passion turned to anger." Fiona recounted Tyrell's painful words and scornful departure. When she finished telling it, some of the shame left her. It no longer clawed at her like a hateful secret trapped in the dark pit of her stomach.

Honore cast a knowing eye over her niece. "I daresay, Lord Wesmont acted very badly."

"Oh, but, Aunt, don't you see?" Fiona held out her hands, entreating her aunt. "It was entirely my fault. I behaved improperly. I goaded him. I hit him. And when he kissed me I ought to have resisted him. But I didn't. On the contrary, I *wanted* him to kiss me more. Truthfully, I hoped he would never stop, even though I knew it was wrong to indulge in such—such wanton behavior."

Fiona's cheeks flamed red, and she feared a fresh bout of tears might overtake her. "I utterly failed to discipline my emotions, and now, not only must I bear this dreadful curse, but I have compromised myself as well."

Honore's lips clamped together into two stiff lines. Her eyelids lowered over dark, boiling eyes. Then her face erupted and flamed majestically. "Oh for pity sake!" Her aunt's voice boomed around the carriage as if thunder had just exploded right inside the coach. Fiona pressed her back against the cushions and held her breath.

"I refuse to hear any more about this wretched curse! Only ignorant Hottentots believe in *curses*. Do not speak of it again."

Fiona tried to speak. "Yes, my lady, I mean . . . no, my lady."

"Never speak of it!"

Fiona nodded.

An invisible wind blew Honore's features back into those of a concerned aunt. In silent astonishment, Fiona watched her aunt's mercurial countenance transform again.

"Now"—Honore's voice softened back to normal—"you've misunderstood the thing, my dear. I did not say there was anything wrong with Wesmont kissing you. Indeed, under the circumstances, I should have thought him half dead had he not."

Honore reached over and patted Fiona's hand. "And you certainly aren't compromised, my dear. Believe me, there is far more to it than that." She laughed gaily.

"But, he—"

"Good gracious, child, if I married every man who had kissed me, heavens, I'd have nearly two hundred husbands. What ridiculous rot."

Fiona looked up at her aunt in confusion, then down at her folded hands. "As I understand it, my lady, society allows widows far more latitude in that respect, do they not?"

"Undoubtedly, and what a great wagonload of hypocrites they are. A flock of bleating sheep in wolves' underclothes— that's what society is—"

"You mean, wolves in sheeps' clothing?"

"Yes, wolves! Ever eager to tear apart the first lamb that missteps. Ignore the lot of them." Honore waved her hand, dismissing the invisible offenders. "That's what I do."

Fiona shook her head. "Then, I confess, I am at a loss. You said Lord Wesmont acted badly. How? In what respect did he disappoint you?"

"The cowardly way he escaped." Countess Alameda stared out the carriage at the dismal landscape. She leaned closer to the window and blew a cloud of vapor over the glass.

A moment passed before she spoke again, almost to herself. "His wretched morals evidently swamped him. He couldn't bear the guilt, so he blamed you for the liberties he took—and then ran away." Honore touched the steamy glass with her finger and scrawled a jagged line cutting across the condensation. "Stupid man, he should have known you wouldn't have forced him into marriage."

Honore threw back her head and laughed. Then she leaned over and grasped the startled Fiona's hand in hers. "No doubt, by now he has come to his senses and realizes that he acted like the veriest cur, running away, like he did, barking insults. It was done completely without honor. Oh, my dear—the poor man. His precious *honor,* Fiona, just think of it."

Honore pulled Fiona's hand to her satin-covered bosom, and striking a pose, like a saint in prayer, she prophesied, "Take heart, Fiona, my child, no doubt, *he* is even more miserable than you are."

Chapter 5
Chasing Regrets

The Earl of Wesmont sat brooding in his library, every bit as miserable as Lady Alameda had predicted he would be. Raindrops streaked down his long windows as he stared blindly outside, not seeing the trees of his park, nor the birds playing in the wet grass. Instead, he saw Fiona's wet hair splayed out on the sand and her dark exotic eyes looking up at him. She haunted him. Her laughing specter teased him as she floated in yesterday's shimmering sunlight and water. He could not escape the image of her face flushed from his kisses as she lay unresisting in his arms. Equally haunting was the image of her stricken face after he had rebuffed her.

Tyrell rubbed his fingers against his temples and forehead and looked away from the window. He remembered Fiona's face when she was a young girl, twirling around in her party frock, looking up at him with those bewitching eyes of hers. It was a Yule party. He was home from Eaton, too old for the children and still too young to be truly interested in his parents' conversation.

The children gathered at the far end of the ballroom to play together and practice dancing. Tyrell remembered wandering between the two groups and finally sitting down near the children. Fiona stood tall for her age, a handsome child, not fussy and frilly like the other girls, but natural and athletic. She caught him watching her and had giggled without missing a step. She skipped merrily along, changing hands and dancing vivaciously to a country dance. He had laughed back at her.

When that dance finished he'd bowed with great ceremony before the little imp, and asked her for the next set. She, with equal flourish, executed a deep curtsy and rose with a teasingly solemn expression on her face. He partnered her for a minuet, and while stepping around her during the dignified turns, he teased her about the time she had forced her pony to jump the creek in his father's pasture and landing, both horse and rider, in the drink. She ignored his jibe and retorted, with some heat, that her horse was not a *pony*. Her mare was smallish perhaps, but assuredly not a pony. She'd been an adorable minx even then.

That seemed like a lifetime ago. Now, Fiona was a woman. The only human being who seemed capable of making him laugh or smile. For a few moments, in her company, he had forgotten about the hellish battlefields of Spain. When he was with her, life did not seem like one endless nightmare. And he had thanked her by humiliating her.

The Earl of Wesmont slammed his fist down on his desk. "Damn me for a coward!" He yanked the bell cord, and paced impatiently. Finally, he flung open the door of his study and yelled at the servants. "Get me that blasted valet my mother hired! Tell him to bring me something to keep this infernal rain from soaking me to the bone. I'm riding out. Now!"

The world smelled of fresh mud as he headed Perseus toward the upper meadow lake. A broad brim hat and an oilcloth kept out most of the moisture, but Tyrell felt confined and hot in it. With any luck at all, he thought, Fiona would be in her boathouse reading a book, or painting a picture of her precious lake enshrouded in clouds. He had to find her alone to apologize. It wouldn't do at all to sit down to tea in Lady Hawthorn's confounded drawing room and say, "Thousand pardons, Miss Hawthorn, for attempting to seduce you the other day."

He grimaced to himself. He most certainly had to find her alone. Fiona might not force him into marriage, but Lady Hawthorn wouldn't hesitate to make him see his duty. And marriage was out of the question. He'd suffocate altogether if anyone added one more ounce of responsibility onto his shoulders. He couldn't do it, no matter how badly his mother wanted him to produce an heir. No matter how far he'd crossed over the line with Fiona, marriage was unthinkable. He had nothing to give.

He found the boathouse deserted. There was no sign that she'd been there that day, no bread, or cheese on the table, no clothes hanging in the corner, just the blue swimming dress, and the dreary smell of dampness. Only rain had entered the old boathouse that day. Tyrell shut the door and climbed back onto Perseus. The big white horse bowed his head in the drizzle, and sniffed at the steamy air. They trudged dismally home together.

Tyrell did not give up. He circuited the upper meadow lake later that day, and twice again the next day. Finding the lake perpetually bereft of Fiona's presence he decided he must, after all, make a call to Lady Hawthorn's stuffy drawing room. Fiona may have decided, as he had advised her, that it was dangerous to stay alone at her beloved lake. Had she drowned herself? Hanged herself? Where was the dratted girl?

He sat on Lady Hawthorn's hot yellow sofa, drowning in a conflagration of garish paisley draperies, and several Chinese vases filled with gigantic, pink, ant-infested peonies.

"And where is Miss Hawthorn?" he asked, unable to circumvent any longer. When Lady Hawthorn answered him, he stared at her in disbelief.

Fiona was gone. Gone with her aunt, Lady Alameda. For pity sake, even he'd heard of the notorious Countess Alameda. What was Lady Hawthorn thinking, allowing Fiona to go away with a woman like that? And for a stay of an indefinite length? Gone! He should be relieved. Instead, Tyrell thought that his cravat might strangle him. He ran his finger around his neck.

Tiny beads of perspiration trickled into rivulets meandering down his chest, mixing with the starch from his shirt, producing a hot, itchy, irritating concoction.

Emeline chattered on like a bothersome parakeet. "They're staying at the Pavilion. Wouldn't that be lovely this time of year? To be near the sea and surrounded by all of the Prince Regent's distinguished guests."

"A rackety crowd," he mumbled and stared at a vase of peonies on the tea table in front of him. The flowers oozed sticky sweet sap, and if one more ant crawled out of one more big pink blossom, he was going to grab the whole disgusting mess of flowers and beat them to pieces on Lady Hawthorn's ridiculous yellow couch.

Tyrell rose suddenly. "Must go."

At their startled expressions, he looked wildly around the room. "Urgent business. Must go."

He scarcely remembered to bow before he stalked out of the room. He did have business, and he was fairly certain that that business was somewhere near the seashore.

Chapter 6
The Sea Air
Makes You Blind

Fiona gazed in amazement at the exotic minarets and domes of the Brighton Pavilion. Her aunt whispered in her ear, "Wait until you see the inside. It's the greatest collection of Chinese pandemonium in the kingdom. Most amusing."

Amusing perhaps, but as Fiona lay in bed that night her head ached. Could she be overwhelmed by all the gold-gilded pagodas and brightly colored peacocks, the red and blue silks, satins, and the elaborate Chinese wallpapers? During her Season, she'd heard an older matron warn a group of debutantes, "Too much stimulus will give a young lady the megrims." Fiona had thought it all a hum until now.

Now, her head throbbed, and a dull ache persisted in her chest. But when she closed her eyes it was not oriental carpets, or bamboo furniture she saw. Instead, the masculine lines of Tyrell's face, a flurry of remembered kisses assaulted her dreams, sending her soaring up to heaven. But inevitably, visions of his warm blue eyes turning to ice and the memory of his stinging words sent her spiraling down into a black pit of despair.

The next morning, she rose, as one does from a restless

sleep, having found no comfort in either waking or sleeping. She walked quietly into Honore's room.

"Good morning, dearest. Good heavens, child! What is that monstrosity you're wearing?" Her aunt looked her up and down, as if she were facing a leper draped in crusty rags.

"This? This is my best morning gown from my Season. I thought you would want me to wear my finest since we're at the palace."

"Lorraine!" Honore screamed for her abigail. "Lorraine!"

A buxom woman, no taller than a twelve-year-old girl, bustled into the room. Her frizzled brown topknot bobbed up and down as she dipped a quick curtsy to Honore.

Honore pointed dramatically at Fiona. "Get that abomination off my niece! Rip it to shreds. I tell you, if I ever see that hideous thing again I'll set fire to her. Do you hear me?" She turned on Fiona. "Lawks, girl! What do you think you are? A marzipan cake? All decorated up with layers of sugar and sprinkled with ribbons, and geegaws. And, mark me on this, white don't become you." She stopped railing and moved closer to Fiona, squinting as if she were inspecting a painting. "Good gracious, child, what happened to your face? A horse trample you in your sleep? Gad. You look positively *bruised* around the eyes. Don't tell me you've been crying again."

"No," she protested. "Of course not." Then, she meekly held out her arms while the dwarf-sized abigail circled around her, undoing tapes, and removing the offending gown. Lorraine held the offending garment out at arm's length as if it had a stench, and without a word she tore the dress in half. Fiona started at the ripping sound.

"I'm sorry, miss, but m'lady has the right of it. It were an awful concoction, it were."

Honore wheeled around. "Of course I'm right. Lorraine, you take the dressing of her. Mind you, no more of those ghastly debutante frills." Honore snatched half of the dress from Lorraine's hand and threw it out the open window.

"Find her something suitable from my wardrobe. And do it quickly, will you? I want to take a walk along the Steine. Later, take her up to North Street and see what you can purchase for her there. We'll just have to make do until we get back to London."

Honore sagged back against the wall, dropping her arms to her side and sighing. She instantly resembled a sad child. "Gad! How I miss Mattie. I've been gone too long this time." This last was said to no one in particular, and she gazed out the window.

Lorraine hustled her charge into the adjoining room and shut the door.

"Who is this Mattie?" asked Fiona.

"She's yer aunt's cook, miss."

"A cook? My aunt misses her cook?"

"Yes, miss. But you see, she's a sight more'n that. Afore she were the cook she were m'lady's nanny, and then she served as her maid. Mattie is her ladyship's favorite. Like kin, they are, except not really, because, of course, your aunt is a grand lady."

The maid babbled on as she held up a pastel blue gown next to Fiona's face, shook her head, and tossed it onto the bed. "And a fine Scottish cook she is. These days with all them Frenchie cooks making them rich sauces with snails and whatnot, it's a rare treat to have her cooking. An' she keeps a finger on everything what goes on in yer aunt's house. That's how the land lays at Alison Hall."

Lorraine rambled on until at last she held up a lemon yellow muslin with lace at the neck. "Ah, Just the thing."

Lorraine dressed her and tied the tapes. Fiona's eyes opened wide at the image staring back at her in the oval looking glass. She put her hand over her breast. "Surely, this gown is too daring. This lace, well, it's nearly transparent. And, the bodice is cut very low. I don't think—"

"Now, miss, mayhaps her ladyship dresses a bit more daring than a young lady like yerself. But this gown is perfectly respectable." She tugged at the bodice and looked at Fiona in the mirror.

"You are a wee bit fuller in the figure than her ladyship is at present, but bless me if you ain't a stunner. Yes, miss, you look a picture, you do. An' see here, here is a perfectly lovely pair of lace mittens to match the gown."

Lorraine slipped a fingerless lace glove onto Fiona's hand. The delicate mitten was made of the same sheer lace covering the bodice. Fiona looked into the mirror and cringed. The entire ensemble gave the illusion of clothing but revealed far more of her than it concealed.

Fiona cleared her throat. "Lorraine, is there, perchance, a shawl to go with this gown?"

"Yes, miss, as a matter of fact—" Lorraine rummaged through a trunk at her feet and produced the desired garment. She held up a shawl sewn out of the same vaporous lace as were the gloves and the neck of the gown.

Fiona lifted her eyes heavenward. "Lovely," she murmured, certain her father would horsewhip her if he ever saw her dressed so wantonly.

Honore opened the door and looked at her maid's handiwork.

"Quite presentable," she declared. "Well done, Lorraine. I daresay even Prinny would be favorably impressed. Too bad he is indisposed today. Now, let us walk down to the sea."

The *haute ton* gathered for their morning ritual in Brighton, a stroll along the Steine in their finery. They waved and nodded to one another, sized each other up, gossiped behind their gloves, and all the while the breeze coated them with briny moisture. Fiona licked her lips and tasted the sea air. A small droplet of saltwater trickled into her eye. She blinked and touched it gently, but it stung. She stopped walking as tears temporarily blinded her.

"It's this ocean air," Honore commiserated. "Burns the eyes. Have you a handkerchief in your reticule?"

They were engaged in a search for the said cloth when a masculine voice interrupted their ministrations.

"May I be of assistance?" He flourished a white handkerchief across his palm.

"Ah! Marcus. What an accommodating surprise you are."

Honore handed Fiona the proffered handkerchief, and the gentleman bent and kissed Honore on each cheek.

Fiona dabbed at her stinging eyes; nevertheless she could not fail to notice even with her blurred vision how exceedingly handsome he was, tall, with a Romanesque profile, strikingly outfitted in a blue morning coat, and his white shirt points set off his dark olive skin and raven black hair.

"And you, dear Mother, are looking as lovely as ever. Although, I nearly failed to recognize you. You are so"—he glanced pointedly at Honore's brilliantly colored hair—"so, very red. Or is it liver-colored?"

The word *Mother* jolted Fiona.

Her aunt thumped the tip of her umbrella against the walkway. "If you ever dare to address me as *Mother* in public again I shall hang you from the nearest tree by your cravat. Any fool can see you're far too old to be my son."

"My apologies." He bowed. "However, I protest, dear lady. Must you punish me because my father married a sinfully young bride?"

Honore shrugged. "Don't flirt with me, you young rapscallion. And pray tell, what are you doing in Brighton? You are supposed to be in Portugal tending to your estates. This is very bad of you, to suddenly appear where you are not expected."

He placed his hand over his heart. "You wound me, my lady. First, I am an 'accommodating surprise,' and now I am 'very bad.'"

"Oh fustian! Don't try to distract me, m'boy." She rapped his arm with her umbrella handle. "What are you doing here? Out with it!"

"At the moment, I am standing along the Steine with two

of the loveliest women in Brighton. And while you enjoy berating me, this silent beauty remains a delectable mystery. Do you mean for me to suffer longer or will you introduce me to your companion?" He bowed toward Fiona and swooped off his hat, grinning like a roguish schoolboy. Fiona could not help smiling back at him.

Honore's voice bit sharply through the damp air. "Don't be a popinjay, Marcus. She's not my companion—what do you take me for? An old woman who needs her hand held? She's m' niece."

"Better and better. *Por favor,* introduce me."

"Oh very well." She sniffed. "But, I had hoped you would never meet. Miss Fiona Hawthorn, this is my late husband's son, Lord Marcus Jose Alehandro Louis Alameda, the new Count de Alameda."

"I'm honored to meet you, my lord." She curtsied.

"Much too formal, Miss Hawthorn. You must call me Cousin Marcus, mustn't she, Honore?"

"Oh, call him whatever you like." Honore waved a gloved hand in the air. "Just beware, child—a greater rascal has never lived."

Marcus took Fiona's hand, smirked at the thin little lace mitten, and then caressed her fingers with his thumb before bowing over her hand. Still holding her hand, he leaned close enough to her cheek to whisper, "She wounds me to the core. Dear sweet cousin, I pray you, comfort me."

He smiled at her teasingly. Fiona felt heat rising in her cheeks and lowered her eyes under his impertinent gaze. He straightened to his full height, which was considerable, and turned to Honore. "My compliments, Honore, your niece is charming as well as lovely."

"Let go of her hand and stop toying with the girl." Honore poked him with her parasol handle. "Mind you, Marcus, step lightly in that direction. I mean to bring her out as if she were my own daughter."

Marcus's eyebrows shot up in momentary surprise. "You mean to give her a Season then?"

"No, I mean to do more than that. I want a daughter of my own. An heir to follow in my footsteps."

Marcus glanced irritably at Fiona, then back to Honore. "You raised me, did you not? Odd you should crave a child at this late date."

"Fah! You were half grown when you came to me. I daresay, you probably sprang from the womb full grown—never needed a mother." She laughed. "I warrant you'd have bit off the teat that suckled you."

Fiona stifled a gasp.

"And that makes us two of a kind, my lady." Marcus hissed the words under his breath, scarcely loud enough to be heard.

Honore thumped the ground with her umbrella and glared at him. "Mind your manners, boy. That insolent attitude disfigures your face. I'll choose whomever I want for an offspring. And furthermore, I won't have you sniffing about her skirts."

He lifted his chin and turned to Fiona. Callously, he raked his eyes up and down her body, assessing every detail of her face and figure. She felt naked and pulled the flimsy shawl to cover herself better. Finally, Marcus's shoulders relaxed, and he chuckled. "I never sniff skirts, my dear. And, I must hasten to tell you, Honore, this child is quite full-grown. You'll have to find another pup to raise."

He delivered this retort through a genteel smile, but Fiona could not help but observe the shrewdness glimmering in his eyes.

"You know nothing about it, Marcus. Aside from which, you very cleverly dodged my first question. Why aren't you in Portugal where you're supposed to be?"

He picked a minuscule particle of fuzz off his coat sleeve and flicked it away. "My dear Honore, Portugal is still in the throes of war. I found the situation there . . . er, rather uncomfortable for my taste."

He presented them with a disarming smile. "Come let us

talk of pleasanter things. Will you ladies be my guests for dinner this evening? I'm lodging at the Four Feathers which boasts of an almost tolerable cook."

"We are engaged for dinner with Prinny," Honore said, sniffing at the air.

"Ah! Excellent. I, too, am invited to the Pavilion later in the evening for the entertainment." He stepped toward Fiona, lifted her hand, and executed a salutatory bow. "Until then, dear cousin."

Fiona watched Lord Alameda walk away. She had never met anyone like him before. When she finally turned back to her aunt, she found Honore's eyes boring into her. Fiona bit her lip and looked at the ground.

"Humph." Honore straightened her back and walked on briskly. Fiona hurried alongside. "You, Fiona Hawthorn, are painfully green. And that young rascal you just met is much too tough a lesson to cut your teeth on. But"—Honore sighed, and slowed her pace—"I suppose, there's no help for it. He will, undoubtedly, remove to London with us when we return. Mark my words, child, be wary of your *cousin*."

"Yes, Aunt. But I'm certain there can be no danger in that quarter. Surely, a man like Lord Alameda surrounds himself with women of rank and beauty. What possible interest could he have in me?"

"What indeed! Don't be a fool. Listen here, my girl, let us have this perfectly clear between us. I refuse to be your *nursemaid,* your *governess,* or your *duenna!* I will not be relegated to the role of an old dragon. And don't you forget it." Honore rapped nervously against her thigh with her umbrella before she pointed it at Fiona. "You cannot afford to be ridiculously innocent. Not in my company, not with the society I keep. Do you hear me? You must guard yourself."

Fiona put her chin in the air. "I have always done so. Indeed, I would not have it any other way."

"Ha!" Honore rolled her eyes and raised her hands to heaven. "Oh very good, very good indeed." Her voice dropped menacingly low. "The greatest danger, my ignorant young beauty, is that you do not see the truth, *especially* the truth about yourself. You have that wild look about you, as if you ought to be standing out on a moor with the wind blowing through your hair."

Honore waved her hand about her head, simulating the wind, ignoring the curious glances of passersby. "Won't the poets just love that," she ranted on. "Nothing stirs a man to passion as quickly as a female who needs taming."

"But, Aunt, I haven't an untamed bone in my body. Quite the contrary, I've spent my entire life trying to do just what was expected of me and failing miserably."

"Yes, well . . ." Honore's skepticism was plain. "You aren't hunting for a husband, that much is clear. Dutiful tame girls hunt husbands. A man can smell a husband-hunter a mile away. So, he steers clear, unless he fully intends to step into her trap for reasons of his own. But naturally, if an eligible young woman isn't hunting *him, he* will hunt *her*. Men are like that."

"I cannot believe men are so predictable as that."

"And there's the danger, my dear. You don't have your moorings. You're all out to sea." Honore thrust her umbrella point in the direction of the ocean.

Fiona tried to muddle through her aunt's metaphors and extract some meaning from them. She finally gave up and shrugged.

"Silly child, you don't have a proper grasp on reality."

Fiona noted the irony of her aunt lecturing her on reality.

Honore stabbed her umbrella point against the boardwalk. "Pay attention! You've shut your eyes to your assets and magnified your failings." She smirked at Fiona. "If you go on like this, my dear, you'll stumble, and land smack in the mud on your face. Then society will delight in roasting you on a spit and serving you up with tea and toast."

Just as if they had been discussing the weather rather than Fiona's social demise, Honore smiled and took her arm. "Come, let us remove from this sea air. I declare, I am crusted over with salt, and wet to the bone. It cannot be good for my complexion."

Lord Wesmont glared at the host of the ship. "Blast it, man! I've been on the road for two days. I'm hungry and covered in filth. I need a room, and a bath."

"I haven't a room to spare. The Regent's birthday was a fortnight ago, and half of London is in Brighton." The host perused Tyrell's dusty boots and coat as if an unwanted rodent had just crawled into his inn. "Perhaps the Four Feathers across town can accommodate you, Mr. . . . ah—?"

"*Lord* Wesmont," Tyrell corrected the man. He took a deep breath and tried to control his temper. No pompous little innkeeper was going to get the best of him. Through clenched teeth he couched his order in as much civility as he could muster. "I'm willing to pay double, if you will kindly find me a room, sir."

The innkeeper sniffed and lifted his nose into the air. "A moment, my lord." He strutted away, and when he came back he opened the guest book and handed Tyrell the quill. "You understand, my lord, it is a very small room."

"Have a bath sent up. Hot water."

Tyrell's valet tromped through the doorway, lugging a valise in each hand, and looking more bedraggled than any other self-respecting valet in all of Britain. He and the innkeeper exchanged haughty long-suffering glances and came to an unspoken understanding before they both turned their resentful expressions on his lordship.

Annoyed with their collective displeasure, he barked orders at both of them. "Don't just stand there, man. You, Innkeeper, which way to our room?"

He realized he'd abused the poor valet's sensibilities, riding like a mad man to get here. But Tyrell had a blot on his conscience, and he intended to wipe it off. Hence, this insane pace. Fiona was here. And now, he had only to find her, apologize, and make certain her aunt wasn't corrupting her entirely. Then he would be free.

Two servants lugged a copper tub up the stairs and poured steaming kettles of water into it. Tyrell stripped off, and as he sank into the soothing water, it never occurred to him to ask himself exactly *what* he would be free of.

Chapter 7

Hens and Their Confounded Chicks

Marcus waited in the long gallery with the rest of the guests who had been invited for after-dinner entertainment. The smell of ducklings in orange sauce, stuffed pheasant, and veal in wine sauce, floated in the air. His stomach rumbled in response. Prince George's table rivaled any in the world for its elaborate dishes and plentiful removes, while Marcus had, out of economic necessity, to content himself with an inferior pork pie from the Four Feathers.

At long last, Prinny ushered his dinner guests into the large gallery. Marcus quickly spotted Fiona and Honore.

The entertainment proved to be the Regent himself circulating throughout the room, doing impressions of members of the *ton*. Marcus observed Fiona closely, watching as she laughed at Prinny's impression of Lord Byron. The Prince limped along and declared his love for three different women all in the same breath. While His Majesty was a very skilled mimic, Marcus would have preferred something more interesting, like one of his indoor shooting exhibitions or fireworks. As his interest waned, he covertly studied Honore and Fiona as they circulated about the room.

As the countess introduced Fiona to her acquaintances, she

made it clear that Fiona was not simply a niece she planned
to puff off on the marriage mart. She proclaimed Fiona her
understudy, her protégée, her new daughter. Women whispered behind their ornate fans and nodded discreetly.
Gentlemen bowed low and peered at Fiona speculatively.

Marcus overheard Lady Bessborough exclaim, "The
daughter you never had, eh?" Then she looked Fiona over as
if the chit were a plucked goose hanging in a market stall.
After a thorough inspection the lady declared to Fiona, "Quite
suitable."

"Just so." Honore whipped open her fan and created a
breeze for herself.

Marcus leaned back against a carved pagoda protruding
from the wall. He felt a vile mood coming on. Honore was
acting like a demented mother hen clucking around her newly
hatched chick. It nauseated him.

As the night wore on toward morning, Lady Everly sidled
up to him, expecting him to charm her. He tossed back more
champagne and brushed aside the lady's ostrich plumes when
they blocked his view of his quarry. Consequently, Lady
Everly went away in a huff. He shrugged and snatched
another flute of champagne from a passing footman's tray.

Finally, Prinny retired for the evening, and his guests were
free to leave. Marcus made his way toward Honore and Fiona.

Honore rapped him with her fan. "Where have you been
all evening, Marcus? I saw you draped against the wall like
a figure in the woodwork, but—"

"Engaged all night, m'dear. I hope you will allow me to
make up for my neglect. Perhaps, you and your niece would
like to walk out on Brighton Pier in the morning." He smiled
with a graciousness he did not feel.

"It's morning now, Marcus, and I intend to sleep through
the rest of it."

"Surely, Miss Hawthorn will not want to miss the ocean
view in morning light?"

The chit actually looked to Honore for approval, just as a dutiful daughter ought. Marcus felt his smile pulling thin.

Honore shrugged. "Oh, very well, you may go. Take my maid with you. And now, don't bother me anymore. I have a headache and want to find my bed."

Marcus strode purposefully out of the ballroom and away from Prinny's noisy Pavilion. He marched toward the sea and out onto a quiet weathered dock. His boots beat a steady rhythm on the boards of the long pier. A crescent moon hung low in the sky, and clouds flirted across its face, sinking the world into a devilish dancing darkness.

Marcus walked to the end of the long-abandoned shipping dock, turned, and carefully paced three strides back. He thumped on the boards until he found one that made a dull sound, as if giving way to age and rot, and sat down beside it. Drawing a knife out from his boot, he plunged the blade viciously into the board, and wormed it back and forth until he punctured the weathered wood.

"How dare she?" he asked the empty pier. "How dare she push her way into Honore's life. Honore's protégée, indeed! And what, precisely, have I been all these years?"

He grumbled on, while chiseling at the pier. "Send me off to Portugal, will she? Consign me to the heap of rubbish that damned French lunatic made of my estates."

Images of his ravished home peppered his thoughts. His castle, looted and burned, was scarcely fit for peasants to live in. But, peasants *were* living in the ruins, skulking in the rubble like frightened rabbits in a warren. He'd taken one look at his estates, sickened, and returned to England. And now, his expectations from Honore were in danger of being stolen. "Usurped, by a backwater chit from nowhere! I won't have it."

He plunged the knife into the board again and sawed with a vengeance. The gray light preceding dawn began to illuminate the horizon. Marcus's legs dangled off the edge of the pier where he sat chiseling the planks. He leaned over to judge how far down it was to the water, and reckoned it to be nearly thirty feet.

"I'll wager Honore's pup dies instantly from the fall." Vapor wraiths slithered up from the sea like warning ghosts from hell. Marcus ignored them and thrust his knife into the rotting wood again, continuing his work.

Chapter 8
The Plunge

"Cousin Fiona"—Marcus lifted her hand to his lips—"my dear, you look delicious."

Fiona drew her hand away and glanced at him skeptically. He looked positively ragged. "Lord Alameda, perhaps you are too tired for a walk this morning. I should be just as pleased to see the pier another morning."

He cleared his throat and smiled, "No. No, today's the day for it." He whirled around. "Where's your maid? We must be off."

Lorraine, their earnest little chaperone, bustled into the room, shawl and bonnet in place, and they set off.

"I know I promised to take you to Brighton Pier today," he began. "But you realize the royal pier is purely ornamental. After some consideration, I thought you might prefer to see one of the actual shipping wharves. Of course, not one that is still in service. But there is one pier in particular that extends far out into the sea. I'm told the view from the end is breathtaking. I've even heard it said that from the end of it one might even see whales spouting."

"Whales? Right here in the English Channel?"

"So, I've heard." His tone was not convincing, and Fiona wondered if he was simply teasing her.

"Well then, that would, indeed, be a wondrous sight. You are right, I would much rather see a real wharf."

"I knew you would." He tucked her arm in his, looking

quite pleased with himself. Somewhat like a cat who had just cornered a mouse, which made Fiona wonder precisely what her cousin might be up to.

The ocean was majestic. The sun had already burned off the mist and presented Brighton with a dazzling morning. The air smelled fresh, and the sun warmth felt pleasant on their backs.

"Tell me, cousin, what did you make of our Prince Regent?"

She smiled up at him, then shook her head slightly and chuckled. "He isn't at all what I expected."

Marcus regaled her with tales of the Prince's idiosyncrasies until they nearly reached the end of the creaking old pier. A warm breeze ruffled their clothing. Fiona turned her face to the soft wind and enjoyed the feel of it against her skin. "Is that not the most wonderful sensation, wind, warmth and water combined in such perfect proportions. I would love to live near the sea, wouldn't you?"

She turned to find him standing closer than she realized and wearing the oddest expression, he looked almost sorrowful and yet there was something else in his demeanor she couldn't quite distinguish.

It startled her when he reached out to tuck back a strand of her hair fluttering beside her cheek. The back of his fingers brushed against her cheek. "Such a pity," he said softly.

"What do you mean?"

"So young. That wild sweetness . . . really ought to be tasted before . . . a shame to waste—" He leaned toward her mouth as though he meant to kiss her. Fiona was completely befuddled. Surely he wouldn't. But his mouth was mere inches away from hers when Honore's maid started coughing wildly.

Fiona turned away from Marcus, blushing, but he put a restraining hand on her arm.

"Pardon me, miss, but I think you should come over here with me." Lorraine went to the edge of the dock and motioned for Fiona to join her. "Well, bless my soul, would you just look at that! Look there, Miss Fiona! It must be one of them whale spouts his lordship was talking about. Come an' see if it isn't. Look there. Way out there." She hopped up and down and pointed at the ocean.

Marcus looked down in horror at the plank the lunatic maid was bouncing on and shouted, "No!"

"Oh yes, there is a whale, I tell you. Come see for yerself, miss. If you was to look out this waaaaaaay . . ."

The plank splintered and broke just as he had planned it should, but the wrong female plummeted into the sea. Her scream seemed to last forever before he heard the splash. He walked to the ragged edge of the boards he had so carefully chiseled into a weakened state, and watched as the maid sank under the dark water far below.

"Wretched bad luck!" he muttered and glanced back at Fiona.

To his amazement, her gloves and slippers lay on the pier and she was removing her bonnet. She handed it to him and stepped to the edge of the boards. His mouth still hung open as she jumped.

"Wait!" he shouted.

There was an answering splash as she hit the water far below. Leaning over the edge, Marcus saw Fiona's head come up from the waves. She began paddling toward the maid, who had resurfaced and started screeching like a cat in a bathtub.

"The chit can swim," Marcus declared to no one in particular. People ran out onto the pier to see what was happening. A crowd began to gather around his shoulders. Then he pointed at Fiona and began to laugh hysterically. "Honore's wretched pup can swim."

Fiona struggled to get her bearings in the rolling motion of the ocean. A wave lifted her up and carried her away from the pier. Her eyes opened wide with surprise, but she quickly adjusted and began making long even strokes toward the panicking maid. She swam as fast as she could, and prayed Lorraine could stay afloat until she reached her.

Suddenly Lorraine's head bobbed to the surface directly in front of her. Eyes bulging the frantic maid thrashed at the water, sputtering and gasping for air. She lunged wildly at Fiona, wrapping her arms around Fiona's neck in a death grip. They sank under the salty suffocating water.

Fiona tugged at the arms strangling her, but she couldn't escape. As she struggled, they sank deeper and deeper. In desperation, Fiona bit down as hard as she could into Lorraine's forearm. The suffocating arms jerked apart. Fiona slipped away and circled up behind Lorraine. Grabbing her by the hair, Fiona made for the surface.

She came up underneath the pier. Waves slapped and pounded against the huge pilings. Fiona grasped the nearest pillar with her free arm. Coated with green slime, it was far too slippery and too big for her to get a good grip. She searched for anything else to hold on to. The crossbeams were up too high. There was nothing except the big pillars. She wrapped her legs and her free arm around the piling. She wouldn't be able to hold on for long, but it gave her a moment's respite. She held Lorraine's head as high out of the water as she could. Lorraine coughed and sputtered and then turned, frantically clawing and trying to grab Fiona again.

Fiona jerked on Lorraine's hair.

"No!" She shouted over the noise of the waves. "Listen to me! Or we'll both die."

The little woman's eyes flickered with a faint light of sanity.

"Lie back in the water and try to hold your breath. I am going to pull you to shore." Fiona glanced toward the beach. It looked so far away. Lorraine darted a glance in the same direction. Her eyes opened wide with panic. Fiona smelled the stench of vomit rising in the maid's throat, and looked away.

The next wave rolled toward them and she knew it would knock them off the piling.

"Lie back!" she shouted. The wave hit. Fiona plunged through the roller, towing Lorraine by the hair until they were prone in the water. It took her a few moments before she could start side-stroking properly. Then she put her arm around Lorraine's neck, trying to keep the woman's head above water. She laboriously swam toward the shore. Their clothing billowed and dragging against the water, slowing them down. Breakers pulled them under instead of carrying them forward. The salt burned her eyes and nose. Still, she swam through the waves, thinking only of reaching the shoreline. Lorraine had stopped struggling. She was either already drowned, Fiona thought, or she was cooperating admirably. Fiona kept swimming.

At long last, she heaved herself and Lorraine onto the beach and collapsed. A throng of cheering onlookers ran toward them. Fiona glanced up, surprised to see such a crowd, and then flopped facedown on the beach, exhausted. A cry went up amongst the spectators to send for a doctor.

Fiona lay in the sand, draped in seaweed, her tattered gown clinging to her body, her straggled hair filled with sediment. She didn't care. Her only interest was in breathing, heaving air in and out of her aching lungs. Vaguely, she registered the sound of Lorraine retching and moaning on the beach next to her. The people stepped aside as a shout went up.

"He's coming."

"Make way for the sawbones!"

"Right here, Doc. This maid here fell from the pier an' like to drown if it weren't for that lady there."

"Miss, are you—"

Fiona waved him away. "Her. Take care of her."

"You must both come to my surgery. Saltwater in the lungs can cause pneumonia, or consumption, not to mention—"

She waved him away again, and he went to tend the maid. Fiona wanted to be left alone while she regained her breath.

A moment later, she noticed the toes of two very polished boots standing directly in front of her face. The owner of these boots squatted down and pulled a string of seaweed from her hair. He gently brushed the sand from her cheek.

She lifted her head and squinted up into the face of Lord Wesmont. "It can't be." She moaned and let her head flop back down onto the sand.

"Good morning, Miss Hawthorn. I thought that just might be you." He chuckled. Obviously pleased with himself.

Chapter 9
An Ogre in Brighton

Fiona was too tired to struggle when Tyrell deftly picked her up and began carrying her away from the beach, apparently following the surgeon to his house. But by the time they reached the boardwalk she felt much better.

Fiona looked up at Lord Wesmont's stern profile as he carried her. "I'm quite capable of walking now."

"I don't doubt it."

"Then, you should set me down." She intentionally didn't remove her arm from around his neck. There was no hurry.

"I can't oblige you on that score."

"Why not? The seawater is ruining your coat."

He shifted her in his arms and, finally, looked at her. "Because, Miss Hawthorn, what little clothing you had on is now torn to shreds and plastered to your lovely body with the very seawater you mentioned. Make no mistake, my dear, your elusive charms no longer elude me. And I have no desire to expose them to this mob you have attracted."

Fiona felt herself turning red under his gaze.

He took a quick breath. "Where did you find this mockery of a gown anyway? Under the best of conditions it is scandalous apparel for a young lady. Your father would horsewhip you if he saw—"

"You needn't lecture me. I thought the same thing myself. But my aunt insists it is eminently suitable. My own wardrobe has been relegated to the trash bin. Apparently, my gowns reminded her too much of baked goods, so she had the maid rip them up."

Tyrell took a deep breath, obviously struggling not to lose his temper. "I cannot fathom your stepmother entrusting you to Countess Alameda's care. I have been on the Continent for nearly five years, but even I have heard of her reputation."

"And it disturbs you?"

He merely raised an eyebrow.

It occurred to her she hadn't asked him the most important question. "Why are you here?"

He didn't answer.

"In Brighton? So far from home."

He still didn't respond, but she noted that the stubborn muscles of his jaw buckled even tighter. That pleased her, and the more wicked side of her character decided to see if she couldn't vex him just a little more.

She toyed with his lapel with her free hand as if she were an innocent child. "I can scarcely believe you're here because you crave the Prince's society. You would hardly find the peace and solitude you're so fond of, here in Brighton. Especially, not at this time of year." She tapped a finger against her lips. "Hmm. No. I doubt you're interested in his noisy parties. Unless, you've suddenly developed a love of dancing?" She smiled coquettishly and waited for a reply.

His stern countenance assured her none was coming.

"No? Well, of course, there are any number of unattached females here. Perhaps you're here hunting for a wife?" She wriggled up, trying to get a good look at his face. "Oh, but my wits must have gone wandering. Aren't you the same fellow who would rather be hung at dawn than get legshackled?"

He came to a short halt and exhaled sharply. "You are an impertinent young woman, aren't you? I've half a mind to drop you on the street and go about my business."

"I wonder why you haven't?"

"Devil if I know."

She suppressed her pleasure at having annoyed him. "And what business might you be going about?"

He exhaled again and continued down the wooden walkway. "Very well, if you must know why I'm here, I came to apologize to you. I owed you that much for my behavior at the lake, but now I expect I have paid even the balance sheet."

She jerked her arm from around his neck and glared at him.

"Paid even the balance sheet? How typically presumptuous of you—"

Just then, they stepped through the doorway of the surgery. The doctor instructed Lord Wesmont to set Fiona in a chair and then shooed him out to the sitting room. She crossed her arms tightly over her chest and smoldered.

The physician hovered behind her, thumping on her back. "Just as I thought. Your breathing is much too rapid and shallow. Lung fever—that's what comes of swallowing seawater."

Lorraine moaned from her position on a pallet.

"I assure you, Doctor, I am quite all right. Do attend to my maid."

Marcus burst into Honore's apartments at Brighton Pavilion, outraged.

"She dove off the pier! Swims like a confounded duck. Rescued that idiot maid of yours who fell into the drink. What sort of niece do you have—goes around diving in after servants?"

"Sit down, Marcus. Have a drink. Explain yourself."

He dropped into a chair and swirled a shot of brandy in the bottom of the glass she handed him. "Hardly the thing for a well-bred lady to do, is it?" He gulped the contents of his glass. "Should've let the maid drown. But no, your young filly jumps in after her and pulls the wretched creature to shore."

Honore sat down and stared at him. "Where are they now? Surely you didn't abandon them on the beach?"

"No. No. Some nob was there shouting orders like he was a demmed general. He had the situation well in hand."

"Who was he? You left my niece in the hands of a stranger?"

"For pity sake, Honore. I know a gentleman when I see him. It was Lord Somebody-or-other. Seemed to know the gel."

"Lord *who*? Exactly."

"Don't take that tone with me, m'dear. I'm not a schoolboy you can take to task. It was Lord Westerly or Wesmont—something like that." He snatched the brandy decanter and refilled his glass.

"So, Wesmont ran her aground already, did he?" Honore chuckled and leaned back in her chair.

Marcus watched her over the rim of his glass. "At any rate, the chit was covered stem to stern with seawater and sand and Lord *Whoever-he-was* carried her around like an infant. And I might add, *your niece* didn't put up much of a fuss. Naturally, I wouldn't have ruined my coat for a snip of girl who doesn't know how to conduct herself properly."

"Where do you suppose he took her?"

"I neither know nor care." Marcus caught her disapproving stare. "He probably hauled her off to a surgery. There was an annoying little sawbones trailing behind his high-and-mighty-lordship, stuttering out a dire prognosis of lung fever."

Honore chuckled, "Oh, Fiona will be well enough once she gets dry. Of that I'm certain. Swims like a fish. But perhaps I ought to retrieve her from the physician."

"Yes, well, unfortunately your maid is no fish. Last I saw, she was a most interesting shade of gray. Bound to feel miserable. Better for everyone if Fiona had let her drown. Really, Honore, how can you countenance the chit's behavior?"

"If my maid had drowned I'd have your head on a platter. Where do you imagine I'd find an abigail half as agreeable as Lorraine?"

Marcus sniffed. "Really, Honore, you ought to be more concerned about the scandal your niece has created, than about your silly twit of a maid."

Honore snapped a shortcake in half and popped it in her mouth. She waved her hand, signaling him to silence. "What scandal? You're kicking up the dust over nothing."

"Well, it's all over Brighton by now. Prinny is bound to hear about it."

"More than likely." She pushed a crumb from the corner of her mouth. "If he hasn't, I'll make certain he does."

"Whyever for?"

"I should think it would be rather obvious. The girl is a heroine. He'll probably give her a medal, or a knighthood, or some such." Honore popped the other half of the shortbread into her mouth.

"Fah. You are all about in your head. Women can't be knights."

"Pity."

"More'n likely he'll send the pair of you packing for making spectacles of yourselves."

Honore laughed. "Balderdash! You mistake him. Our Regent enjoys a little excitement, especially when it reeks of bravado. He'll admire her for it. Mark my words. It's the best thing that could've happened to her."

Marcus shook his head. "Eccentric behavior is one thing coming from you, Honore, but the *beau monde* will not tolerate it coming from a débutante."

"Ha! They tolerated it well enough coming from you."

"I ain't a deb."

"No, but you're a foreigner."

"I *am not* a foreigner!" He thumped his glass down on the side table. "You know perfectly well my mother was English. I was raised in England—for pity sake. *You* raised me. I do wish you would stop using that tired old quip when you run out of arguments. We both know Fiona has overextended her credit. Nothing for it, but to send her back to the country where she belongs."

"Nonsense, can't you see, she's wasted in the country. Let Prinny decide the matter. Apart from that, I have no doubt that her credit can stand today's adventure and tenfold more." Honore stood up and shook out her skirts. "After all, she's not a débutante, she's *my* protégée."

"So, she is." Marcus seethed. "I nearly forgot."

"Will she recover?" Fiona leaned next to the doctor while he fussed with a listening cone at Lorraine's back.

"Yes, as nearly as I can tell through this wet dress," he answered sourly. "Provided she doesn't get pneumonia, or lung fever, or consumption. I'll need to observe her more thoroughly."

A commotion sounded in the hallway, and her aunt burst into the room, with Lord Wesmont standing behind her.

"There you are my dear!" She swished across the floor and laid her gloved hand against Fiona's cheek. "I've been worried half out of my mind. Marcus told me the most alarming story—and now I see it is all too true. How dreadful for you. Come, dear, I'll take you back to the palace. My carriage is just outside the door."

The physician cleared his throat. "I'd advise against it, m'lady. They've suffered a terrible trauma and I must watch them both for lung fever. Especially your maid, here."

Honore's laughter trilled through the room. "La, sir. I'm certain they are both quite fit." She dug into her reticule and produced a gold coin. "Here you are. Now, come along, my dear." She motioned for Fiona.

The doctor waved his hand in Lorraine's direction. "But your maid, just take a look at her, she shouldn't be moved."

Honore glanced back over her shoulder. "Come along, Lorraine."

The bedraggled woman heaved herself off the cot and shuffled after Lady Alameda.

Tyrell leaned against the doorframe, his jaw flexing, and an unreadable expression on his face. Honore breezed past him without so much as a nod, and Lorraine slogged after her.

Fiona stayed back and stopped beside him. She lifted her chin and in tight whispered tones said, "Consider your debt paid, my lord."

Tyrell took no pains to guard his volume. "Listen, my little seaweed princess, I'll decide when my debts are paid."

"Once again, how very presumptuous of you."

"Undoubtedly."

"And irritating."

"As you say." He brushed sand from his stained coat sleeve.

"Overbearing, and detestable—" She huffed in an unladylike fashion.

"Probably." The corners of his mouth curled up in an evil smirk. He was obviously pleased with himself.

Her hands knotted into fists. "You are truly the most arrogant, ungracious—" She couldn't lay her tongue on a suitably degrading word, and the one she finally found rang out sounding childish and weak. "Ogre!"

"What?" His eyebrows shot up in mock alarm. "You mean, one of those big ugly hairy creatures with the bumpy noses?" He wriggled his fingers by his face and then slid one finger down his straight patrician nose. "I think not—"

"Oh yes!" She stepped away from him. "A great loathsome ogre. And I never want to see you again."

She mustered up as much dignity as she could while dripping seaweed and saltwater across the floor, and flounced away to her aunt's carriage.

Chapter 10

Treason Is A
Hanging Offense

The next evening Fiona stood mesmerized in the Pavilion. A hundred candelabras created a brilliant light in the Prince Regent's huge ballroom. His band, from the Tenth Light Dragoons, played an Italian rococo melody, one of the Prince's favorite pieces of music. Guests stood together in small circles along the gilded walls and in the ornate vestibules, looking like brightly painted birds clustered in golden nests, ladies wore purple and pink plumes, colorful shimmering silks, and on their arms and necks sparkled jewels of every kind.

His Royal Highness moved around the room, greeting his guests and amusing each group with *on-dits* and witticisms.

Honore nudged Marcus. "See how he does not limp so heavily this evening. His gout must not be bothering him tonight. How lucky for Fiona that His Highness is in a good humor. Would you care to wager on her success?"

Fiona looked at them, annoyed that they spoke of her as if she weren't standing beside them.

"Fa. He's not feeling the gout because he's foxed. Look at the way he lurches about. He's one hiccup away from passing out. If he makes the connection, he'll censor her, see if he doesn't. Whoever heard of a lady diving in to rescue a servant? Demmed peculiar, that's what it is. He can't like it."

"We shall see." Honore smiled.

Fiona did not share her aunt's optimism. She guessed Marcus probably had the right of things, but still, one could hope that the highest personage in the land would not send her packing in shame. Perhaps it would all escape his notice.

Prince George, decorated like an ornate red-and-white ship, drifted ever closer to their party. Beaded with sweat, he dabbed at his florid brow with a handkerchief and then stuffed it into the lace at his sleeve. Clearly, it cost him a great deal of discomfort just to travel from guest to guest. Yet, Fiona observed, he remained animated and jolly. Everyone smiled and laughed at his anecdotes, and seemed genuinely amused.

When at last he came and stood before them, flushed and beaming, Marcus bowed low. Fiona's knees nearly failed her, as she and Honore sank into deep curtsies. The Prince tut-tutted, and commanded them to rise. "Lady Alameda, a story has reached our ears. A story about this niece of yours." He waggled his ringed fingers at Fiona.

Here it comes, Fiona thought and swallowed hard, struggling to keep her breathing regular, as the Prince of England prepared to give her a set-down.

"We must know. Is it true? Did she jump off a pier to rescue a mere maidservant?"

"Oh yes, Your Highness," Honore gushed. "It is true. The woman who fell into the sea was my own personal dressier. My niece, knowing how much I rely upon the woman, did not hesitate. She dove into the crashing waves, and pulled my abigail by the hair all the way back to shore, saving the woman from certain death. I don't have to tell Your Highness how much it would have distressed me to think of my poor devoted servant being eaten by fish in a watery grave."

The Regent, who obviously enjoyed a good story, nodded sympathetically. Then he lit up as if struck by a brilliant flash of inspiration. "What!" he declared, "What. What. The chit is a hero!"

He looked around himself with delight. Other guests clustered around them. Assured of an audience, he launched into a loudly broadcast speech. "I daresay not many men would have dared such a brave rescue."

He beamed at the crowd, then turned and reached for Fiona's hand. His corset creaked as he leaned forward and Fiona feared he would topple over onto her. Before she knew it, he had her hand in his and had lifted it up into the air. "Yet, here it is, gentlemen. This young gel rescued Lady Alameda's maid from the sea and has set us all a brave example."

He put his hand over his heart and turned to her dramatically. "Oh, that We had been there. We would have leapt into the sea and saved the woman m'self."

Fiona, recognizing the climax to the Prince's dramatic moment, lowered herself into a curtsy. Thus, she honored him and simultaneously left him to bask in the glow of center stage.

The guests, as if on cue, began to murmur and exclaim over the Prince's bravery, his amazing courage, and his equanimity in any situation.

Marcus did not comment other than to let out an exasperated puff of air. Fiona noted that the corners of Honore's mouth were twitching up and down, obviously stifling a loud guffaw, instead her aunt blurted, "A more heroic monarch never lived!"

To which, other guests added, "Huzzah!" The Prince Regent basked in the praise of his guests. Beaming, he gestured for Fiona to rise. "We would be pleased to dance the first dance with our brave Miss Hawthorn."

"I am deeply honored, Your Highness." But really, she was not. The truth was, she wanted to throw herself at his feet and beg him not to make her dance.

But Fiona had the good sense not to throw herself on His Majesty's royal feet and beg. So, the Prince waved aside the crowd, and with regal pomp and a great many huffs and puffs escorted her to the middle of the ballroom floor. The guests fell silent as the Prince raised his hand to signal the conductor of the Tenth Light Dragoons' band.

"A waltz," he shouted. "We shall have a waltz."

"Oh, dear," Fiona murmured.

The music started to play, and the Prince Regent, with surprising agility, whirled her across the polished floor. Rivulets of sweat rolled down his jowls, while Fiona tried her best to produce a smile that didn't betray her teetering nerves. Glancing with feigned casualness over the Prince's shoulder and out at the guests, her attention snapped sharply into focus when she caught sight of a familiar face with ice blue eyes staring back at her.

Tyrell! Her feet faltered.

Prince George sputtered. "What? What? Just follow me, m'dear. Nothing to it. All be over soon enough."

Fiona tried to compose herself. Where was the bravery the Prince had admired in her? Gone. Her knees turned to jelly and her wits to mincemeat. What was she doing on a dance floor with the Prince of England? And why must the most aggravating man in all England be standing across the floor watching her?

The Prince wobbled precariously as Fiona endeavored to correct her graceless footing.

"Here now." He wheezed. "All this attention is unnerving you. We can't have that." He waved his hand at his guests along the wall, signaling them to join in the waltz.

As he waved his hand, his silken handkerchief slid out of its hiding place in his sleeve and dropped to the polished floor beneath his feet. Time seemed to slow down to an unreal pace. Fiona watched, helplessly frozen, as his shiny white kerchief fluttered down, and gracefully slid underneath the toe of Prince George's shoe just as he stepped down. She knew, in that moment, which stretched into an agonizing eternity, what would surely happen next.

The Prince's foot slipped out from under him, and his rotund body crashed into her with such force that Fiona was knocked off her feet and hurled backward, where she landed in someone's arms. The Prince Regent finished his spectacular somersault, a great mass of waving arms and flailing feet, and fell, with a great thud, landing on his back on the ballroom floor.

Fiona caught her breath and looked up uncertainly into Marcus's astonished face. "Thank you for catching me."

"I had nothing to do with it, I assure you. Not every day a young lady comes flying into your arms." He pulled her to a standing position and patted her shoulder sympathetically. "Well, my girl, I'd say you've done it now. If diving off the pier in your morning gown didn't put you in disfavor, nearly killing our monarch on the dance floor ought to do the trick. You'll be demmed fortunate, if they don't hang you."

Fiona panicked and fled from the room. She ran out into the foyer and found her way into a small anteroom, where she huddled in the corner to have a good cry. If she could have crawled under the oriental carpet to hide, she would have. Everything had gone wrong. Tears streamed down her face so hard she could scarcely catch her breath. Maybe the Prince would hang her for attempted murder. Then, at least, her life would come to a merciful close.

After what seemed like only a handful of minutes, Aunt Honore stormed into the room with Marcus close behind. "Fiona! What is the meaning of this? How dare you run away like a sniveling coward."

"Because I am a coward!" Fiona wiped angrily at her tears. "Perhaps you didn't notice, but just now"—she pointed in the direction of the ballroom—"I nearly killed the Prince Regent. I have it on good authority, my lady, that murdering heads of state is a hanging offense. Naturally, no one would dream of chopping your head off, but I assure you I am not immune to charges of treason or—"

Honore stomped her foot and planted her hands firmly on

her hips. "Don't be ridiculous. Prinny is fine. He said so himself, not a moment ago, after he had enough of everyone gushing over him. Lady Bessbourgh offered to make a garlic and mustard poultice for his poor head. He recovered with miraculous speed. Popped up and promptly took over conducting the musicians. He has everyone bounding around the room like a gaggle of mad rabbits trying to keep pace with that dreadful German galop he's playing."

Marcus shook his head and attempted to correct Honore. "No, my dear Honore, you see, *geese* are found in *gaggles*, not rabbits. It's a *warren* of rabbits. Or a *down* of hares."

Honore stamped her foot again. "What are you prattling on about, Marcus? He has them jumping up—not down. Bouncing around like a pack of antelopes."

"A herd of ante—oh, never mind." Marcus shrugged and rolled his eyes.

Honore flicked open her fan and cooled her face. "In any event, by morning Prinny won't even remember falling down."

"Care to wager on that?" Marcus studied his fingernails and smiled archly at Honore.

Tears recommenced running down Fiona's cheeks. "Marcus is right. I'll catch the next mail-coach back to Timtree Corners. I should never have come."

Honore grabbed Fiona's chin and forced her to look up. Her gloved fingers held her firmly. "No you won't. Dry up, child. I will not tolerate this missish behavior. Now, you simply must reappear in that ballroom with your chin up and your eyes dry. I'll not have you skulking in this room like an ordinary criminal. Furthermore, if you're determined to be a criminal, put some backbone into it."

Fiona blinked at her aunt. Honestly, the woman was a complete bedlamite sometimes.

"Good. See here, I can tell you are already beginning to collect yourself." Honore patted Fiona's cheek and stepped back. "We'll return to the ballroom and all will be well. Marcus will partner you for the next set."

Marcus cast Honore a wounded look. "So, now I'm to be sacrificed, am I?"

Honore squinted, pursed her lips, and glared at Marcus.

He smirked and cocked an eyebrow defiantly. "Really, Honore, you ought to give some consideration to my reputa—"

A man standing in the doorway cleared his throat. "I would be pleased to accompany Miss Hawthorn for the next set."

Fiona moaned. Just when she thought things couldn't get any worse, the devil would walk in.

Honore raised her quizzing glass to inspect the interloper. "Hmm. Lord Wesmont, isn't it?"

"Make him go away," Fiona muttered.

Her aunt chuckled. "What's that, dearest? You don't know what to say." Honore let her quizzing glass drop down and swing on a velvet cord pinned to her bosom as she extended her hand to Tyrell. "My niece is speechless. I accept your offer on her behalf."

Honore turned around, clasped Fiona's shoulders, and pulled her to her feet. "There, my dear, you look almost normal again. That pout is quite fetching. Although, you might contrive to look slightly less willful, and a trifle more penitent. Come, take Lord Wesmont's arm."

Fiona glared at her aunt. "I cannot go back. Surely, my eyes are still puffy and red."

"Oh, a little red becomes you." Honore tugged her forward, took Fiona's hand, and set it firmly onto Tyrell's sleeve. "Now go. You really must do this, Fiona. I insist upon it. No protégée of mine is allowed to behave like a timid doe afraid to return to the watering hole. Show some spine, dear. Pride. Yes, that's it."

Fiona looked Tyrell squarely in the face, holding her chin in the air in an effort to restore some of her dignity. "You needn't do this, my lord."

"Of course, he must." Honore prodded them toward the door.

Tyrell's voice had a patient, soothing quality. "I want to do it. Aside from that, your aunt is right. It's much better if you face the situation here and now."

"You see, Fiona. Such a sensible fellow."

"I'm not your responsibility, Lord Wesmont. As I told you yesterday, I've absolved you of your obligation."

Honore clucked her tongue. "*Absolved*? Fiona, really, you talk as if you're the pope. Let the man alone." She maneuvered them into the ballroom like children being herded into a classroom.

Tyrell covered Fiona's hand with his own and held it there. "I'm your neighbor, and your friend. Do you recall the time I pulled you out of the hedgerow after your pony threw you?"

"Not a pony. My mare. And I was only ten then, my lord—"

"Ah, but you didn't expect me to leave you tangled in the briars, did you?"

"Well, I hardly think this—"

"And did I not pluck thorns and burrs from your hair and clothing."

Fiona winced, remembering. "Yes, and the whole time you rang a peal over my head for attempting to jump a hedge my mare was not up to."

Tyrell half chuckled. "Well, she was a very small mare. Come now. I wasn't as severe as all that."

She chanced a wary smile at him. "No? Didn't you punish me by making me hold my skirt out so you could fill it with raspberries."

"Ah that. Well, who could have known you would land in such a ripe patch of berries. In another day, the birds would have devoured the entire lot."

"Yes, but I was covered with scratches and bruises from my fall. Hardly ideal circumstances for berry picking."

"You seem to forget that you feasted on those berries as eagerly as I did. In fact, you went home happy and with a bright red stain around your lovely lips." He looked at her lips, and an embarrassing heat crawled up his neck and into his cheeks.

Warmth flooded her own cheeks in answer. She looked away and realized that her aunt had maneuvered them to the far end of the ballroom, near the musicians, right beside where the Prince Regent stood directing the band with highly exaggerated movements. The lively galop ended, and he turned around to take a bow for conducting the music.

The dancers were so winded they could scarcely clap, but Lady Alameda made a great racket with her applause.

Prinny smiled. "Ah, Lady Alameda! You and your delightful niece have returned. Good! Now, I think, we shall have a nice sedate minuet." Belying his promise of tranquility, he ordered everyone in a booming voice, "Dance! Everyone dance!" And although the minuet is usually performed by one couple at a time, everyone danced.

Tyrell led Fiona to the floor and held her hand up as he circled around her. She felt anything but tranquil as they played out the restrained flirtation of the minuet. As Tyrell circled her, looking intently into her eyes, her heart rapped wildly against her chest. Her breathing came in shallow bursts, which could hardly be put down to the exertions of the minuet, since the dance required little more than a walk on her part.

He did not seem unaffected either. At one point, his hand trembled, and he let go of hers prematurely. When they stood face-to-face, he exhaled sharply and looked away. She saw the same heat that warmed her cheeks reflected on his neck. It was her turn to circle him, she curtsied and tried to school her response to his nearness as she slowly dipped under his arm and let her arm trail across his shoulders to return and face him again. He bowed, but as he raised his head, she saw a look in his eyes that startled her, a look of desperate confusion. Knowing he suffered from the same turmoil she felt only served to endear him to her all the more.

What was happening? Blinking like a dazed child, she placed her hand on his forearm and relied on him to guide her as they crossed the circle and changed positions with another couple. For the first time in her life, she felt as though she were drowning. Was there no way to stop herself? She glanced up and caught sight of the strong handsome lines of his profile. If only he *were* an ogre. If only she hadn't loved him since she was five years old. If only he loved her. But he didn't. She *was* drowning, and the only way to save herself was to get out of the water, get away from him.

Chapter 11
Does Running Away
Ever Solve Anything?

"Damned unsettling that's what it is. She twists me up inside, muddles my thinking, turns me into a mindless sop." Tyrell muttered to himself as he tromped through the dark streets of Brighton on his way back to the Ship Inn. He'd chosen to walk rather than hail a hackney in the hope that a brisk walk would cool, what he surmised, must be brain fever. But it didn't help. He stopped at the door to the Ship and rubbed his temples with both hands. Something had to be done.

He yanked open the door and rattled the bell for the proprietor. When the man didn't appear immediately, he rang the bell again. The host stumbled out of the back rooms with his nightcap askew and a candle in his hand.

"Tally my bill, sir. I'm leaving this place."

"But, my lord, you took the room for the entire week. I've turned away several—"

"I'll pay you for the week."

"But, my lord, it's three in the morn. Surely you can't mean to—"

"I most certainly do. I mean to leave just as soon as I can rouse my blasted valet, and get packed."

"Won't he be delighted," muttered the host. "I'll gladly send an accounting to your estate, my lord, if you—"

"No. I'm going to London. I plan to find someplace uncluttered by memories of raspberry-stained lips, or troublesome imps with long eyelashes. You'd best settle with me now. I'm going to find a gutter someplace and crawl into it. And I may never crawl out."

The innkeeper rolled his eyes and minced away, mumbling, "A suitable abode for his lordship, I'm sure."

Tyrell stared after the man for a moment before climbing the stairs to awaken his valet. He should wait for morning, but he knew that if he stayed he would be in eminent danger. The exact nature of the danger eluded him, but the image of her face threatened something fragile inside him. Something he had to protect at all costs. He felt instinctively that she had him outgunned. A simple touch of her fingers on his sleeve had the power to unnerve him.

He nodded sagely, while climbing the stairs; all of the artillery appeared to be lined up on her side of the field. A hasty retreat was sometimes the best battle plan. Particularly, if the foe threatens to touch one's reliably stone heart. The sooner he got away from here—away from her, the better.

The following afternoon, Fiona sat in a wicker chair, staring vacantly at the pages of a book. Honore came into the sitting room and flopped into the chair next to her. "I grow weary of Brighton. What say you, we remove to London?"

Fiona nodded without enthusiasm. "Any plan that suits you, Aunt, suits me."

Honore snorted indignantly. "What banality. You aren't still upset about that silly episode last evening are you? Everyone thought it a great lark. Prinny's friends are not so hen-witted as those rustics in your part of the country. No one here is going to think you are cursed, jinxed, or anything of the kind. On the contrary, it was the greatest fun they've had in days. Prinny spiraling through the air like an acrobat, truly was . . ."

Fiona ignored her aunt and stuck her nose back into her book. She did not want to think about last night.

Honore folded her arms across her chest. "Whatever are you reading?"

Fiona sighed, "It's Miss Hannah More's latest sermon. I had hoped it might improve my mind."

"Is that the reason for this humbug attitude of yours? Throw that Methodist folderol into the fire. I won't have her turning you into a mope."

"It's August, there isn't a fire anywhere in sight." Fiona glanced about the room in a mock search for a fire.

Honore squinted. "Hand it to me then, I'll just throw it out the window."

"I'm well aware of your propensity for tossing things out the window. But you mustn't blame Miss More for my bad temper."

Fiona thumped the book closed and let it drop into her lap. "You may be pleased to know, Miss More would probably dislike a milk and water miss as much as you do. It's precisely that banal, care-for-nothing attitude she writes against. She finds fault with rote religiosity, claiming that God wants people to genuinely love him. Moreover, she applauds passion—"

"Enough! I'll go to church if I want to hear a sermon." Honore waved Fiona's lecture aside. "If it isn't that book bedeviling you, then what?"

"I can't say." Fiona lifted the book and inspected the binding. "Perhaps, I, too, would like to leave Brighton."

Through the open drawing room doors stepped Lord Alameda. "What's this, Honore? Planning your retreat?"

Both women looked up at him with a start. "Folderol! I retreat from nothing." Honore snapped her fingers at him.

"Neither, do I," said Fiona with a lift of her chin.

"Oh. Begging your pardons." Marcus bowed. "I merely overheard—"

"Eavesdropping, a shabby practice, Marcus. Beneath your dignity."

"Come down from your high horse, Honore. I merely heard you say you wanted to leave Brighton as I stepped into the room."

"Well, and so I do. We both do." She rose and slapped her hands to her sides. "It's time to go home to Alison Hall. We shall leave in two days' time." She looked at them as if she were the general and had just issued orders to her troops.

"Two days? I had thought to accompany you back to London. But, two days is such short—"

"You are welcome to travel with us, Marcus. However, now that you mention it"—she put her finger to her chin—"two days seems excessively long to me. We leave on the morrow. Early."

Marcus grumbled, but inclined his head in reluctant acceptance.

"Good." She turned and walked out of the drawing room, shouting for Lorraine to begin packing.

They started their travels too early the next morning to agree with most aristocratic temperaments. Marcus staggered into the coach as if he had not slept at all that night. But the early hour assured them of little traffic on the roads and the miles rolled rapidly by, with only brief stops at hostelries to change the cattle. Marcus drowsed and made irritated noises on the seat across from Fiona. Honore, on the other hand, was as jubilant as a small child starting out on her first journey. She was going home.

"A delightful day to travel, is it not?" She rapped Fiona on the thigh. "You'll love Alison Hall, my dear. It is unlike any other house in the world. And your rooms are well suited to you. I redecorated them for you in yellow and green and oh . . . all the colors of summer. I'm certain you'll enjoy it."

"You redecorated rooms for me? And you did it before you even knew I was coming?" Fiona looked at her aunt in amazement.

"Of course." Honore pinched her brows together. "Don't be absurd. I planned for you to come. And, so naturally, you have." Honore folded her hands in her lap, self-satisfied.

"But, Aunt Honore, you couldn't have known for certain that I would actually decide to come."

"Nonsense. I saw you last Season, when you were in town with that tiresome old hen your father married. I knew right away you belonged here, with me. I'm childless. You have no mother. What could be more simple?"

Marcus twitched uncomfortably in his seat.

Honore grinned and patted Fiona again. "Only think, Fiona, we will storm London together! Like Cosmas and Damian."

Obviously perturbed, Marcus exhaled loudly and sat up. "Cosmas and Damian were beheaded."

"Never mind, I can never keep all those Greek heroes organized in my mind." Honore waved at the air, swatting at bothersome Greek mythology as if it were an invisible fly.

Marcus shook his head. "For pity sake, Honore. Not Greek—they were *Arabian* martyrs. Arabian brothers, who were stoned, burned, and who knows what else. But in the end, they were beheaded." He smirked at Honore and turned to Fiona. "It sounds as if Honore is promising you a delightful stay in London."

Honore kicked her foot at Marcus's calf. "You're in a decidedly foul mood."

"Yes," he snapped. "You may credit it to the inhumane hour in which you chose to depart."

"Oh fustian. Be happy. We are almost home."

At long last the coach rolled up in front of Honore's London town house. Fiona looked out of the window in wonder. The facade of her aunt's town house looked like a Greek temple, with steps stretching across the entire face of the building and six sleek columns rising skyward, leading the eye up to the third-story dome.

Honore leapt out of the coach before the footman could let down the steps and rushed through the open door.

A woman's voice boomed out a greeting. "O' me pet! Finally ye're home!"

Fiona stepped timidly through the front door in time to see Honore embracing a large, imposing woman whose hard square features were framed by fire red hair tucked under a white cap. Her husky shoulders were draped with a lightweight plaid shawl, but apart from the green and blue tartan plaid, she was entirely garbed in starched crisp white.

"Let me have a look at ye!" cried the woman. She grasped Honore by the shoulders and turned her around. Clucking her tongue she asked, "What hae ye done to yer hair? It's as purple as a plum."

"It's red, Mattie, deep red. I wanted a change."

"Nae, child, that's not red. Red be this color here, on me old head." She bent her head and pointed at her own hair and then straightened, planting both hands on her hips. "That there be purple hair, Honore. Purple as a plum. An' it ain't natural on a human."

"Piffle. I don't give a fig for natural. Now, don't make a dust up over that. Come, see what I have brought us."

"Ah. The lass has come, 'asn't she. An this be her." Mattie motioned for Fiona to come closer, and both women walked slowly around her as if appraising a new piece of furniture. Mattie nodded her head at Honore.

Honore clapped her hands together. "Did I not tell you, Mattie. She's a rare one, isn't she."

"Aye, but not so like ye as ye thought. Nay, but she's a fine-looking gel. Aye, she'll do." Mattie opened her arms and gathered Fiona into a powerful embrace. "Welcome, child. Ye may call me Mattie."

Fiona felt herself crushed against the woman's bosom, and

had no choice but to respond in kind. She smiled with the enjoyment of such unabashed affection. She began to understand Honore's remarkable attachment to this odd woman.

Behind Fiona, boots clicked on the marble floor. Mattie dropped her arms from Fiona and stepped back. "I see the black devil hae returned."

Marcus bowed. "A pleasure to see you too, Mattie."

"Fie!" She whipped around to Honore. "I thought ye packed this cur off tae Spain."

"Portugal, Mattie." Honore examined something trapped under one of her fingernails. "And, as you say, the devil has returned."

Marcus laughed and planted a loud sloppy kiss on Mattie's cheek. "The devil craves his own kind. I couldn't bear to be parted from your delightful company. Nor your cooking."

"Fah!" She brushed her cheek dry. "Ye're naught but a teasing scoundrel." With that she whirled around and marched imperiously out of the room.

Honore stamped her foot. "Now see, Marcus. You've upset her."

He shrugged, donning a helpless expression. "What did I say?"

From the wall a silent onlooker stepped forward, an ancient man, whose white hair neatly contrasted with his black attire. He did not wear a powdered wig. A wig would have been superfluous. His own white hair was far more impressive. He moved deliberately and with caution. Fiona half expected to hear him creak as he bowed to Honore. "Welcome home, madam."

"Thank you, Cairn. This is my niece, Miss Hawthorn, our new protégée."

The very correct butler bowed so low Fiona could see his pink scalp underneath the waving white hairs.

"Put her things in the green apartments in the east wing next to mine." Honore shook out her dusty carriage dress.

"And have Lord Alameda's things taken to his rooms in the west wing."

Honore placed her arm around Fiona's waist and led her up the marble staircase. "Come, my dear. Come see your new home."

Her aunt's house was the complete antithesis of the Brighton Pavilion or Fiona's home at Thorncourt. Here, there were no heavy tapestries, or conflicting patterns. The walls were oyster white, except for a life-size frieze of Greek water bearers in the foyer, and light seemed to reflect everywhere. The walls of the circular foyer rose all the way up to high-domed ceiling. The dome contained six oval windows, each adorned with paintings of naked cherubim. The balustrades on the great winding stairway were carved of white marble and decorated with large Grecian urns set at intervals.

Honore smiled at her niece's wide eyes. "As you can see, my dear, Alison Hall is very comfortable."

"Comfortable was not the phrase that came to mind, Aunt. Rather, I should say it is breathtaking."

Honore lifted her chin and made smug noises that indicated she agreed. "After Francisco died I was restless. I commissioned Alison Hall to distract my mind from grief. It turned out rather well I think."

Honore ushered her into the most handsome apartment Fiona had ever seen. A huge Turkish carpet covered the floor. It was forest green, decorated with cream and rose in the design. Everything else in the room had simple clean lines. The windows ran from the floor to the ceiling, and filled the room with sunshine. Fiona turned to her aunt and hugged her.

Honore tut-tutted. "Come now, must you always turn into a watering pot? I declare, you'll smother me." Her smile belied her words as she patted Fiona's shoulders. "Tomorrow, when you're rested we'll send for the dressmaker, and we shall see about turning you out in a style that becomes you."

Chapter 12
Ghosts in London

Tyrell chose not to hail a hack, instead he walked down the streets of London like a man possessed. He'd spent a restless night, waking up from nightmares in a fevered sweat, and then unable to get back to sleep, because her confounded face kept dancing up in front of him like a relentless specter. A good walk was what he needed and a drink at White's.

By the time he reached the corner of Piccadilly and Fleet, his vehement strides had relaxed into a more rational pace. He glanced occasionally into the windows, glancing at the caricatures.

Fleet Street was home to scores of printers whose shop windows displayed half a dozen new caricatures for sale each week. These lampoons provided the browsing masses with political and social commentaries and a lively dose of humor. They also furnished the printers with a handsome source of additional income. Patrons purchased the cartoons to amuse their friends and acquaintances, and at two pennies apiece, it was a bargain. The more scandalous the lampoon, the better.

Lord Wesmont strolled from window to window. While he didn't actually laugh, a wry grin formed on his face as he perused a caricature of the Prince Regent drawn as a big whale spouting water from his mouth. The whale was eyeing the buxom Lady B. Her busty figure was portrayed as a voluptuous fish floating alongside the great Prince George whale. Her husband, Lord B., sketched as a skinny little fish wearing cuckold's antlers on his head, swam precariously underneath the whale's upraised tail.

A large crowd gathered in front of the next print shop, Laurie and Whittle's. Tyrell heard loud guffaws as someone read out a verse in a mocking singsong voice. As the group chuckled and pointed at a caricature set prominently in the window, he strained to see what drew so much attention. When, at last, he caught a glimpse of the cartoon, he felt as if someone had punched him in the stomach.

"It can't be." He muttered, pushing and shoving his way through the crowd to get closer to the drawing. He planted both hands on the glass, and stood blocking everyone else's view. He didn't care about the complaints from the crowd behind him. He stared down at a caricature of an all-too-familiar face. It could not be. It should not be. Nevertheless, it most assuredly was Fiona Hawthorn. It had to be, because in the corner stood the Dowager Countess Alameda with some jackanapes crawling under her skirt. He closed his eyes and then reopened them, but the cartoon remained.

It featured Fiona center stage with Prince George, who had obviously been dancing with her. The Regent was shown comically flipping through the air in one direction, while Miss Hawthorn appeared to be flying backward in another direction. Count A., clearly identifiable as Count Alameda, held out his arms in anticipation of catching her. Furthermore, Tyrell could not like at all the way the cartoonist depicted Lord Alameda staring lecherously down Fiona's bosom while he waited for the girl to come flying into his arms.

"Blast his eyes," he snarled out loud. The woman next to him giggled. He glowered down at her, and she clamped her mouth shut. Then Tyrell read the limerick captioning the drawing.

> *Beware the Duchess of Disaster*
> *She ought to have a dancing master.*

She wounds our soldiers on the ballroom floor,
And if that ain't enough, there's more.
Britain is in jeopardy, Ladies and Gents,
For now Lady Fiasco trips our Prince!
A lovely young girl, as Count A. observes,
A succulent beauty, with pleasing curves—

He'd read enough. Tyrell growled again and followed it up with some rather colorful oaths, much to the astonishment of the other people standing at the window. He elbowed his way through the crowd and flung open the door of Laurie and Whittle's printing establishment.

The people outside the shop watched through the window with interest as his lordship waved his arms emphatically toward the window display. Muffled shouting seeped out of the shop as he argued with the proprietor. Groans of protest issued from the crowd as Mr. Laurie walked to the window display and removed the entertaining cartoon of the Duchess of Disaster. He placed it on a stack of similar etchings and plopped them on the counter in front of the complainant, who slapped down a handful of coins, stuffed the caricatures under his arm, and tromped out of the shop, seething.

Tyrell felt like a bear on a rampage as he marched down the street in a tornadolike fury. If King George and the entire royal family stood naked in the street singing and waving red ribbons, he would not have noticed or cared. Therefore, it must have been divine intervention when he stumbled across Robert Anbel, and actually took notice.

At first, the two men merely grunted when they collided. Tyrell still couldn't see anything but the red angry cloud enveloping him. The man he bumped into shifted to the side and passed by. When he did, an empty coat sleeve flapped against Tyrell's arm. That empty coat sleeve riveted his attention.

He stopped abruptly. As quick as lightning, he felt as if he were back at Badajoz. He could almost smell the gunpowder, see the flashes of gunfire, feel his hands slick with blood.

He turned. At the same moment, the other man glanced back over his shoulder, and froze in his footsteps. Both men squinted at each other, as if straining to see through a dense fog and bring into focus an important image.

"Ty?" Robert Anbel turned slowly around.

"As I live and breathe, is that you, Anbel?"

"Most of me."

They stood silently comprehending each other for a moment. Then he shot out a hand toward Robert, who immediately clasped it. Tyrell wondered if his heart had suddenly remembered how to function, because it erupted with gladness. It just bubbled up and spilled out like a dam bursting. He was overwhelmed and very pleased to see this man. "This is the confounded-est day of my life. Robert, you must surely be an apparition because nothing this good could possibly happen today."

Robert laughed. "Well, I don't mean to disappoint you, but I haven't stuck my spoon in the wall yet. My arm, mind you, may be in heaven or hell, don't know which, but I remain here, in the world of the living—if you can call it living. Leastwise, I ain't no ghost.

"Now, shall we stand here on the street shaking each other's hand like a couple of lovesick monkeys? Or shall we retire to a quiet table and have a glass of Madeira like civilized men?"

"Lead on." Tyrell laughed and murmured. "I'd forgotten how you do prose on." Robert shot him a quelling look. Tyrell chuckled and lifted a hand to signal peace. "More welcome prose there never was."

In a private corner at White's they raised their glasses to one another.

"I must admit, Robert, I thought you must be dead."

"Oh, I suppose I was dead once or twice." He smiled into the red liquid of his cup. "There were times, Ty, when I certainly wished I were dead. Ah, but that is past. Mainly." He lifted his glass again. "You, Captain—excuse me, I mean Lord Wesmont—I'm deuced sorry about your father—are just as great a surprise to me as I am to you. I left you at Badajoz more than two years ago. In truth, I thought your chances for survival were somewhat less than mine. I was safely ensconced in the surgeon's tent. You see, some foolhardy hero hauled my worthless carcass off that wretched battlefield." Robert raised a sardonic eyebrow in mock disapproval of his companion. "Or don't you remember?"

This time Tyrell lifted his glass, but said nothing. Like a waking nightmare, he felt once again, the warm blood drenching his uniform, covering his hands as he slung Robert over his shoulder and fought his way back through the ranks to find a surgeon.

Robert shook his head. "Never fear. I know I ought to thank you, you damn fool, but I won't."

"Don't." The image vanished and Tyrell felt the momentary tension ebb.

"No. Well then, tell me, why is the Earl of Wesmont sulking around London with a stack of cartoons under his arm. For that matter, what are you doing in London? Oughtn't you to be cloistered in that country manor of yours with a fertile young wife, begetting heirs? I believe that is what it's called, *begetting*. A delightful pastime, or so I'm told."

Tyrell smacked his hand down on the table. "Don't you start! Arm or no arm, I'll serve you up a facer!"

"Oh, I am fairly certain there is no arm." Robert lifted his coat sleeve, pretending to search for the missing appendage. "However, if you must bash me in my nose I stand awaiting your pleasure. Or rather, I *sit* awaiting your pleasure, too much bother to stand. Not a favorite subject, eh, the begetting of heirs?"

"No," snapped Tyrell. "That's why I'm in London—to avoid the subject." He picked up the caricatures from the floor and plopped them on the table. "It would seem, that I have not run far enough. I cannot walk down Fleet Street without being reminded of plaguey females."

Robert Anbel took a cartoon from the top of the pile and set it aside, only to find that the next etching contained an identical drawing. "Bought the whole lot did you?" He chuckled as he perused the caricature, and laughed again when he read the limerick. "But this is delightful."

Tyrell merely scowled at him.

"Ahh"—Robert tapped the edge of the cartoon—"now let me guess. This cartoon disturbs you because it insults our Prince Regent. No, no, that cannot be it. For there are hundreds of even more insulting caricatures of his Royal Largeness. No, perhaps you are annoyed because it depicts your friend, Lord Alameda, as a lecherous scoundrel. However, I cannot remember you ever mentioning he was your friend. Aside from which, all of London knows that the man is actually proud of his dubious reputation."

Robert baited Tyrell further. "Can it be that you have formed a *tendre* for the fascinating Lady Alameda? I understand she has pots of money—such a captivating woman. See here, it shows Lord M. groveling at her hem and straining to peer up her gown. It must upset you terribly." Robert schooled his face into an expression of mock sympathy. "Chin up, old man. It does look like Lady Alameda is about to kick the lusty fellow in the eye."

Tyrell refused to rise to the bait. Robert grinned derisively and set the cartoon in front of his sour companion, pointing to the corner of the drawing. "See there. She most certainly is about to kick him."

"I hadn't noticed." Tyrell sat with his arms folded.

"Oh, I see. Well then, that eliminates the intriguing countess, doesn't it?" He pulled the cartoon back and made a great work of studying it again. "That leaves only this mysterious Duchess of Disaster. Hmm, yes, how does the poet phrase it? *A succulent young beauty*—"

"Enough!" Tyrell snatched the cartoon from Robert's hand. When the wretch threw back his head and laughed, Tyrell glowered at him. Robert made a feeble attempt to contain himself, but his shoulders shook and tears of mirth trickled from his eyes until at last he burst out laughing again. "Oh, my friend, I haven't had such a belly-shaker since before the war. Come, have another glass. You must tell me who she is." He signaled to the porter for service.

"I should have left you on that field."

"Ah, but then, who would be here to persecute you?"

"Have no fear, I am quite loaded down with persecutors. Thank you. Lady Fiasco, here, heads the list." He tapped the offending cartoon.

Robert shook his head skeptically. "She looks like a complete innocent in this drawing. Tell me, has she wounded *you* on the ballroom floor?"

"No." But then, Tyrell remembered being tangled up with her on his balcony and smiled crookedly. "No, but it was a near thing."

"I see."

"No, you don't see." Tyrell raked his fingers through his hair. "This little baggage keeps putting a spoke in my wheel. I came to London to get thoroughly dissipated, to forget her, forget the war, and everything else. I fully intended to become a lecherous scoundrel m'self.

"I'm not ready to set up a nursery full of whining brats. Had enough of 'em on the Continent. What I *plan* to do is gamble away my inheritance, like all these other care-fornothing fribbles loitering about London. I'm going to ravish beautiful women, follow the hounds, get roiling drunk every night—"

"Hmm. Sounds like a course the vicar would recommend."

"Well, an' the vicar ain't been to Badajoz has he?" Tyrell answered harshly.

"No. Although, I have. And I heartily endorse this plan of yours. In fact, it parallels my own to an amazing degree."

Robert lifted his glass high. "Come, let us go forth and dissipate together." He gulped the contents of his glass and slammed it down on the table. "Let us find a gaming hell to gamble away our fortunes in. Forget that chit with the *pleasing curves*. Let us away to a brothel! We'll ravish the lustiest high-fliers we can find." He purported to rise, while Tyrell slid deeper in his chair.

"What? Not coming?" A smirk played on Robert's lips.

"Didn't I just say she put a spoke in my wheels? It's no good, Robert. She's ruined me. Don't want anyone else. Dratted female."

"Oh, this is bad." Robert shook his head mournfully. "Very bad. I suppose you are besotted with joy knowing that she is in the company of that rascal, Alameda."

"The vulture, I'd like to cut his heart out. However"— Tyrell smoothed his waistcoat and ordered his emotions—"I have no claim on the chit." He paused. "Nor, do I want one."

"Of course, you don't. Why, it's a common thing for you to carry several hundred cartoons of a young lady around with you. Did you buy them to give to your friends? I'll take one. After all, she is a rather good-looking female."

Tyrell grumbled, snatched the stack of cartoons from the table, and slapped them onto the floor beside his chair. "This is serious, Robert. And as usual you can do nothing but roast me."

"Now that is odd. I have not roasted anyone since we parted in Spain. I must confess, however, it does my weary soul good to make light of your problems. Forgive me."

Tyrell waved his hand, dismissing his friend's apology. "Happy to be of service. Only tell me one thing, Robert, how do I purge *my* weary soul of this vexatious female and that nightmare of a war?"

"That's *two* things, my friend. Two very different things— a woman and the war." Robert Anbel toyed with his empty glass. A shock of straw-colored hair fell across his brow. For a moment he looked like the young man he had once been, before they'd both seen too much bloodshed. Then he squared his shoulders, and with a slight movement of his head the hair flipped back into place. "Napoleon changed us forever, Ty. I think that if you try to cut out that part of your soul it will leave you a crippled man. You'll lose more than an arm or a leg. The war, with all of its gore and cruelty, as well as its small triumphs, became a part of us. The green young bucks we once were, the ones who bought our colors and rode off to fight the Corsican, they're gone forever."

Tyrell stared at the dark paneling beyond Robert's head. He saw nothing of the club walls. Instead, he saw the mists swirling around himself as a young man, before the war. He wanted that innocence back, but Robert was right. He could not go back.

Robert laughed abruptly, a short cynical snort. "Oh, I suppose they're not exactly gone, those green boys. It's rather like a sapling turning into a tree. Can't scrape the bark off, and whittle it down until you find that sapling again, now can you? No, of course not. The tree *is* the sapling. Simply changed forever. The realities of that war will remain inside of us through heaven or hell. Best to face it, Ty. It's part of us. Running from it won't help. You're never going to turn back into the innocent sapling you once were." Robert lifted his glass and grinned. "My friend, we've become a pair of gnarled old trees."

Tyrell tried to smile. "Anbel, I swear, I can't ascertain whether you've taken up gardening or sermonizing. Gnarled old trees, indeed." Tyrell swallowed the last of his drink. Then he bowed his head and added softly, "Although I think you probably have the right of it."

"Ain't taken up gardening or sermons. I've turned into a demmed nursemaid. My grandmother cajoled me into escorting m' two cousins all over town. The old dragon is too ancient to do the pretty through all the late hours. So she's enlisted me, the merciless old crow. I tried to beg off. Told her I wanted to ship out with the East India Company, but she gave me her worst '*how-can-you-abandon-me-in-my-time-of-need*' glare. Bless her pointy old beak. So, I folded."

"My sympathies. The East India, eh?"

"Yes, and as soon as I puff off the chits, I'll be aboard the first ship going. Say, Tyrell, you wouldn't want to take one of 'em off my hands, would you?"

Tyrell's eyebrows shot up in alarm.

Robert taunted him. "Come to think of it, you're just the man for Diana. She needs a grumpy old husband like you, the chubby minx. She's so cheerful I often want to slap her. Yes, she'd suit you admirably. She has some wits too, or at least I think she does, under all that bouncy hair and incessant chattering. Say you'll marry her—I can't stand much more of this squiring-them-around-town business." Robert dropped back into his seat and sulked.

It was Tyrell's turn to laugh. "I'd like to help you out, Anbel. But, like I said, I ain't getting leg-shackled to anyone." His hasty declaration spun his mind back to the sunshine and water and Fiona's torn face when he had shouted those same words at her. He lowered his eyes.

Robert studied his friend and then leaned forward, suddenly serious. "And why not, Ty? Might be pleasant. Lord knows, *I* wouldn't do it. But you're the type what does. You're a country fellow, with country character and ideals." He glanced sympathetically at Tyrell. "Truth is, Captain, you couldn't sink into dissipation if you spent a thousand years on the effort. Your conscience wouldn't let you. Even in Spain, you didn't trifle with the camp followers like most of the men. And you aren't like me, with a burning desire to go haring off to India or parts unknown. Why not marry?"

"Why not?" Tyrell grimaced. "Because it ain't *pleasant*. It's a great wagonload of responsibility. That's why!" He picked up the stack of caricatures and stood up to leave.

"Oh, don't go off in a snit." Robert followed him toward the door. "Very well. I'll not say another word about it."

Tyrell lifted a skeptical eyebrow.

"See here, I will change the topic entirely. Do you go to Lady Sefton's ball tomorrow night?"

"Whatever for?"

"Well, you might come keep an old soldier company. We'll

retire to the card room as soon as we see that my cousins are properly ensconced along the débutante wall. Who knows, I might even let you win back some of the blunt you lost to me in Spain."

"I never lost to you. It was the other way 'round, as I recall."

"Then your memory is sadly deficient. Why I cleaned your purse out regularly."

"Folderol. Shrapnel must have nicked your brain box. I recall a rainy night in Lisbon . . ."

Thus, they headed down St. James's Street bickering as amiably as children.

Chapter 13
Improper Ballroom Etiquette

Lord Wesmont and Robert Anbel arrived at Lady Sefton's doorstep, accompanying two pudgy débutantes decked out in frilly white gowns. Dragging behind them was an old woman, who served as lady's companion to the girl's grandmother. Their party stood in line on the stairs waiting to enter the ballroom.

When Lord Wesmont, Mr. Robert Anbel, Miss Diana Anbel, and her sister stood framed in the ballroom doorway, they were announced by a footman with excellent diction and a booming voice. Tyrell overheard a gasp from someone in the crowd to his left. He glanced over the crowded ballroom, and amidst the sea of faces he caught sight of the astonished features of Fiona Hawthorn.

His sudden intake of breath and inability to move forward on cue, alerted Robert, who leaned forward and remarked, "Steady on, Wesmont, stairs ahead. Try not to trip my cousin."

Tyrell silently damned himself for getting flustered so easily and made his way down the steps with Diana on his arm. As they stood in line waiting to greet their hostess, Robert teased him in furtive voice. "I hadn't realized the Duchess of Disaster was in town. How very convenient for you."

Tyrell couldn't think of a suitably quelling reply. He was still too stunned at finding her here.

Across the room, Lady Alameda leaned closer to her niece and spoke in cool, authoritative tones, "My dear, compose yourself. One would think you had seen a specter. And what was it? Naught but a mere man. A mere man, dearest, and two pitiful powder puff debs. Now, stop making a cake of yourself." Honore flipped her fan shut with a snap. "Come, I wish to speak with Lady Haversburg. Oh, and *do* remove that apprehensive expression from your face."

Fiona trailed meekly behind her imperious aunt. Tonight her aunt's hair, now dyed a silvery white, and piled up like a crown, was almost matronly; it complemented her shimmering gold gown beautifully.

Their two gowns contrasted with each other, as Honore had planned that they should, saying that when they walked across the room, they would resemble the sun and the moon parading across the sky. Fiona's gown was a light winter blue, shot through with silver threads. It draped elegantly from one shoulder, leaving the other exposed. Lorraine had tumbled Fiona's hair into a Grecian arrangement, with strands of seed pearls woven through it, leaving a brace of curls to drop softly onto Fiona's bare shoulder.

Fiona didn't feel like anything so glorious as the moon. She felt more like Marie Antoinette approaching the guillotine. What on earth was Tyrell doing here? Why was he with that young woman? She felt the urge to be sick, to run away, leave the room, leave London. At least when she wasn't in the same town with him her heart would behave properly.

Honore halted in front of a sturdy matron and a buxom young woman. Fiona smiled dutifully at Lady Haversburg and her daughter, Maria. Sadly, the lovely Maria Haversburg's musk pills were unable to cover up a hideous odor emanating from her mouth. She smiled timidly at Fiona, revealing several yellow and brown teeth. Fiona struggled to keep from wincing. Not only did her breath smell like twelve-day-old

meat, but surely such a mouth must be painful. It troubled her
to see such a pretty girl disfigured by a few rotting teeth.
Fiona smiled as if she hadn't noticed and commented on the
vastness of Lady Sefton's gathering.

Across the room, she spied Tyrell's broad shoulders as he
bent over Lady Sefton's proffered hand. When he straightened
and turned to walk away, he caught Fiona's glance. She
looked away quickly and tried to stop the rising flush that
must be turning her cheeks scarlet.

"Miss Haversburg, what a lovely gown you are wearing,"
Fiona rushed to say with more enthusiasm than she felt.

Miss Haversburg glanced down at her rather exposed
bosom bulging out of the low neckline and tried to tug the
fabric up a little more. "Do you truly think so? Don't you find
it, well, just a trifle too daring? Mama thought—" She suddenly flushed red herself and whispered conspiratorially
behind her gloved hand, "I rather think my mother sought to
distract the gentlemen from noticing my teeth."

"Oh. I . . ." Fiona didn't have the slightest idea what to say.
All she could think about was the man across the room who
made her feel like a newborn filly with wobbly legs.

Fiona closed her eyes and rubbed her brow. Miss Haversburg
touched her arm solicitously, "Are you ill, Miss Hawthorn?"

"Yes. Yes, that's it. I am very sorry, but I seem to have developed a terrible case of the megrims. I really must go home
and rest."

Miss Haversburg tapped her mother's arm and signaled in
Fiona's direction. Lady Haversburg and the countess stopped
talking and took note of Fiona's obvious anguish. The countess frowned impatiently, but Lady Haversburg made a great
show of concern.

"Yes, yes, quite right, you must return home and lie down.
A pity you must leave. And with all these eligible young gentlemen in attendance tonight. Ah, well, more admirers for my
Maria, eh, Honore?" She laughed rather too boldly, but then
caught herself. "I recommend a cloth soaked in lavender

water, and have your maid rub your temples, very soothing. Yes, that would be just the thing."

"Nonsense," argued Honore. "There's nothing wrong with the gel." She waylaid a footman passing by, snared two glasses of champagne from his tray, and handed one to Fiona. "Here, drink this. You'll feel better in a trice."

"But, Aunt, I really think—"

"Drink it."

Obediently, Fiona tipped the delicate flute to her lips. The champagne bubbled into her mouth and trickled down into her empty stomach. She drained her glass and felt the heat spread from her middle. A footman appeared at her elbow to take the flute. She placed it on his tray and took another filled with champagne. She quickly disposed of the contents of that glass, too.

It was amazing how much better she felt. The room seemed to settle into a comfortable warm haze. She noticed the dark coat of a gentleman standing at her elbow. Fiona looked up into his face. "Oh, good evening, Marcus."

"Ah, *Ma belle chère*." He lifted her hand and kissed it. Fiona looked loosely around her, as if trying to find the right person to concentrate on. She settled on Maria Haversburg. "Don't you find it odd, Miss Haversburg, that a Portuguese nobleman should speak French? I confess I cannot get used to it."

Miss Haversburg fluttered helplessly. Marcus answered for her. "It is because, dear cousin, I was raised in England. As I have said before, my mother was an Englishwoman. Naturally, I learned French, as do most English gentlemen."

Miss Haversburg stood speechless during this discussion and kept her lips clamped shut in front of the handsome foreigner.

"Still, it is odd." Fiona parried. "I think the ladies would prefer it if you would impress us all with a bevy of Portuguese compliments, instead of this French bibble-babble."

"French *bibble-babble,* as you call it, is similar to my native tongue. And, unlike the French, if I spoke to you in Portuguese you would not understand a word I said. I might make all kinds of lurid suggestions and you would simply nod and say, thank you, kind sir."

The musicians struck up the opening bars of a promenade. "Ah, I hear the strains of the first set beginning. You might remember, fair cousin, Honore assigned this set to me. It appears to be a wretched country reel." He exhaled with exasperation. "We can look forward to hopping around like a pair of mountain goats. I hope you appreciate my sacrifice on your behalf."

"Oh, really, Marcus, you know I have no desire to dance."

"Odd you should attend a ball." Marcus bowed at the waist and smiled appreciatively at Miss Haversburg's abundant *décolletage*. "And alas, cruel Fiona, you cause me to suffer indescribable agony by neglecting to introduce me to this delightful young lady."

"Well, I had thought to spare her." Fiona laughed, unconsciously mimicking her aunt. "But I refuse to have your agony on my head. Miss Haversburg, prepare to meet the Count de Alameda. Lord Alameda, Miss Haversburg. And as my aunt would tell you, he is a rascal of the first water, so beware."

Maria sank into a deep curtsy. Unfortunately, she smiled at Fiona's saucy remarks. This exposed Marcus, however briefly, to her yellow teeth and a cloud of foul breath. He abruptly inclined his head, and without taking any further notice of Miss Haversburg, declared himself, "Charmed," and promptly whisked Fiona out into the promenade before the set.

"You were rude to her, Marcus."

"I find her offensive. And you, my succulent cousin, must learn to temper your impertinent remarks. You have had too much of Lady Sefton's excellent champagne."

"Nonsense, Marcus, I have had only two small glasses. You are becoming a grouchy old nursemaid."

"Then you have no head for it, my dear."

She tossed him an impish smile. "I promise, Nursie, I shall not swallow one sip more."

"Ah." He nodded genially at an acquaintance as they passed by. "So, you taunt me, delectable one. Shall I teach you just how unlike Nursie I can be?" He clasped her hand tightly, twisting it, until she was drawn up toward him. With hooded eyes, he examined her body as if she were naked. His lips parted, displaying his perfect straight teeth, set in an unnerving leer.

She tried to pull away. "No, Marcus. Truly, I meant nothing." She quickly tried to recoup the situation. "You are right, of course, I have no head for champagne."

Marcus relaxed his hold on her, and they continued the promenade.

Tyrell stood with Robert's party, observing every nuance of Fiona and Alameda's exchange. His fists were clenched like two iron hammers ready to strike. He thought he was holding his emotions in check, but holding oneself as stiff as a granite statue was not quite the kind of self-control he hoped to achieve. His instinct to engage the enemy took over. He turned to Miss Diana Anbel and offered her his arm for the forming set.

Following the promenade, the dancers twirled and cut their figures in sets of four couples. Tyrell glared across the ballroom at the quadrangle containing Alameda and Fiona. Diana stamped her foot loudly in front of Wesmont as she faced him in the turn. She curtsied, he bowed, and they looped arms.

Through a false smile Robert's cousin hissed at him, "Lord Wesmont, you look as if you are about to murder someone. Everyone will think I am a most disagreeable partner. Please do try for a little more pleasant countenance. After all, this is not a battlefield."

"I had forgotten. My apologies."

Diana beamed up at him approvingly. "See there, you have a most agreeable smile. And that mischievous glint in your eye is very attractive."

"Young ladies should not comment on such things," he admonished her as they separated to form a line, all the ladies on one side and the gentlemen on the other.

They came back together and joined upraised hands to create an arch for the couples to promenade through. Tyrell held Diana's hands up as the other couples passed under. He tried not to stare at Fiona, tried not to think about thrashing Alameda senseless, but it was no use. Frustration twisted his stomach into a knot. He wanted to knock Alameda's arrogant face into Hades, where it belonged. It was not right that such an malevolent cur should be endowed with such deceptive good looks. Women were so easily fooled by outward appearances. It galled him the way the bounder indecently raked his eyes over Fiona. Fury churned and coiled inside Tyrell until he felt ready to explode.

Fiona and Alameda crossed hands and capered forward underneath the raised arms of the other dancers. Alameda was tall and had to stoop more than most to go under the arch. Tyrell tensed as they started to pass under his arms, he trembled with the force of his emotions, and let go of Diana's fingers. It all happened in a blink. He clenched his fists, and drove down on Alameda's neck, thumping the wretch to the floor.

Marcus lay sprawled on the ground by Tyrell's feet. Diana stood squawking like a wounded goose. Fiona stumbled to keep from falling atop her partner. The music screeched to a stop. The entire company of Lady Sefton's ballroom turned to stare at the spectacle. Fiona looked up into Tyrell's face. He knew he couldn't hide the rage blazing there. She shook her head and started to close her eyes as though she might swoon. Marcus stumbled to his feet, looking like one of Satan's minions about to spear his quarry.

Diana stopped squawking. The crazy chit began hopping

up and down, grabbing at her ankle and crying out. "Oh, Help! Help me! I've twisted my ankle. Oooh—"

Everyone turned to look at her. Diana reached out to Lord Alameda and grasped his forearm for support. "You must forgive me, my lord. I'm dreadfully sorry I knocked you down. I twisted my ankle, you see, and stumbled—just as you were passing under. I'm so short and you are so very tall. I leaned up as high as I could and—" She looked sweetly up into his face. "I lost my balance and fell on you. Can you ever forgive me?"

Alameda narrowed his eyes at her skeptically, but he inclined his head and murmured his acquiescence. Diana smiled gratefully, released his arm, and turned back to Tyrell. "My lord, would you be so kind as to lend me your arm? I fear I am in no condition to finish the set." She waved at the other dancers. "My sincerest apologies. Pray continue."

In scratchy discord the musicians struck up their instruments, found the right measure, and the music flowed forth once again. Dancers shuffled back to their places.

Tyrell silently escorted Diana to a chair near her sister and Robert. As she sat down, Diana commented in firm undertones. "Lord Wesmont, the next time you plan to commit mayhem on the ballroom floor, I wonder if you would be so good as to choose a different partner?"

Robert laughed. "Diana, you are a Trojan. And here I had you down as a frilly little jabber muffin with nothing but fluff for brains."

Diana folded her arms across her bosom and harrumphed. Robert laughed and turned to his friend. "You have to admit it, Ty, she pulled your fat out of the fire. What were you playing at out there?"

"A simple accident, just as Miss Anbel says."

"Folderol. Although, I hope for your sake Alameda swallowed Diana's Banbury tale."

"Let him call me out. Nothing would give me greater pleasure than to shoot off one of his legs."

"Ah, how gracious of you not to mortally wound the fellow. Unfortunately, I hear the Lord Alameda is also an excellent shot. He, not being as chivalrous as your lordship, might prefer to put a sizeable hole between your scowling eyes."

"He wouldn't dare." Tyrell adjusted the lace at his wrist.

"No?" Anbel spotted a scuff on the toe of his left shoe. "By all accounts, the fellow is rather unpredictable. Some say mad as a hatter."

"Do you think I care one whit about his sanity? He was leering at her. Needed a lesson in manners."

"Oh, naturally." Robert chuckled. "Your manners being as exquisite as they are, makes you just the man to tutor him. Yes, thrashing a fellow in the middle of a set—done every day in the ballrooms of London. A perfect tutor—"

A low threatening rumble from Tyrell silenced his friend's jibes.

Across the room, the notorious Lord Alameda abandoned Fiona and left her to sit with her aunt.

Honore leaned over and whispered into her ear. "Watch how Marcus is flattering Sally Jersey. Watch her blush and strike him with her fan." A moment later, Honore's prediction came true. "Yes, there it is. Now observe how the scoundrel will tease her until she is nearly pink with pleasure. Next, they'll be off to find a dark corner." She sat back and sighed. "It's all an effort to restore his bruised dignity after being walloped to the floor by your swain."

"Lord Wesmont is not my swain."

"Ha! Well, he's not indifferent to you, my dear. Mind you, I cannot approve of a man who, in plain view of society, is foolhardy enough to knock Alameda to the floor. Still . . ." Honore chuckled under her breath. "I cannot quite dislike him for it either. He has bottom. I give him credit for that. And, unless I am mistaken, the young fool is approaching us now."

Alarmed, Fiona glanced anxiously toward Tyrell. She saw him heading across the room in her direction, his familiar scowl set in striking contrast to his brown angelic curls. She sprang up out of her seat. "Aunt, I beg to be excused. I must go to . . . er, uh, mend my flounce."

"You don't have a flounce, Fiona."

Looking around desperately, she blurted, "It's Miss Haversburg, *her* flounce is torn. I must go and help her at once."

Honore rolled her eyes. "Coward," she said to her retreating niece.

"Prudent. I prefer to think of it as prudent," Fiona murmured, looking back over her shoulder. She scurried off to Miss Haversburg, snared that young lady by the elbow, dropped a curtsy to Lady Haversburg, and fled toward the entrance. She glanced over her shoulder and saw that Tyrell had adjusted his course and was likewise heading for the ballroom door. He arrived at the doorway just after Fiona rushed through it.

"Miss Hawthorn."

She ignored him and tried to hurry Miss Haversburg along with her. However, Maria gestured toward the handsome gentleman, hailing them, and began to drag her feet. Tyrell caught Fiona's arm, halting her at last. She looked up at him, infuriated. How dare he run her to ground this way.

"Don't pretend to cut me, Fiona." He inclined his head at Miss Haversburg and returned his attention to Fiona.

"I am not pretending."

"Nonsense. At the very least, you owe me the courtesy of a few words. I am your neighbor, after all, a friend of your father's, and, until I saw that ferocious look on your face, I thought you also counted me a friend."

"Friend? By what definition? I had not thought a friend would knock down one's dancing partner. Indeed, you seem to do a great number of things I would not find listed under the desirable characteristics of a friend. How dare you lecture me on courtesy." She pulled her arm out of his grasp.

He stiffened. "I don't expect you to understand my reasoning. I wouldn't bother speaking to you now, if it were not for the fact that you are without sensible counsel, and I feel I am duty-bound to warn you about the company you are keeping."

Fiona's mouth opened involuntarily. She snapped it shut and shook her head. "This is outside of enough, Lord Wesmont. I told you before. You owe me nothing. You have no duty toward me whatsoever. You may refrain from bashing any more of my true friends to the floor."

"Friend? I hardly think Alameda should be counted—" He grimaced apologetically at Miss Haversburg. "This is exceedingly awkward, Fiona. It would be much better if I called on you tomorrow to discuss your situation privately."

"That isn't at all necessary. I am quite satisfied with my situation. Now, if you will excuse me."

She turned to leave, but Tyrell reached out and caught her bare shoulder. The sensation of his fingers touching her skin rushed through her like a blast of heat on a cold night. She couldn't breathe, couldn't move. With a great effort she forced herself to turn slowly back to face him, and clearly she was not the only one startled by that moment of contact.

His hand slid hesitantly from her shoulder, and when he spoke his voice had softened, and held a bewildered quality. "I would appreciate the opportunity to explain. If you will permit me, I should like to call on you."

She bit her lip for a split second, hopeful, loath to think she might never again feel that delicious warmth he seemed to possess. But then she remembered how painful it could be to get too close to Lord Wesmont. An iron door slammed shut on her foolhardy emotions. She lifted her chin, defying him to ever hurt her again.

"You surprise me, Lord Wesmont," she said, straining to sound contemptuous. "Do you truly require my permission to call? For I am convinced that you, my lord, are the sort of man who does precisely as he pleases."

He straightened, visibly irritated, but the light of challenge flashed in his eyes. "Very well, then. It *pleases* me to call.

Shall we say tomorrow at four o'clock for a drive in the Park."
He bowed curtly to both women and turned on his heel.

Fiona's mouth fell open, astonished at his audacity. She breathed out an annoyed little huff. Stamping her foot on the marble floor, and grabbing Miss Haversburg's arm with a vicious jerk, she marched down the hall to find the ladies' repairing room.

Maria blinked at her irate captor. "Miss Hawthorn, I must say your conversation with Lord Wesmont leaves me baffled, and more than a little astonished."

Fiona muttered under her breath. "Then you are not alone."

Chapter 14
A Scandal by
any other Name

The next morning Fiona sat with her aunt at the breakfast table. Of course it wasn't really morning, the giant clock in the hallway chimed twelve times, marking the hour as noon. Nevertheless, they sat breakfasting together in companionable silence until the butler presented Honore with a silver salver stacked high with mail.

"Oh, bother, what a pile." However, Honore didn't actually seem annoyed as she eagerly slit open the first missive. She was used to hostesses vying for her company at their evenings "at home." A rout was sure to be a crushing success if word got around that the notorious Countess Alameda might be in attendance.

Honore pulled out the first invitation. Extending her arm, she held the card up, squinted, and adjusted the distance until she could read it clearly. Grunting, she flipped the petition onto the table and ripped open the next card, read it, and tossed it down. Her brows pinched together as she looked over at Fiona.

"What is it, Aunt? Is something amiss?"

Honore's forehead cleared, but her eyebrows lifted, and her gaze floated up toward the ceiling. "Do you know, Fiona, I can see the ceiling with perfect clarity, but if I hold a letter closer than the end of my arm I can scarce make out the words."

"How bothersome that must be. Would you like me to read your morning correspondence to you?"

"Heavens no! I'm not as aged as all that."

"Of course not. I merely thought it might be more convenient—"

"Convenient? Convenient is being able to read the demmed things m'self. It is *my* correspondence, after all."

She tore open another invitation, read it, and flicked it aside. She grabbed a handful of letters from the silver tray, turned them over, and perused the seals until she found one that interested her. Running her finger over the large blue wax seal, she broke open the invitation. She read it, smiled sardonically, and let the card fall out of her hand.

"How perfectly extraordinary," she said, contemplating Fiona with a frown.

Fiona stuck a forkful of kippers into her mouth. She wasn't going to ask.

"It seems, m'dear, that you are no longer riding on my coattails."

Fiona wondered what she had done now; obviously her aunt was upset with her. The fish she was chewing suddenly tasted crusty and dry and became difficult to swallow. When at last she was able to clear her throat, she ventured, "I don't understand your meaning?"

Honore pulled her breakfast plate back in front of her and primly lifted her fork. "No? You don't understand?" She stabbed an orange and twirled it on the end of her fork. "Well then, let me explain. Society has crowned you her latest attraction. Judging from this stack of cards"—with her left hand she flicked the envelopes sitting on the tray—"every hostess in town is hoping *you* will attend her next ball. And can you guess why, m'dear?"

Fiona shook her head and carefully set her fork down on her plate, no longer hungry.

"Oh, I should think the answer obvious. Come now, whatever other failings you might have, you're not stupid. Can you not guess?"

Fiona took a deep breath. "I should think if I am invited anywhere it is simply because I am connected to you. I cannot possibly fathom any other reason."

That answer seemed to mollify Honore slightly. Her tone became less sarcastic. "Yes, I would have thought the same thing until last night. Now, it seems you are the one in demand. Without a doubt, they are all hoping you will come and create one of your famous incidents at their party."

"No. That can't be." Fiona's eyes opened wide. "You must be mistaken, Aunt. No one could wish a disaster on their own friends and family."

Honore snorted. "How little you know, my dear. Consider Lady Sefton's ball last night, do you recall the most interesting thing that happened? You need not answer, because everybody knows it was when Marcus got himself thumped to the floor. No matter it was Wesmont what thumped him, Marcus was dancing with you. Coupled with the news of your previous mishap with the Prince, society appears to have concluded that you are the harbinger of interesting scenes."

Fiona clapped her hands together in her lap and gritted her teeth. It was nonsense, just more of her aunt's insanity. It must be.

Honore chuckled and sliced open her orange. "Think, Fiona. If you go to Louise Haversburg's rout and a catastrophe occurs, Louise can be confident that her gathering will be talked about for weeks."

She frowned at her aunt. "This is ridiculous. It's extremely difficult to believe anyone would be so callous as to wish something to go wrong. Aside from the distress to one of their guests, what if someone is harmed, or worse yet, killed?"

Honore sucked the orange slice on her fork. She licked the juice off her lips. "That doesn't appear to have troubled anyone in the least. See here"—she gestured to the large invitation with the blue seal—"the Countess Lieven is most insistent that you appear at her ball. And the deuced thing is more than a month away." She lifted the gilt card and considered it for a moment. "You know, Fiona dear, I think she must have written this card out the moment she returned home from Lady Sefton's." Honore looked at the pile on the silver tray. "They all must have done so. How perfectly odd; they didn't think it could wait until morning."

"Well"—Fiona lifted her chin—"I shan't go! They may as well have gone to bed and saved their ink and paper. I refuse to be fodder for society's entertainment."

"Stuff and nonsense. What difference does it make?" Honore scoffed at her. "Consider Miss Phoebe Ritwater, is she not invited everywhere simply because she is beautiful? Yes. It's certainly not for her conversation. The moment the chit opens her mouth she becomes a dead bore, a lisping dead bore at that. But she is a lovely ornament, and gets invited everywhere simply because she is a spectacle for folks to gawk at, much like a walking flower arrangement."

Fiona shook her head; more of her aunt's wild ramblings. "I thought it was because she was well connected."

"Heavens no, child. Do you know how many well-connected gels sit home with only a few invitations for the whole Season?"

Honore picked up a small brass bell and jangled it. Her butler appeared at her elbow. "Send a footman to collect Monsieur Renellé. I want him here this afternoon, without delay. Tell him I am not at all pleased with the hair color he has inflicted upon me. Tell him I look older than the Queen Mother thanks to his ministrations. Silver, indeed. I ain't blind. It's gray. I want something youthful. Youthful, I tell you, more in keeping with my age."

The butler's mouth quivered almost imperceptibly, but his voice remained steady and even. "Very good, my lady."

Honore brushed the rest of her post out of the way with a

huff. She spread open a newspaper and ate the remainder of her breakfast in silence.

That afternoon, Maria Haversburg came to call and sat fidgeting on Lady Alameda's sofa. Her mama rapped her smartly on the leg. "Sit still," she said under her breath. Lady Haversburg looked anxiously at the mantel clock. "I daresay, Lady Alameda must be unavoidably detained. Perhaps, we ought to take our leave."

Fiona earnestly shook her head. "Oh no, I'm certain my aunt will appear at any moment. You know how unhappy she'd be to learn she missed you." She lifted a plate of Mattie's shortbread. "More biscuits, Lady Haversburg?"

"Well, just one more; they *are* tasty. I often say, Honore is most fortunate in her Scottish cook."

Lady Haversburg plucked a large biscuit from the plate. Maria looked hopefully at the plate Fiona held out, but her mother gestured it away, shaking her finger from side to side. "No, no." She sputtered crumbs. "Maria has had quite enough, thank you."

Fiona smiled sympathetically at her friend and looked up at the clock as it pinged four times for the hour.

Maria spoke, and the odor of musk and fetid teeth wafted toward Fiona. "Miss Hawthorn, were you not engaged to go driving with Lord Wesmont this afternoon?"

"I'm not quite certain." She smiled and acted as if it were of little or no importance.

"But didn't I hear him say he would call for you at four o'clock?"

"I don't know, did he? Lord Wesmont jests so often, one never knows if he is sincere or simply bamming." Fiona bit the corner of her lip, hoping her lie was not evident.

"Odd," said Maria. "He appeared to be such a serious man. I wouldn't have thought him one to jest about anything."

"I daresay, Maria is right." Her mama fanned at the air to

dispel her daughter's dental aroma. "Did you not see that beastly scowl Wesmont wore last night? Enough to give anyone the impression he is naught but an ill-tempered grudgen."

The butler stood in the open doorway and cleared his throat. Behind him stood the ill-tempered grudgen himself. "Lord Wesmont." He bowed, presenting the guest in the doorway.

The ladies turned to face the subject of their discussion standing before them, dressed in a perfect-fitting blue cutaway, and buff form-fitting unmentionables.

"However, one could do worse," muttered an admiring Lady Haversburg, nudging her daughter, not at all abashed about the disparaging comment she had just made.

Lord Wesmont's thick eyebrows were not set in his famous furrowed scowl. His eyes were shuttered halfway, and the corners of his mouth appeared to be twitching.

Fiona rose, struggling to control her breath and pulse. "Lord Wesmont, such a surprise."

He took her hand and spoke softly enough that only she could hear. "I see. So you thought I was merely jesting when I told you I would call at four."

She ignored his jibe and introduced him to Lady Haversburg and her daughter. He bowed politely over each lady's hand, and Fiona noted that, as he bowed over Maria's hand, he did not recoil from the blast of fetid air that surely must have assaulted him when the girl smiled. It pleased her that he took pains to be kind, and again, when Maria spoke to him and revealed even more of her unfortunate teeth, he maintained complete composure.

Honore startled everyone when she burst into the room. Fiona's mouth dropped open. Her aunt's hair was yellow, not ordinary fair hair, but the hue of a great yellow cheese, nearly orange. Shocking, as it was, her vivid new coiffure was eclipsed by her scanty gown of green transparent muslin. Although artfully designed, the neckline exposed far more than it concealed. The only covering over Honore's bosom was a diaphanous layer of mint green muslin leaves, emerging from a line of dark green silk which extended from floor to midriff, curving around the sides of each breast and up over her shoulders. The muslin bodice was cut in the shape of leaves waving like wispy feathers over Honore's nakedness.

Lady Haversburg stood up to greet her hostess while Maria dropped back down onto the sofa, too astonished by Honore's gown and hair to rise, until her mother's foot connected with her ankle, and she sprang to her feet.

Honore bustled forward, clasped Lady Haversburg's shoulders, kissed her cheek, and lisped as if she were an infant. "Louise, what a delightful surprise! I had no notion you were waiting for me." She turned on her niece. "For shame, Fiona, you should have informed me that I had guests."

Fiona blinked. Hadn't she sent word with the butler that her ladyship had company? Yes, and Lady Haversburg had seen her do it.

"Ah! And here's our Lord Wesmont." Honore lisped coyly and moved to him with mincing steps. She stopped directly beneath his gaze and lifted her hand up to him. "How good of you to call."

Fiona flushed livid pink as Tyrell bent over her aunt's hand. Surely from that position he must have been exposed to all of Honore's naked bosom.

Fiona's pink flush turned red and then hot. She spoke with a sharp authoritative tone that she hardly recognized as her own. "It is cool today, Aunt. I'll fetch your shawl so that you do not catch a chill."

"Nonsense." Honore continued to stand flirtatiously close to Tyrell. "It's a very warm day. Is it not, my lord?"

"Quite warm." He answered evenly.

Honore threw back her head and laughed.

Lady Haversburg reached out as if to clamp her hands over her daughter's ears, but then caught herself just in time. She cleared her throat. "Honore, dearest, I had hoped to stay and solicit your opinions about Maria's upcoming ball. But, oh heavens! Just look at the time. We've been here upwards of an hour, most unseemly of us. How time passes. We have so many calls to make. Must take our leave. I daresay you know how it is."

"I daresay," Honore said, waving them away while still smiling seductively at Tyrell.

"Come, Maria." Lady Haversburg yanked her daughter by the arm and whisked her out of the room. Fiona tried to see them to the drawing room door, but they were too quick for her. As they bustled down the stairs, Fiona heard Lady Haversburg mumbling and Maria's innocent question, "What did you say, Mama?"

"Nothing. Nothing, at all. A near thing that's all. Oh, do come along, Maria."

Fiona crossed her arms sternly across her chest. Her aunt was out of control and someone had to do something.

Honore pointed to a parcel under Wesmont's left arm, and then clapped her hands together. "What's this? Have you brought us a present?"

"Of sorts." He glanced at Fiona standing by the door.

"Delightful!" Honore pressed a finger against her cheek. "Let me guess. It must be a book."

"No, Lady Alameda, not a book."

She arched her eyebrow at him. "How mysterious. Whatever can it be? Surely it's not chocolates wrapped in plain brown paper."

"Nothing so amiable."

"No?" she said. "Well then, I cannot guess. You mustn't keep teasing me like this. I am quite overcome with curiosity." Her hand fluttered seductively to her breast and then to his arm. "Come, Wesmont, I insist you indulge me."

Fiona wanted to indulge Honore by throwing a blanket over her ladyship's nakedness and tossing her down the stairs headfirst. But she contained her murderous desires and glared at Tyrell as he led her lascivious aunt to a chair.

"Perhaps, my lady, you would like to sit down first. Unfortunately, my gift is not calculated to please."

Honore dropped unceremoniously into the chair. The petals on her bodice fluttered, revealing her dark nipples and covering them up again as the fabric settled back into place. "Very well." She patted her hands against her lap. "Give it to me. I am prepared to be displeased."

He handed her the package. She pulled off the string and folded back the brown paper to reveal a stack of cartoons. She lifted the first one from the pile, muttering under her breath as she struggled to bring it into focus.

"Aha! It is drawn by that fellow Cruikshank! What a wit he is." She sounded delighted.

Tyrell frowned at her. "Yes, I suppose he is, but look closer, Countess. Observe the identity of the characters."

She squinted and brought into focus a drawing of herself, kicking Lord Maverly in the eye, Marcus catching Fiona, and Prince George flipping through the air like a pinwheel. Honore's mouth quivered. She sputtered, guffawed, and then broke out in loud high-pitched laughter. Tears ran down her cheeks. Her laughter escalated until it became a howl echoing through the house.

Mattie bolted into the room. Her apron was covered with bloodstains and flour. She waved a butcher knife in front of her as if she were wielding a broad sword. Whipping her gaze around the room, she squinted suspiciously at Honore, who was doubled over in the chair, hysterical, crying, and stamping her small slippered feet against the floor. Mattie charged forward, her red hair flying about her like a madwoman. She stopped in front of Lord Wesmont and shook the knife in his face.

"Hie, ye rascal! What ha' ye done to m' babby?"

Wesmont lifted both hands, surrendering to the Scottish demon fishwife. "Nothing, madam, I assure you. Lady Alameda, please call off your she-bear."

"Yes. Yes. Oh, Mattie, do come away from Lord Wesmont."

Honore sputtered and giggled as she waved away her protector. Wiping at the tears running down her cheeks, she said, "Only just look at this." Laughing again, she handed a cartoon to her bristling former nanny.

Before she accepted the paper, Mattie glared suspiciously at each occupant of the room. She bent her head and studied the cartoon. "Och! What's this then? This 'ere is disgusting, that's what this is. Ye cannot stand for it, me girl. Ye must have whoever drew this filth horsewhipped."

Honore's lips pinched into a thin line, and she snatched the cartoon out of Mattie's hands. "Nonsense! It's merely a bit of fun."

Lord Alameda strolled into the drawing room, wearing little more than a dressing gown and breeches. Lord Wesmont stiffened as the rogue walked over to Fiona, took her by the elbows, and kissed her cheek proprietarily. "Good morning, my dear." He glanced casually around the room. "What's all the commotion?"

Fiona answered him curtly. "Officially, the day is well into the *afternoon,* Marcus. And I haven't a clue what the commotion is about. Lord Wesmont appears to be entertaining my half-naked aunt with a lampoon. And she—well, observe for yourself." Fiona waved her hand with disgust at her wayward guardian.

Honore grinned up at Tyrell. "My dear Lord Wesmont, not only did you fail to displease me, you have entertained me famously. This etching is utterly diverting. Oh, Marcus, come see, it is a most hilarious cartoon."

With the barest acknowledgement of Lord Wesmont's presence, Marcus went to Honore's side and took the print. He pulled a quizzing glass from his pocket and surveyed the caricature.

He chuckled and dropped his eyeglass. "This is exquisite. Might I have one?"

"No." Tyrell pulled it out of Marcus's hands.

Honore chuckled again. "Oh, but it is vastly amusing, Lord Wesmont. Wherever did you find it?"

"In the window at Laurie and Whittle's on Fleet Street. May I say, that I do not think the rest of the *ton* would take it in as favorable a light as you do. Not only does it make Miss Hawthorn into a figure of ridicule, but it casts dispersion on both of your virtues. As a precaution, I purchased all of the cartoons remaining in the shop, and Mr. Whittle assured me he would break the plate. We may hope that the scandal is averted, but I've no doubt that, at least, some of the caricatures were purchased prior to my arrival at his shop."

"You bought them all? To protect our virtue? How very stuffy you are. The *ton* don't care. On the contrary, half of 'em were there when it happened." Honore pointed over her shoulder at Fiona. "There stands the reigning attraction of the *beau monde*. This lampoon would only have increased their interest."

"I don't follow your reasoning."

"No, you don't do you. Ah well, how tiresome. I leave it to her to explain it."

"Very well, I came to take Miss Hawthorn driving in the Park, with your permission of course."

Honore stood up and brushed out her skirt. The movement set the diaphanous petals to fluttering again. Her nipples were once more exposed.

Mattie, who had been standing nearby, with arms folded across her chest like a disapproving general, gasped. She put her hands on her hips, her nostrils flared, and her eyes blazed like an enraged mother's.

Honore sidled up to Tyrell and ran her finger under his chin and cocked her head. "How do I know I can trust you with Fiona? I've heard some *very* alarming reports about you."

"I assure you, Countess—"

"No, don't bother." She waved away his explanation and closed her eyes. She rubbed her temple and flashed her eyes open again. "Just go. Go on, Wesmont. Take Fiona to the

Park. I'm certain it will be a very proper, very dull drive." She shooed him away.

Tyrell brusquely inclined his head and strode across the room to Fiona, and offered her his arm.

She wasn't sure she would go anywhere with him. After ogling her traitorous aunt like any common rake, how could he expect her to accompany him on a drive.

As Fiona considered how best to set down Lord Wesmont, she heard Mattie ordering Honore to cover herself up.

The towering woman removed her apron and thrust it at her ladyship. " 'Ere, use this."

Honore lifted her chin in defiance. "Take that smelly thing away. I'll wear anything I like."

Mattie started huffing and puffing like a bull about to charge, and it looked as if they were about to come to blows.

Fiona suddenly decided it would be prudent to accept Tyrell's offer to leave the house. Without speaking, she placed her hand on his arm and gestured toward the door.

They had nearly escaped when Honore called to Tyrell in a shrill voice, "Lord Wesmont! I'm giving an informal little soirée Thursday evening. Do come. I believe it will be an education for you." Her laughter rang false in the charged air of the room.

Tyrell nodded his acceptance. As they hurried to leave, Mattie's voice exploded behind them. "What are ye about, wearing a tart's dress like this? It scarcely covers ye." There was a loud ripping sound. "Oh, begging yer pardon, m'lady! I guess it won't even do tha' no more." The nanny-cum-cook's voice rang out triumphantly.

As Fiona and Tyrell retreated down the hall, they heard Marcus's sardonic laugh, and Honore screaming, "Get out of here, Marcus! Out!"

"Aye, you heard her ladyship," echoed Mattie. "Now, pet, put m' apron around ye. We'll take ye up an' put something decent on ye. And what hae' ye done to yer hair? It looks like a great yellow peach—"

"You can't treat me like this, Mattie! Give me that knife! I have a good mind to run you through, you interfering old busybody! I'm a grown woman. And I'll wear what I like!"

Honore was shouting so loudly that Fiona shuddered involuntarily. She and Tyrell quickened their steps. They couldn't walk down the stairs fast enough to miss hearing Mattie's booming response. "Not while I live under the same roof—ye won't!"

"As to that, you would do well to remember precisely whose roof—"

Fiona and Tyrell were almost at a dead run by the time they reached the foyer. The butler opened the door for them and calmly handed Tyrell his hat as they rushed out. Tyrell boosted Fiona into his curricle, grabbed the reins from his tigers and whipped his horses away from the curb.

A moment passed before he had his horses and his self-composure restored to order. He glanced over at Fiona. She looked up at him, and they broke out laughing.

Tyrell shook his head as if to clear his mind. "I feel as if I have just narrowly escaped from bedlam."

She smiled apologetically. "Yes, she is a trifle unusual. And, I fear, not very predictable."

"You've vastly understated the matter. The woman is a veritable lunatic."

Fiona nodded, "And yet, at other times, she seems so understanding and almost motherly."

Tyrell sputtered. "Motherly? I'd be hard-pressed to believe that."

"No, it's true. Sometimes, she can be very affectionate. Did you know, she completely redecorated a bedroom in anticipation of my arrival? It's true. And what's more, she even guessed correctly what my favorite colors might be."

"Astonishing."

Fiona heard the skepticism in his voice. "You don't believe me, and I can't blame you. She can be so rational and loving one minute, and then turn quite dangerous and irrational the next. I fear you've not seen the more noble side of her character. Today was certainly not a good example."

"I'll have to take your word for it. Still, her radical shifts in conduct cannot be safe. Didn't I just hear her threatening to run her cook through with a butcher knife? Your aunt is hardly a fit chaperone for a young lady. I cannot be pleased about you staying in her household."

Fiona crossed her arms and exhaled loudly. "It seems, my lord, that you are never pleased with me. I show marked skill in disappointing you."

"You misunderstand—"

"No, I don't think so. Aside from that, I hardly think you are the one who should be concerned about my welfare. After all, I cannot be in any greater danger with my aunt than I was with you at the lake."

Tyrell's jaw tightened. "I've already apologized for that, Fiona. Believe me, I thoroughly regret my behavior that afternoon."

Fiona grabbed the curricle seat and squeezed the leather until she could compose herself. She faced Tyrell, and words flew out of her mouth. "Exactly *which* behavior do you regret, my lord? Pretending to drown and nearly frightening me out of my mind? Or perhaps you regret kissing me? Or was it the humiliation you heaped on me afterwards?" Immediately, she regretted her outburst. She peeked self-consciously back at the young tiger standing behind them.

Tyrell looked over at her. "You needn't worry about my tiger. He's deaf as a doornail. Ain't you, Kip?"

"Right you are, guv, been deaf since the day I was born." The young lad riding on the back of the curricle winked at her. Fiona smiled uneasily.

Tyrell shifted the reins to his left hand and with his right reached over and covered Fiona's hand. "Fiona, I'm sorry, I said those things to you. Truthfully, the entire episode baffles me. I cannot comprehend why I acted like such a madman. I have no excuse for my actions, and I only hope that you will forgive me."

He dropped his guard and looked at her with all the tenderness he felt. Specks of sunshine glimmered in her eyes, and her cheeks blushed an endearing pink. She seemed to question him without even speaking. He answered with a half smile. *She is doing it again,* he thought. *Pulling me toward her as if by magic.* Unbidden, his fingers caressed hers, and his eyes traced a path across her velvet cheek to her lips and then down her ivory neck.

Confusing man, Fiona thought, blushing under the intensity of his gaze. *You are no more predictable than my aunt. But, please, don't take your hand away. I like how your fingers play with mine. Your very touch makes me feel as if I've stepped for a moment into heaven.*

Just then, a young blade driving a high-perch phaeton skidded around the corner, headed straight toward them, out of control. Tyrell jerked his hand away from Fiona's and pulled the reins. He swerved his team out of the way with only inches to spare.

Kip whistled. "Nice work that, guv."

"Yes, well, perhaps we ought to take a turn about the park, away from young jackanapes who shouldn't be allowed to hold a whip."

Tyrell's brows drew together in a silent brood, under which he cast sidelong glances at the woman seated next to him. Why did his traitorous body respond so quickly to this female? He fixed his eyes straight ahead and concentrated on controlling his cattle, controlling them perfectly. After taking one turn about the park, he headed back in the direction of Alison Hall.

"My lord," said Fiona, "you are wearing your famous scowl."

The corners of his mouth twitched. "Ah yes. The beastly scowl that makes me appear to be—how did Lady Haversburg phrase it?—an ill-tempered old grudgen."

"I don't believe the word *old* was mentioned."

"No? Well, that's a comfort." He laughed. "You may as well know the truth, Fiona. Lady Haversburg is right. I am an ill-tempered grudgen."

"I am quite aware of that, my lord."

"Are you, indeed?" He frowned down at her. "Unfortunately, I must risk provoking you even further. Fiona, it is impossible for you to continue living with Lady Alameda. Not only is she a woman of questionable character, but sharing the same roof with Lord Alameda is . . . well, it's reckless in the extreme. Dangerous."

"What can you have against Marcus?" She noticed his brows pinching together even tighter, and something inside her registered a triumph.

"The man can't be trusted, that's what. You shouldn't be anywhere near the wretch."

"But, my lord, Marcus has been everything that is kind to me. He is affectionate and generous with his time. Without his attentions, I fear I would be sitting against the wall at every event."

A grumble came from deep within Tyrell's throat. "I see you use his given name."

"Of course." She smiled and lifted her chin. "The man is practically my cousin."

"Nevertheless," he growled, "you ought not to be staying under the same roof with him. Cousin or not. He's a known rakehell, a scapegrace, and a scoundrel!"

"Really, Lord Wesmont." She feigned offense, but the muscles in her cheek quivered with mirth. She found his hostility toward Marcus extraordinarily amusing.

Tyrell was too busy managing his team and fuming to notice. "I tell you, he cannot be trusted. You say he is affectionate. Ha! It's his *affectionate* nature that troubles me. Exactly how affectionate is he?"

It was Fiona's turn to glare at him. "Pray, don't trouble

yourself on my account, my lord. As I told you before, my welfare really isn't any of your concern."

"It most certainly is my concern. You are"—he stopped—"you are—I am a friend of your father's. Yes, and your neighbor. I would be derelict in my duty if I didn't concern myself with your welfare."

"Oh fustian! You think I'm a little fool who can't manage her own affairs. Well, I am not nearly as green as everyone thinks."

Tyrell arched one brow and cast his eyes knowingly over her. "Are you not green? I seem to remember having very little difficulty trapping you into a compromising situation. Or don't you remember?"

"That is unfair, Lord Wesmont. That was a completely different situation. Besides you tricked me."

"Yes, but that is precisely my point. It was easy to trick you. And, if memory serves, you are rather susceptible to kissing. I don't recall much resistance from you, quite the contrary—"

"Stop it!" she ordered, knowing her face had turned red. She bit her lip in an attempt to steady her voice. "My lord, you have passed over unfairness and gone directly into cruelty. Do you really think I would have allowed anyone but you to kiss me like that? I'm well aware of how foolish it was. How can I forget? Especially when you remind me of it at every turn. I realize I was gullible. But that day"—tears trickled out freely from her eyes—"it was unlike any other."

Tyrell felt his chest tighten and part of his stubborn heart rip open. He shifted the leather and tried to grab her hand, but she pulled it away.

He sighed heavily. "I've done it again, haven't I? I've said everything precisely the wrong way?"

She nodded, wiping at her eyes.

While trying to manage his team, he grabbed her waist and urged her toward him. "Listen to me, Fiona. I don't mean to be unkind. I don't understand what happened to me that day. You were so beautiful in the water and sunshine, so earnest and sweet. I lost my head. I acted like a scoundrel and took advantage of you. Perhaps that's why I worry that Alameda, who is most assuredly a shameless scoundrel, might also try to take advantage of you."

He patted her tenderly. "Do you understand?"

She looked up at him, her dark eyes swimming with softness and a tentative trust that melted him to the core and made him start to burn. Her mouth was just a heartbeat away. *Gad,* he thought, *I've got to stop this nonsense!* He snatched his arm away from her and snapped the traces to make the team pick up their speed.

Fiona looked down at her hands and twisted the finger of her glove. "If I left Alison Hall, where would you have me go? Timtree Corners is only too glad to be shot of me. Truthfully, I am happier living with my aunt than I was at home. She may be eccentric, but she doesn't accuse me of being forever underfoot. She doesn't think I'm cursed. And, while Marcus may be a rascal, he is quite securely under her thumb. Nothing goes on at Alison Hall without her approval. So you see, whether I am painfully green or not, Aunt Honore keeps me safe enough."

His brows remained knitted together. "I see," he said and meant precisely the opposite. He thought she was flat wrong, but right now there was nothing he could do about it.

They pulled up in front of her aunt's town house. Tyrell handed the leads to Kip and jumped out of the curricle. He helped Fiona down, but did not linger holding her. He set her on the ground and stepped away without giving his treacherous body a chance to respond to her exotic smell, or the curve of her waist under his hands, or the small dimple on her left cheek that came and went with each smile. He stepped back so he could properly ignore all of those things.

Fiona wondered if he had developed an aversion to her. But she had endured enough of Lord Wesmont's fickle nature.

She'd had enough of him being loverlike one minute and distant the next. Right now, she wanted nothing more than to deliver a swift kick to his shin. Instead, she stamped her slippered foot on the sidewalk, winced briefly at the pain it caused, and proceeded up the stairs.

The front door opened, and the butler waited like a mute vigil. Lord Wesmont tipped his hat to Fiona's retreating figure and said formally, "I'll see you Thursday evening at your aunt's soirée."

"As you please." Fiona bobbed a less-than-gracious curtsy, without turning around, and continued to march up the stairs.

Tyrell set his hat back firmly on his head and muttered as he climbed into his curricle, "Damnable girl."

Kip's mouth spread in a knowing grin. "Quite right, guv, a very damnable girl."

Lord Wesmont snarled, "Thought you were deaf, Kip."

"Yes, sir, quite right, deaf as a doornail."

"Well, see that you stay that way."

Chapter 15
The Soirée from Hades

Honore floated down the stairway in a purple gown. Marcus perused her figure at length. Her breasts mounded up out of a very low neckline, and a huge garnet nestled between them. The entire gown was beaded, not beads sown onto fabric, but strung together like a coat of mail. If one caught precisely the right angle and looked carefully through the glittering network of beads, Honore's anatomy was quite apparent. Shafts of beaded material hung from the bodice to the floor, where they ended in triangular points. These flowed over a transparent purple underskirt. Past the flimsy underskirt she wore nothing at all.

He dropped his glass and drew in a loud breath. "My dear Honore, you will simply devastate the gentlemen."

She tossed her nose into the air. "And why should I not?"

Marcus looked at her speculatively. "No reason at all, my dear. You are a stunner."

She inclined her head.

"Why, the poor fellows will go blind just straining to look at you." He glanced up at the chandelier and twirled his glass faster. "Poor Fiona, she'll quite fade into the woodwork. She's naught but a mouse next to you."

Honore glared at him. "What is that to me? She looks after herself well enough."

"Certainly. I merely thought, that as her chaperone—"

"I am not her dragon!" She poked her finger at his chin. "Not an old biddy consigned to the wall! Do you hear me? I am not." Honore stepped back and straightened her shoulders.

Marcus hooded his eyes, surveying her body appreciatively. "Perish the thought, Honore. Hiding your superior charms away, buried in the role of duenna, it's unthinkable, a tragic waste. Yet, my dear, you have mentioned, *many times,* that Fiona is your protégée, the offspring you never had?"

"Well, that was before I really knew the chit. I've changed my mind. She's not at all of my ilk. She's as stuffy and dull as that lovesick earl who pants after her. No, she doesn't serve the purpose. Thank goodness, I haven't gone to all the bother of changing my will, yet."

She flipped her hand backward against her forehead and briefly struck a pose of one of the seven muses. Then she patted his cheek as if he were eight years old. "It doesn't matter. My brother in Hertfordshire had a daughter—her mother died some years ago. I may look into that when I've a mind to. As for now, I've had enough of schoolgirls, haven't you? Excuse me, Marcus, I must attend to my guests."

As Honore walked past him, Marcus glared at her undulating backside and muttered, "How many motherless nieces can the woman have?"

No point in killing Fiona now, he thought, his inheritance was safe for the moment. But what if Honore changed her mind again, or found a new orphan to donate her wealth to? Damn. One solution seemed to elevate itself above the others—get the inheritance now. Tonight's scheme to eliminate Fiona would have to be altered. He had a new target.

Tyrell looked down the long table at the unusual collection of faces seated at Countess Alameda's dining table. He was placed halfway down the table, and perversely, Honore had seated him across from Fiona, where he might glimpse her but not be able to speak to her. Equally annoying was the mountainous centerpiece of flowers that obscured Fiona from his view unless he craned his neck sideways.

The perversity of her aunt's table arrangement was not lost on Fiona either. On Tyrell's right sat a voluptuous young actress. For some reason Fiona wanted very desperately for the footman to spill something hot on the young woman's head. Where were her accursed catastrophes when she needed them? On Tyrell's left sat Maria Haversburg.

Fiona noted how pleased Maria looked. She was fortunate Honore had placed her next to the one man in society who did not act repelled by her unfortunate breath. Fiona strained to hear their conversation.

She heard Maria say, "It is a great relief to be seated next to you, Lord Wesmont. Mama warned me that the company might be a trifle fast tonight. But she said we must come and bear it. One dare not risk offending Lady Alameda. She gave me strict orders, to be on my guard. But, nothing prepared me for this— poets, actors, and artists—my goodness." Maria gestured toward the other side of the table, and Fiona quickly averted her eyes so that they would not know she had been eavesdropping. "The man sitting next to Miss Hawthorn is said to be friends with Lord Byron. And, Lord Wesmont, when the tenor began to sing that song about—about country maidens, I tried not to listen. Truly, I did. But of course, I heard every word. I suppose I should have put my hands over my ears, but that would've been rude, wouldn't it?"

Tyrell nodded, only half listening, and tried to steal a glance at Fiona. She looked like an enchanting sea nymph, with a wreath of tiny blue flowers encircling her head and tendrils of escaping hair floating around her cheeks and whispering across her bare shoulders. Her dress was the color of seawater in sunlight, neither green nor blue, but it made her eyes appear as dark as the ocean during a storm.

The young man sitting next to Fiona bent too close to her, and Tyrell frowned. Blast the bounder! Why did Honore invite that rabble here? Poets! He cursed the lot of them—nothing but a pack of dissipated dandies. Tyrell coughed loudly and glared at the poet insinuating himself on Fiona. The young puppy took no notice.

"My lord"—Miss Haversburg touched his sleeve and glanced in the poet's direction—"I think the young man is foxed. Indeed, he and his friends were rather well into their cups long before dinner began."

"It would seem so," Lord Wesmont agreed and stuck a fork of something into his mouth. He chewed. The something had no taste.

After dinner, Lady Alameda's guests were invited to wander into various rooms as they pleased, much like an indoor circus. Musicians played in the ballroom, so that those who wished might dance. A magician entertained in an anteroom, and there were several card rooms available, port, claret, and champagne flowed liberally throughout the house.

The actress on his left laid a proprietary hand on Tyrell's arm and asked him to escort her to a drawing room, where she'd heard there would be a snake charmer of amazing ability. When Tyrell glanced across the table, Fiona had already risen and was leaving the room. He could not possibly catch up to her without vaulting over the table, so he reluctantly led the actress to her destination.

He scanned the audience in the drawing room for any sign of Fiona. She was not there. The woman at his side squealed with delight as the snake charmer allowed what appeared to be a live viper to crawl into his mouth. It looked as if he swallowed the creature, but when he opened his mouth again, the lethal snake slithered out.

"The fool," grumbled Tyrell.

"Oh, how can you say so?" The actress protested. "It's just the most fantastical feat I've ever seen!"

"Suppose the blasted thing bites him? What then? We have a dead snake charmer and a house crawling with vipers."

"Ooh, how dreadful. Oh, what shall we do?" She squealed

and clutched at his arm, looking desperately about the floor as if the snakes were already loose. Tyrell rolled his eyes.

The Duke of Cumberland stepped forward, a cruel scar marred the side of his face and was only partially concealed under a black velvet eye patch. His thick wiry side whiskers did nothing to soften his harsh appearance. "Do not concern yourself, miss."

Cumberland sneered at Wesmont before he blatantly examined the shapely little actress's assets. The dark duke puffed up his chest and spoke. "No viper will escape, but I shall take great pleasure in blowing its head off." He opened his coat to reveal a small pistol housed in the sash around his waist. "I never go anywhere unarmed."

Wide-eyed, she sank into a deep curtsy. "Oh, Your Grace, how very brave you are." Then she tilted her chin and fanned her eyelashes at the notorious duke.

Tyrell left them to it. He stalked out of the room, mumbling that the house was indeed crawling with vipers, and the Duke of Cumberland was one of them. *The mad Lady Alameda probably has bear-baiting in the next room. It's a demmed asylum—that's what it is.*

Fiona and Maria Haversburg sat together on a sofa in a quieter part of the house, hoping to avoid the raucous company. Relaxed somewhat by all the rum punch and champagne, Fiona asked Maria a question that had been on her mind since the day they met. "Why does your mother not take you to a surgeon to fix your teeth?"

Maria sighed wearily. "Oh, I have begged her to do so several times since we came to London. But it's useless. She swears by our family physician, Dr. Klimes. Honestly, the man must be a hundred years old, quite the most ancient fellow I've ever seen. Which only goes further toward convincing Mama that he is the best doctor alive."

"Will he not do something for your poor mouth?"

"Oh, Fiona"—Maria put her hands up to cover her face and tried to hold back the tears—"you can not imagine the ghastly cures he puts me through. He forced me to drink boiled pikes' eyes. Can you imagine?"

Fiona shook her head.

"On another occasion he smeared my gums with alum and lime and seared them with a hot iron. He even put leeches in my mouth. Leeches! I didn't think I could bear it. And no matter how I scream, or cry, Mama will not listen. She's known that wretched old doctor since her birth. His cures are sacred to her. I swear, she reveres him more than the King himself. I dare not think about when we return home, and what remedy he will try next."

Fiona flexed her jaw. "But that's barbaric."

"The worst of it is, Fiona, I have been praying, *praying to God,* that Dr. Klimes will die before the Season ends. Do you think I will go to hell for that?"

Fiona's brows knit together. She looked at Maria and bit her lip. "I don't know. It is a very bad thing to pray for someone's death."

Both girls sat in silent contemplation.

"Come." Fiona decided they needed a diversion. "Take a turn with me in Aunt Honore's garden. She has some roses that will look lovely in the moonlight. They might cheer us. And perhaps, Maria, we can think of a way to get you to a proper doctor. Then you won't have to fear that wretched old Dr. Klimes, and you could stop praying for his death."

They looped arms and headed out into the summer night. A few moments later, Tyrell, still searching the house for Fiona, passed by the empty sofa they had just occupied.

* * *

Maria and Fiona wandered among Honore's rosebushes. The cool crisp air smelled sweet with the rich perfume of new blooms and dying blossoms. Autumn would be here all too soon.

"I love the fragrance of summer roses, don't you, Fiona?"

"Yes," she agreed absently and pulled Maria's arm tighter to her. "But listen, I think I've devised a plan. Let us suppose that I were to pose as your older sister, I am much taller than you are, you see, so it would be quite believable. Then I could escort you to a surgeon for a consultation about your teeth. We might escape Lady Haversburg by telling her we are going to visit Hatchard's together."

"Oh, I don't know if Mama can be persuaded to let me out alone in your company. It is not you, of course. I'm never allowed to go anywhere without a maid."

"Of course." Fiona studied the stones on the pathway and looked up suddenly. "I have it! I'll call on you with my aunt's maid with us. She owes me a small debt, so I'm certain I can obtain her promise of silence. We'll have a maid with us and all will be right with your mama."

"Yes, it might just work."

They stopped to admire a huge white rose. The spray from a nearby fountain adorned the rose with minuscule drops of moisture and set the rose petals to glimmering in the moonlight.

In back of them a shout went up. "There she is!"

Three young bucks stumbled and staggered up the path behind Fiona and Maria. Mr. Rupert, the amorous poet who had sat next to her during supper, waved his finger at Fiona.

"That's her. My enchantress! Look at her, you mere mortals! Be captured as I am, by her wild—her wild, engulfing spirit. That's it—engulfing spirit. I am swallowed up." Rupert swung around, nearly knocking down his fellows. "There is no escape for me. I am consumed by the—by the liquid fire in her eyes. She calls to me like a siren song. Behold me, I am drowned in the elixir of her mouth."

"Kissed her, did you?" jibed one of his companions, slapping Rupert on the back.

The poet stumbled forward, almost falling at Fiona's feet. He turned around to his companions and placed his hands on his heart. "No"—he shook his head—"though her lips beckon me like ripe—ripe plums—no, that's not it, I have it! Her lips beckon to me like ripe pomegranates." He pointed up at the air like a statesman. "I have not yet tasted—nor yet partook—partaken." He hiccuped.

Fiona squeezed Maria's arm. "I think we'd best leave quickly." She edged away down a side path.

"Hold!" cried the young man. He reached out with surprising speed and snared Fiona's arm. "Would you leave me to suffer the endless torment of unrequited love? Can beauty be so cruel?"

"Mr. Rupert," she said while trying to pry his fingers loose, "you are foxed. The only thing you will suffer from is a violent headache in the morning. Now, please let go of me."

"Nay," he said. "I will not release you until you have freed me from your spell."

"Ho, now," said one of his less-inebriated companions. "You'd do well to remember that the chit is the countess's niece, la Hawthorn, the Dangerous Duchess. Come away, Rupert. Think, man, Lady Alameda will have your guts for garters."

"I don't care. Go away you—you—gutless sheep. Better yet take away this other charmer and leave me alone to worship at the feet of my goddess."

"Nah! You're balmy. You'll have hell to pay." The dissenter waved his hand at the group and staggered away. "I'll have no part in this, thank you."

The third young man stepped forward and waved his hand in the air as if answering his teacher's summons. "I'll oblige you, Rupert." He eagerly snatched Maria by the waist and pulled her away. "Come, my beauty, let's away in the moonlight."

Maria shrieked as he put his other hand on her bottom and hurried her along.

"Kick him, Maria! Run!" Fiona called after her. Maria only answered with a squawk before disappearing into the darkness.

Fiona stomped down on Lord Rupert's boot, but her slippered foot did little to penetrate his inebriated senses. He pulled her close, and his rum breath turned Fiona's stomach. "Mr. Rupert, I insist you stop this nonsense immediately."

"I cannot help myself, my siren. It is you who must release me—from this exquisite bondage I am in." He dropped to his knees, still gripping her arms, and buried his face against her abdomen. "I worship you."

"Sir, I beg of you."

On the pathway behind them, Fiona heard scuffling noises and a rustle of bushes. Then Mr. Rupert's friend bellowed. "Gad! What an odor! *Foul,* does not do it justice. Fah!" The man spit noisily and cursed again. "I've been cheated, I have. Thought I was kissing a woman and it turned out to be a chamber pot."

Fiona heard Maria's wounded exclamation and a resounding slap as the man must have received his just reward.

"Gads, well, I deserved that. Pr'haps, it'll bring me to m' senses and I won't asphyxiate from yer breath. That's right, dearie, run away, does me a favor it does." He, too, fled the scene, but in the opposite direction.

Poor Maria, to be doubly insulted in such a way. Fiona wanted to console her friend. Her patience with the poet clamped against her belly ran out. She grabbed a sizeable chunk of his hair and began to apply a painful twist.

Maria skittered away down the dark path toward the lights of the house. She burst through the first open doorway, looking like a frenzied lunatic. Fortunately, she collided with Lord Wesmont, who was just on his way outside, having exhausted all of the interior rooms in his search for Fiona.

He grasped her by the arms. "Miss Haversburg, you're overset. What's happened?"

"Oh, my lord," she sobbed, "it was horrible!" She sniffled and tried to stop sobbing. "Those wretched poets—they—they accosted us. I escaped. It was awful—truly awful. Oh!" She looked up, suddenly alarmed, "But you must come quickly! Lord Rupert still has Fiona. I can't say what he is doing to her. Oh—it's all too dreadful—"

"Where?" demanded Tyrell. "Where is she?"

"Out there." She pointed at the dark garden. "Near the fountain."

"Stay here," commanded Tyrell. "Better yet, your mother is in the next room, tell her what's happened. She'll undoubtedly want to take you home."

She nodded obediently. He marched out with his fists doubled, planning to knock the randy poet all the way to perdition. He would have, too, if he hadn't arrived at the fountain just in time to see Fiona thrust her knee into Rupert's private parts and shove the blighter backward into the fountain pool.

Fiona planted her hands on her hips and watched the poet thrashing around in the fountain pond. Tyrell strode up beside her. She turned and glanced up at him as if it were the most natural thing in the world for him to be standing at her side. "Do you think I've killed him?"

"No. He'll live. Which is more than I can say if I had reached him before you politely pushed him into the drink."

"He became annoying."

"Yes, so I heard. Miss Haversburg bolted into the ballroom looking like the devil was after her."

"Is she all right?" Fiona put her hand on his arm.

"Yes." Tyrell covered her hand with his. "She appears to have come to no serious harm."

"Thank heavens."

Just then the poet sat up in the fountain. He shook his head, sending a spray of water over Fiona and Tyrell, and beamed up at them like an idiot. "I will be famous!" he shouted. "Yes, famous! I have been vanquished—nay, nearly drowned, by the Duchess of Disaster. I'll be the talk of all London by morning. Help me out, sir." He held out a hand to Tyrell. "I must compose a verse to send the *Post*."

Tyrell's eyes narrowed dangerously. He approached the enthusiastic young buck, placed a firm hand on the fellow's forehead, and pushed him back under the water. Fiona's laughter bubbled out behind him. He let go, and the bewildered young man popped his head up out of the water, coughing, gasping, and spitting.

Tyrell gave him a moment to recover before speaking to him like a tutor to an erring pupil. "I suggest you go home, Rupert. Sleep off the excesses of this night, and forget you ever met Miss Hawthorn. 'Else you'll find yourself in a very uncomfortable state. Nay, a painful state. For I've not thrashed anyone in several days. I must admit I am fairly itching to do so. If you were not too drunk to be of any sport, I'd beat you to a bloody pulp this moment."

"What!" cried the young man. "Not tell a soul that I, Rupert, have fallen prey to London's latest enigma? Why, it's the perfect showcase for my poetry. How can you expect—"

Tyrell grabbed the poet's head and thrust it back under the water. He thrashed about until Tyrell let him rise, gulping for air. "Not a soul, is *precisely* what I expect. You will carry the burden of this night to your grave. Think of it as poetic torture, exquisite suffering. Whatever you like. However, you will not tell anyone. Do we understand one another?"

Rupert nodded his head reluctantly. Strands of dripping hair flopped over his forlorn face. "Nary a soul. You have my word."

"Just so," said Tyrell, shaking the water from his cuff. He inclined his head at the soaking poet, turned, and took Fiona by the arm, guiding her down a side path.

She smiled and shook her head. "You needn't have nearly drowned the poor wretch."

"Needn't I?" His voice rose. "Forgive me, Miss Hawthorn, I forget that you don't mind being the subject of the latest gossip. If you prefer I can go back and invite him to ridicule you in any manner he—"

She yanked her arm away from him and stopped walking. "Do you truly think there is anything I can do to escape my reputation? No matter where I go, no matter how quiet and unobtrusive I try to be, something extraordinary always happens."

She threw her hands into the air, frustration overwhelming her, making it impossible to speak calmly. "It's hopeless. I accept my fate. What else can I do? I'm cursed, jinxed, or maybe just plain unlucky. Whether you choose to believe it, or not, my lord. The *ton* believes it. They find me vastly entertaining—a novelty. Well, and why shouldn't they? Am I any different from a bearded lady at the fair, or a two-headed calf?"

She stopped for a moment and lowered her voice. "I'm just another spectacle like—like that horrid snake charmer Aunt Honore hired." Tears ran down her cheeks, and she lifted her hand up to cover her trembling mouth.

Tyrell's heart lurched uncomfortably. He gathered her into his arms, and she sobbed against his chest. Smoothing her hair and stroking her back, he wondered what he should say. The moonlight wrapped them in a comfortable silence. He said nothing. After some time, she stopped crying.

Fiona grimaced and whispered self-consciously, "I've flattened your cravat."

He lifted her chin up and rubbed it with his thumb. "Yes, I expect you've given it a good wash, too."

"It seems I'm always ruining your clothing."

Her smile made his insides tumble, and the familiar heat began to rise.

"Fiona, you must not look at me like that." His gaze washed over her, lapping up her beautiful face and lithe form. "You have no idea how tempting you are." He kissed her cheek and stroked the inviting curve of her back.

Fiona sniffled again. "How can you say I tempt you, my lord, when I have been nothing but an annoyance to you."

"True," he whispered, as if murmuring love words to her. "You *do* annoy me. You drive me mad. You couldn't possibly know how much you annoy me." He spoke softly into her ear and gently brushed her wayward curls away from her cheek. "You even bother me in my sleep. You refuse to leave my dreams, and you haunt my waking mind as well. It is all very annoying."

She tried to push back from him, to see his face, to try and understand what he meant, but that only brought them face-to-face.

"Yes, Fiona, that's it—push away. Run away, while you can. I'm about to behave like that ridiculous lovesick poet I wanted to drown."

She felt his warm breath on her face, and as he held her firmly in place, he slowly bent toward her, covering her mouth with his. Then his restraint vaporized. Unleashing a ravenous hunger on her lips, he kissed her again and again with an open searching mouth as if he wanted to devour her.

Fiona put her arms around his neck. He was right, she ought to run away as he had ordered her to do. But, just now, she couldn't. She wanted to kiss him, for a very long time, melt into him, wrap her being around him. So she pressed closer and kissed him as wildly as he kissed her.

It was happening again. That sweet all-consuming euphoria was overtaking her. Fiona remembered falling into this same trap at the lake. He had kissed her senses into sweet oblivion and then hated her for it later. She had to stop him this time. Better to suffer without his kisses, than to suffer the disgust he would feel later. Fiona slid her hands onto his chest and gently pushed away.

Tyrell stopped and looked into her downcast eyes. "I'm sorry." His voice came out husky and sounded harsh in the quiet night air.

Her response was barely audible. "Are you?"

"No." He cleared his throat and stepped back from her. "No. Yes. No! I'm not sorry. I wanted to do that and much more. I get near you and a kind of insanity takes over. It's all I can do to keep from throwing you down and having my way with you right here in the garden. I can't explain it. You are like a strange wine, one taste, and I am drunk to the point of madness."

He raked his hands through his hair. "Fiona, I've known you since you were a child, and it isn't my desire to hurt you."

She studied the pathway stones as they reflected the whiteness of the moon. A cool breeze blew against her hot face, sending gooseflesh down her arms. She prayed that her voice would not choke. "Then, my lord, I think we should return to the house."

He nodded and offered her his arm. She accepted quietly, and they turned toward the noise and lights of Honore's soirée.

Fiona stopped. "I think I would prefer to make a less public entrance. My aunt's study is just down this side path. I'm certain the doors are unlocked. You needn't accompany me. I can find the way without help."

"Undoubtedly." Tyrell's voice sounded gruff even to his own ears. "If it's all the same to you, I intend to make certain there are no more inebriated poets lying in wait. Regardless of how capable you are, I'll see you safely into the house."

"Very well, I know it's of little use to try and change your mind, my lord." She walked briskly up the path, and he matched his steps to hers.

The doorknob of the study turned easily, and the door opened. Silently Fiona and Tyrell slipped into the dimly lit room. A scuffling noise came from the corner of the room. Tyrell held his finger to his lips, signaling Fiona to silence.

An indignant gasp followed a woman's voice. "Get off me, you great oaf. Stop it!" A loud thwack resonated through the room.

"Slap me, will you! You mean to make this difficult, eh, my little courtesan? Well, I'll teach you not to tease a man. Parade around like a doxy and you'll get—"

The man never finished his sentence. Tyrell jerked the fellow up by his collar and slammed his fist squarely against the offender's chin.

Fiona sucked in her breath and covered her mouth with her hands. The flickering candlelight illuminated the face of the woman lying on the floor. Her Aunt Honore jumped up, features twisted with rage, and grabbed the fireplace shovel. She walloped her attacker on the back. "You arrogant, thick-witted, pig! Roast in hell—" She raised the iron shovel over her head, preparing to club the man, but Tyrell grabbed it midair.

"Countess, murder is still a hanging offense. I will gladly take the miscreant outside and punish him further for you. But I don't recommend you hit him again with the shovel. Think, my lady, your neck is far too beautiful to want stretching at Tyburn. Aside from that, consider how this worthless cur's blood would stain your lovely carpet."

The man in question rubbed his bruised jaw, and sat in a daze, staring up at the raised shovel, awaiting judgment.

Honore's arm remained positioned to strike. Tyrell still held the iron rod firmly in his fist. "I await your direction, my lady." His voice was calm and soothing.

Honore's features cooled slightly. "Yes," she hissed, relaxing her arm. "He's not worth it. Take him out and thrash him."

Tyrell bowed to her. He removed his coat and handed it to Fiona. The other gentleman remained on the floor. Slowly, with resignation, he stood up and struggled out of his coat. Tyrell grasped him firmly by the collar and pushed him through the door.

Outside, the two men circled each other, squaring off. Tyrell sized up his opponent. The man was younger than he, broader, bulkier, but not taller, and probably not quicker. The fellow flashed out with his right. Tyrell neatly dodged it, boxed him on the nose, and heard the sound of cracking bone. The man yelped in pain. It took a moment before he regrouped and began to circle Tyrell.

"Get on with it!" screamed Honore. "Don't wait for him to recover. He's no gentleman. Punish him!"

The culprit shot out again with his right, leaving his middle section unguarded. Tyrell blocked with a left and sent his right slamming into his opponent's belly. The man doubled over, and Tyrell followed through with a left to the man's jaw. A stream of blood arced through the air as Honore's assailant twisted under the impact and collapsed in a senseless heap on the grass, blood running out of his mouth and nose.

Tyrell rubbed the knuckles on his left hand and watched warily as Honore walked over and stared down at the prone man. The reprobate's white shirt was splattered with red blood. He moaned, and lifted a hand up to his face, the jaw had already begun to swell. Honore kicked him viciously in the ribs with her slippered foot. He groaned, his eyelids fluttered as he tried to focus.

"Good, you're awake. Now listen to me, you gutless worm." She drove her foot into his side once more. "I never want to see your repulsive face again. Should you ever cross my path anywhere, I will tell the entire *ton* what a vulgar little piece of pig excrement you are, and I will send men after you who will not be nearly as gentle as Wesmont was. Now get out."

Honore held his finely tailored coat up by two fingers, as if it were infested with vermin. She let it drop down onto his chest and face where it would surely pick up bloodstains. "Come, Fiona, Wesmont. There's a foul odor in the shrubbery. I'll send a footman to make sure the stench is removed." Honore strode majestically back to the house. She locked the study doors after them and turned to Tyrell. "Neatly done, Lord Wesmont. I am indebted to you."

"Not at all, my lady. You have provided me with some much-needed exercise this evening." Tyrell used the mirror above the fireplace to straighten up his appearance. "My cravat is a sad mess. However, if you ladies are not too ashamed to be seen with me, I would be pleased to escort you back to the ballroom."

He turned to take his coat from Fiona and noted her ashen complexion. She stared out of the window at the bloodied man lying in the grass. Her brow was furrowed when she handed him the coat. Tyrell put it on, studying her face the whole time. "Are you unwell, Fiona?" he asked in a low voice.

Honore answered for her niece. "Of course, she ain't well. She isn't used to seeing a fellow bashed about. Blast that insolent upstart for causing all this upset. It's the blood and whatnot. I daresay, she'll recover in a few minutes."

Fiona's jaw tightened. "No. I don't believe I will recover, not tonight, in any case. I have had quite a full evening. If you will both excuse me, I believe I will go up to my room and lie down."

She turned and fled. Tyrell made to go after her; but Honore grabbed his arm. "Hold, Wesmont. Let her go. Pray tell, just what have you been up to this evening? It's more than that brawl that's upset her."

Tyrell looked down at the eccentric lady. She was dressed like a courtesan, topped with absurd orange hair mounded up like a turban, yet somehow she managed to look as severe as a vicar's wife, fully qualified to chastise him for mistreating her charge.

He said nothing.

She scrutinized his face. "Yes, that's what I thought. Hear me out, Wesmont. I appreciate how you handled yourself tonight, in my behalf. You have my respect, which is not a thing I give lightly. Now, having said that, I must tell you, you haven't handled my niece well at all. In point of fact, you have bungled the entire affair. Now, walk with me back to the ballroom. I intend to call you to task."

With great self-restraint, Tyrell allowed Lady Alameda to lecture him regarding his behavior toward Fiona. She further subjected him to completely scurrilous advice on how he ought to proceed in the future. His brows were drawn together in a choleric scowl as he and the countess stood wrangling in the corner of the ballroom, completely oblivious to the music and laughter floating around them.

"Your suggestion is scandalous. Worse than that—it's heinous!" Tyrell slapped his hand against the wood paneling.

"Ha. So, you think it's kinder to knock the chit's feelings around as if she were a croquet ball?"

"You know perfectly well that's not my intention."

"Well then, take her to bed and have done with it."

"How can you suggest such a course? She's your niece. She'd be ruined."

"Fah! She won't be ruined unless you go boasting about it at White's, or Brook's, or wherever the devil you go to brag about your conquests. What archaic notions you have, Wesmont. She won't be ruined at all—she'll be seasoned. You want her. That much is obvious. I seriously doubt you'll be able to stop sniffing about her skirts until you've had her properly."

"There's nothing proper in what you propose." He folded his arms across his chest.

"Oh, well"—she tilted her head and dragged out the word—"if *proper* is what you want—court my niece and marry her?"

"You whittle everything down to the bone, don't you?"

She shrugged. "I'm not one for roundaboutation."

"Truly said."

"You're avoiding the question, my lord. What's it to be. Are you going to bed the gel, or marry her?"

"You can't force my hand like this."

Honore's eyebrows shot up. "Oh, can't I? Are you challenging me? Just see if I can't. I tell you what, Wesmont, you make up your mind, or I'll take matters into my own hands. I'll banish you from her circle until she discovers there are other men who might please her. Perhaps her cousin, Marcus, he pants after her occasionally—"

Tyrell growled. "If Alameda lays one finger on Fiona—I'll have his bloody head on a plate."

"How daft you are, Wesmont. It ain't his finger I'm thinking of." The countess laughed wickedly.

Tyrell tried to moderate his breathing, his fists knotted, and he very much feared he might pummel his hostess in her own ballroom if she didn't stop mocking him.

As if knowing her cue, Honore stopped teasing him, smoothed down the sides of her gown, and looked up at him in deadly earnest. "I see you are not much pleased with the thought of Marcus having her."

He glared at her.

"Then, my lord, I have trumped you. I win. I give you two days to decide whether you intend to take her to bed or marry her. You have my permission either way. Otherwise, I tell Alameda he may do as *he* pleases with her."

Tyrell stared at her, consigning the woman to burn in Hades. "You belong in a sanatorium."

She smiled, refusing to rise to the bait. "Perhaps, but I mean what I say."

"You leave me little choice."

"No. No, I didn't, did I? Don't intend to. Be warned, Wesmont. I never make idle threats. Call for Fiona early Saturday morning. Take her riding. When you return, give me your decision. Oh, and bring a spirited mount. I have it on good authority Fiona enjoys—"

A bang followed by a whizzing sound splintered the air. Honore screamed and her hands flew to her head. "My hair! My head. I've been shot. I've been shot!"

She blanched. The music screeched to a halt, and the guests on the dance floor gaped at her.

Tyrell grasped her arm to support her. "Are you hurt?"

"I don't know. No." Honore felt her head in various places

just to make sure. "I'm not bleeding. I think it went through my hair."

Tyrell frowned. It did, indeed, look as if something had flown through her odd coiffure. He grabbed a candle from a wall sconce and used it to illuminate the paneling behind where they'd been standing. He ran his fingers along the wood until he found a small dark ball embedded in the wall. He glanced across the room to an empty doorway, from where, he surmised, the shot must have been fired. Dashing across the ballroom, he found the gallery crammed with guests, all laughing and bantering with a magician who challenged the audience to guess which box held his rabbit.

Tyrell returned to Honore and shook his head. She waved at the musicians, ordering them to resume playing.

"I'm sorry, my lady. It is impossible to tell exactly where the shot came from. Perhaps, someone was carrying a pistol and it misfired. Just this evening the Duke of Cumberland showed me his firearm concealed under his coat. Such a thing is not impossible."

"I suppose not. Some ladies carry small revolvers in their reticules for protection. I do. If the bag were dropped then, perhaps . . ." She shrugged.

"Perhaps."

Chapter 16
Decisions

"Excellent claret, this."

Tyrell swirled the ruby liquid in his glass. "Yes. Well, the least I could do was bring a bottle, since I planned to consume most of it myself."

Robert Anbel sat in a leather chair across from Tyrell, lounging in his robe. They were ensconced in Robert's comfortable rooms, surrounded by piles of books, with outdated copies of *The Scourge* and various other newspapers strewn about. Two mismatched hounds lay snoring on the hearth.

"Ungodly mess you have here, Anbel."

"Yes, I know. Wonderful, ain't it. I'd shoot my man if he were to touch a thing. So, of course he leaves it all alone."

That almost won a chuckle out of his surly visitor.

"Stop brooding, Ty. Lady Alameda's household can't be as bad as you say it is."

"Oh, can't it?" Tyrell glared at him. "It isn't a fit place for any young woman. It's bedlam, pure and simple. No, I'm wrong. It certainly isn't *pure,* and it isn't *simple* either. It's depraved and chaotic. The woman completely lacks any moral character. And we mustn't forget her salacious stepson. And her soirée, did I tell you Cumberland was there?"

"Yes. Yes, you mentioned the duke, two or three times."

"Well, I ask you, what kind of woman invites that vile old lecher to a gathering where her own niece will be in attendance? Not to mention letting loose a parcel of Byron's would-be-cronies on the company."

Tyrell slammed his empty glass down on the end table. "And this is the woman who had the audacity to ring a peal over my head about *my* behavior. Oh, and what an interesting peal it was. I still cannot fathom her offering me *carte blanche* with Fiona. 'Make up your mind,' the insane countess commands me. But under no circumstances may I to continue confusing the gel. 'Take her to bed,' says she, 'Or court her properly and marry her.'"

Robert choked and nearly sputtered his claret. "Good heavens, man! You didn't mention *that* before." He regained his composure. "An unusual proposition, to be sure. Knowing your strong predisposition against marriage, as I do. I wonder, what will your decision be? Have you decided to ruin the lovely Lady Fiasco, or have done with her?"

Tyrell cast him a murderous look. "Don't be an ass. I plan to get her away from that asylum she's living in."

Robert ignored Tyrell's thunderous expression and smirked. "Ah, I see. And how do you plan to accomplish this feat?"

"I don't know. I planned to write a letter to her father, but the mad countess only gave me two days, before she lets Marcus have a go at Fiona if I don't come up to snuff. That's not long enough for the post to get back and forth from Spain."

"Alameda? Good God. The woman is deranged."

"It gets worse. This morning, I was astonished to receive an invitation from Lady Hawthorn, Fiona's stepmother. She's giving a ball for her daughter, Emeline. So, obviously they're in town."

"Then what could be simpler? You need only remove the chit from the madwoman and place her in the bosom of her family."

"That's the rub. I don't think Fiona knows they're here. When I told her she ought not be under the same roof with Alameda, she claimed she had nowhere else to go, just as if she hadn't any notion her family was right here in London. Further to the point, she didn't mention the Hawthorn ball."

"Oh, now that's a bit much. Surely, she's had an invitation to her own family's ball. It would be socially damning not to invite their own daughter."

Tyrell lifted the crystal decanter and poured more liquid into his glass. "Exactly. Think how Fiona will feel when she finds out."

"Rubbish. They wouldn't intentionally exclude her. Just isn't done." He tapped his glass. "Unless she had a falling out with them. In that case, she might be prepared for the slight."

"Slight? It's hardly a slight. More like a back-handed slap in the face."

"You're jumping to conclusions, my rash friend."

"Well, as to that, I'm taking her riding tomorrow morning. I intend to find out more about it then."

"Riding, eh?" Then he added under his breath, the corners of his mouth twitching in silent mirth, "Decided to pay court, did you?"

Tyrell frowned at him. "Don't be daft. The countess ordered me to do it."

"So, naturally, you must obey."

"No choice."

"Hmm."

While Tyrell and Robert lounged in Anbel's cluttered apartments, Fiona and Maria stood in front of a town house, screwing up their courage to knock. While behind them, the maid, Lorraine, scuffed obtrusively at the sidewalk, obviously disapproving of what her young mistress was up to.

Fiona smiled at Maria, grasped the brass knocker, and rapped briskly. "Chin up, Maria. I have it on the best authority that this doctor knows the very latest medical techniques. He teaches at the university. There are rumors he might even be granted a knighthood for his extraordinary service to the wounded soldiers. I'm certain he can do something for your poor mouth."

"What if Mama finds out? She'll murder me."

Just then a young maid opened the door. Fiona looped Maria's arm under hers and in her haughtiest voice addressed the maid. "The Misses Hawthor—er"—the smell of baking ham wafted to her nose—"Hawthornham, to see Dr. Meredith."

"Yes, miss." The maid curtsied and showed them up the stairs.

Dr. Meredith was younger than Fiona had anticipated he'd be, and a trifle too handsome to fit his distinguished reputation. She sat down beside Maria, in front of his cluttered ink-stained oak desk, while Lorraine annoyed her by hovering in the back of the room like a nervous specter.

He smiled patiently. "It is customary, Miss Hawthornham, to send round for an appointment. You're fortunate that I was not with another patient or at hospital."

She shifted uneasily in her chair. "Yes, well it was a matter of the utmost importance, an emergency, of sorts."

The doctor pinched his lips between his teeth, as if trying not to betray some hidden amusement. Brushing an errant lock of black hair away from his forehead, he cleared his throat. "What exactly is this urgent matter?"

Maria and Fiona exchanged anxious looks. Fiona straightened her shoulders. "It's my sister, sir. Something must be done for her mouth. She has some rotten teeth, a foul odor, and I expect she has diseased gums."

Dr. Meredith looked them both over carefully. "For sisters, you are not much alike."

Fiona smiled confidently. She had anticipated this line of questioning. "Maria takes after our dear departed mother, and I look more like Father"—she drooped her head to the side and added in a mournful timbre—"more like our father *did*."

"Oh, I see. Both of your parents have passed on?"

Fiona looked up and nodded. "Yes. I, alone, must care for

little Maria. Please, Doctor. I have heard from several of my friends that you are the best surgeon in London. Won't you take a look at her teeth? I'm prepared to pay you twice your normal fee." She extracted a small stack of coins from her handbag and set it on the corner of his desk.

He frowned. "Put your money away. You ought to have taken your sister to a dentist."

"A tooth-puller? I don't think you understand. It's far more than just a rotten tooth. Her gums are dreadfully sore. Indeed, her whole mouth is in a very painful state. I'm afraid a dentist just isn't knowledgeable enough for this job."

He shrugged. "Very well, I suppose it wouldn't hurt to look at the problem." Then he added in a wry tone, "Have *little* Maria come sit in this chair under my lamp."

Maria dutifully trod over to his examining chair. Fiona thought her friend looked like a beautiful martyr walking bravely to her execution. It pleased her to note Dr. Meredith's reaction. He flushed slightly and ran his finger nervously around his collar, before stammering a reassurance to his patient. "Don't worry . . . we'll just have a look here, shall we."

He flinched when Maria opened her mouth and pungent gases fluxed out at him. He stepped away, cleared his throat, took a deep breath and bent over her with a flat metal instrument, not unlike a long thin spoon. He pushed and prodded, thoroughly examining her mouth, throat and cheeks.

"Good grief!" He exhaled and tossed the probe onto a steel tray. The clatter made Maria's shoulders jump. She blinked up at him. "What has been done to your mouth? Your gums are hashed up like dog meat."

Maria's chin began to quiver and her eyes filled with tears. Fiona tapped the surgeon's shoulder. "You mustn't speak to her in that manner. It isn't her fault. A beastly old doctor set leeches on her gums, and put alum and lime on them. Why the horrid old man even seared her gums with hot irons."

Dr. Meredith turned a steely glare onto Fiona. "How could you allow such barbaric treatment? It may be common practice among the poor. But you are obviously quality, and at least somewhat educated, how could you stand by and watch your sister being tortured with such primitive cures?"

"I?" Fiona gasped. "I didn't, sir. I wouldn't. How can you say such a thing?" Then she remembered their ruse. "Oh. You think—yes, of course you do. But, you don't understand. It was, uh, our father, uh, before he died. He doted on that horrible Dr. Klimes. There was nothing I could do."

Fiona noted the skeptical set of his brow. She stamped her foot. "There was nothing I could do, I tell you. Don't you see? The damage is done. Now, it's up to you to help her. Surely, you can do something?"

He looked back at Maria. Tears shimmered in her enormous blue eyes. He shook his head. "I cannot understand why anyone would do such things to so beautiful a creature." Meredith picked up his instrument. "Open your mouth. Let us see what can be done."

When Fiona and Maria left Dr. Meredith's surgery, Maria's cheeks were packed with cotton wadding. She tried to speak. Translating the garbled speech, Fiona ascertained that Maria did not think it a good idea to go directly to her home with her cheeks puffed out like a fat walrus.

"No, I quite agree. We'll go to Alison Hall and perhaps the swelling may go down before long."

Maria rolled her eyes. Lorraine, tripping along behind them, contributed her opinion. "I wager a chunk or two of ice on them gums might help. When we get home, I'll go straight down to the kitchen an' chisel some nice pieces o' ice for you. An', miss, may I say, you were that brave, you were. I near fainted myself, what with that doctor prying them two teeth clean out like he did. Why you never even flinched. Ooo, miss, all that blood—"

Fiona cast Lorraine a quelling frown. "Now, Maria, you must remember to apply Dr. Meredith's salve to your gums every night, and to use this special tooth powder exactly as he directed. No more musk tablets. Truly, they do not improve mouth odor. I know other members of the *ton* use them, but I think they create a worse stench than the original odor."

Fiona fell quite thoroughly into her role of older sister, and lectured Maria all the way home. They arrived at Alison Hall with Maria mumbling of a head-splitting megrim, and a fear she might lose the contents of her stomach.

"Whatever have you done to the child?" Honore asked her niece. "She looks ghastly."

Fiona led Maria to a divan and propped a pillow under her head. After settling her patient, she turned and looked at her aunt. "I like your new hair color, Aunt Honore. It is quite the loveliest shade of auburn I have ever seen."

Honore smiled and put a hand up to her new, dark tresses. "Thank you, dearest. Monsieur Renellé, was here this morning. I'm pleased with the new style." Honore checked the mirror and twisted one of the short curls surrounding her face back into submission.

Then she clucked her tongue. "Clever diversion, dearest. But, you haven't answered my question. What ails Maria? She looks as if her face has been bludgeoned with a hammer. Where have you two been all morning?"

Maria moaned and cast her eyes heavenward.

Fiona squared her shoulders. "I took Maria to a proper surgeon to have something done about her dreadful mouth."

Honore crossed her arms and regarded her niece from under a cocked eyebrow. "Did you? Did you, indeed?"

"Yes." Fiona's face remained impassive. "It needed doing. She deserves better than a mouth full of rotting teeth and festering gums."

"And, I suppose Lady Haversburg approved of this experiment."

"No. She did not. I don't doubt that when she finds out

what I have done she will turn quite livid. I offer no defense for my actions."

"Humph. You had better devise one, my dear. When Louise discovers what you've done, she'll eat your liver for breakfast."

"I don't care. I simply could not sit idly by while Maria's life was ruined by her mother's misplaced confidence in that old quack she calls a doctor. What he has done to her mouth, in the name of medicine, is criminal. He ought to be hung. I am not sorry. Nor, will I pretend to be." Fiona folded her arms across her chest and waited for Honore's wrath to fall.

Honore surprised her by clapping her hands together and laughing. "Why, child, bless me, you *do* have a backbone. I knew it all along. You've got gumption, my girl, just like me."

"Does she?" The question came from Marcus, who stood in the doorway, flipping open and snapping shut a silver snuffbox.

"Of course she does. Why, only look how she has turned Maria's life upside down. Oh, and that's not the half of it. She's willing to face Lady Haversburg's wrath into the bargain."

"*That's* what you call 'backbone'? How very curious." He sauntered into the room. "The Haversburg chit looks as if she might die. Of course, you're right, death will certainly turn her life upside down."

He paused in front of Honore. "You changed your hair again. Too bad, I quite liked the yellow stuff." Marcus scanned Honore's sedate morning gown. "Very proper dress, my dear, quite matronly." Although he smiled, his expression looked as deadly as that of a snake, hypnotically weaving, while preparing to strike.

"Yes, well, my solicitor is coming this afternoon. We have urgent matters to discuss." Honore looked fondly over at Fiona, then back to Marcus. She lifted her chin into the air and marched off toward the door. "I'll be in my study."

She paused and called over her shoulder. "Fiona dear, I forgot to mention, Lord Wesmont is taking you riding early tomorrow morning. He arranged it with me last night."

Fiona started, caught off guard, but her aunt merely waved a dismissive hand in the air and pranced out of the room.

Marcus stared at Honore's departing back. A puff of air pushed through his lips and made a small popping noise. He wheeled around, looked at Fiona, and snapped his snuffbox shut again.

"Oh, well," he muttered and flung himself into a chair across from the divan Maria reclined on. "It looks as if you're the heir of choice for the moment."

"Pardon." Fiona looked at him quizzically, not quite comprehending his words.

"Nothing." He waved her question away. "By all means, continue nursing your victim." He lounged back, watching them, stroking a finger back and forth across his lips.

Fiona ignored him and bent over her patient, ordering the girl to open her mouth. "It looks as if the bleeding has stopped."

With the toe of his boot Marcus lifted up the back of Fiona's skirt. He tilted his head slightly to scrutinize her ankles and calves. The chit was nicely shaped, he would give her that much. Lifting her dress still higher he cocked his eyebrow and grinned wickedly.

Fiona felt the air under her gown and whipped around. "Marcus! What are you doing?"

His foot dropped to the floor, and his leer collapsed into a lazy boyish smile. "Don't scold me, cousin." He tapped his fingertips together and raked his eyes over her figure. "It's your fault, you know. You're forever enticing me. You tempt me and tease me, unmercifully."

"I do not."

"Yes you do—you tantalize me by your very closeness."

"You're being ridiculous."

"No, it's true." He protested. "My passion for you is nearly uncontrollable. Every night I thrash in my bed for want of you. I can't eat. Can't sleep. I'm beside myself. Marry me, Fiona, or go away, someplace where I cannot see you. Someplace where your presence will not torture me with longing." Marcus tapped his fingertips together, and in a decidedly different tone continued his speech. "Otherwise, I cannot be responsible for my actions."

Maria gasped.

"Ignore him, Maria." Fiona laughed and shook her head. "Marcus, stop being absurd. If you are thrashing in bed, it's with some ballet dancer somewhere, for you are never at home till dawn. And then, I declare, you sleep like the dead until well after nuncheon."

"Oh ho, so you lay awake listening for my return, do you?"

"Heavens no. Everyone living at Alison Hall knows when you return. You are always so loud, and generally foxed, that the entire household is roused and the servants must help you to bed. I confess, I am forced to hold my pillow over my ears until you are settled in."

"Ah well"—he raked his eyes over her—"as my wife, you could reform me. Think of it, Fiona. You might devote your entire life to changing me into a respectable gentleman."

"Ha! That would be a life destined for disappointment." Fiona turned back to Maria. "Now, Maria, it is time to remove the wadding. Lorraine will be here soon with some ice. Perhaps it will help reduce the pain and swelling."

Maria's enormous eyes were even more enormous than usual.

Chapter 17
Lies One Tells
to One's Self

Early the next morning, Tyrell stood in Countess Alameda's foyer, tapping the white marble floor with the toe of his black boot. He glanced with irritation at the hall clock ticking away the minutes. He uncrossed his arms, straightened his shoulders, and schooled his glowering expression into one of pleasure. He had no wish for Fiona to think of him as the ill-tempered old sourpuss Lady Haversburg had described. Not three more minutes passed before his dark brows pinched together again.

Tyrell paced, his black polished boots clicked against the white marble. His riding crop thwacked rhythmically as he rapped it against his leg. The hall clock ticked on with deafening loudness. Where was she?

A splash of green moved past one of the white Grecian urns on the marble balustrade upstairs. Tyrell caught sight of her. Without any conscious effort, his scowl changed to an expression of delight. Soon, the swishing of Fiona's green riding habit and the sound of her boots pattering down the stairs filled the foyer with pleasantness.

"Lord Wesmont, forgive me for making you wait. Aunt Honore did not tell me what hour you were coming. We were out very late last evening, at Lady Castlereigh's card party and I'm afraid I overslept."

"I can hardly call you to task for oversleeping if you didn't know at what hour to rise." He inclined his head in an assenting bow and smiled at her.

She laughed. "You are right." Linking her arm in his and catching up her train in the other hand, she said, "Did you bring Kip to act as groom. I asked Aunt Honore if I might borrow one of hers, but she refused. She said she doesn't tax her grooms with such nonsense, and that I am perfectly safe with you." Then she added with equal lightheartedness, "Of course, my aunt doesn't know you as well as I do."

He felt a thud in his stomach. Her words, true though they might be, pummeled him. He realized he'd lapsed again into his trademark scowl, and decided he would give her a dose of her own medicine. "I brought Kip, but, not to act as your groom. I brought him to hold my cattle while I waited for you. I didn't bring a mount for him. But if you're that afraid of me, Fiona, we might put Kip up on your horse behind you."

"You know perfectly well that would be ludicrous."

"Yes. And, since it is ludicrous, let us dismiss the subject altogether."

"As you please." But he saw to his satisfaction that her feathers were now just as ruffled as his.

Kip whistled softly at the surly set of his master's face and Miss Hawthorn's stubborn expression. Tyrell set Fiona up into the saddle of a roan mare with white socks. The mare danced to the side and snorted.

Kip handed Fiona a riding crop, which she looped over her wrist. "She's a mite fresh, miss. But she'll settle down if you show 'er who's master."

Tyrell swung up and threw his leg over Perseus's big white back and trotted off down the street. Fiona cast an angry look at his backside as she tried to control her excitable mount. He posted to the end of the street without so much as a backward glance. Fiona exhaled loudly and dug her heel into the roan's side, the animal lurched forward and sprang past Tyrell.

When she was able to rein the horse back in, Fiona laughed at herself. *What a balmy thing to do,* she thought. *This feisty mare might have bolted. A great fool I would have looked, hanging on to a runaway horse as it tore through London.*

Tyrell reined up beside her. "Can you handle her? I thought for a moment she was bolting with you."

"My fault entirely." Fiona smiled at him. "You see I was angry with you and I must have kicked her a trifle too hard."

Tyrell cocked an eyebrow at her and chuckled.

He could be so dratted appealing when he laughed, Fiona thought. Her heart beat a little faster. "I am sorry, my lord. It seems we are forever at odds with one another. Perhaps we can start anew today." She shifted the reins to one hand and extended her other to him. "Friends?" Just then the mare skittered sideways and Fiona had to regain her seat.

Tyrell chuckled again and touched the brim of his hat in a salute. "Friends," he said.

"Good." She beamed back at him.

The warmth of her smile sent an electric charge through Tyrell's body. It caught him off guard. He took a deep breath, stiffened his spine, and posted tautly over to where she struggled with her mare. He grabbed the harness of the recalcitrant animal and brought it under control.

She looked up at him apprehensively. "I must confess a dark secret to you, my lord. I am accustomed to riding astride at home. A shameful practice, I know, and even worse, I appear to be a rather inept horsewoman riding sidesaddle. Just see how I must fight to hold her."

"Nonsense, she's been standing in the stable too long. She wants her head. I might have guessed you still race about the countryside riding like a boy." He smiled. "Can you manage her till we get to Hyde Park? No one will be about this time of morning. I think it will be safe for us to have a gallop there."

"Oh yes. That would be wonderful." Enthusiasm flashed in her eyes like glittering waves splashing playfully against the shore. Lady Alameda was right. Tyrell felt an urge to pull Fiona off her horse and kiss her senseless right here in the street. Instead, he concentrated on finding the shortest route to Hyde Park.

The park, he postulated, would be deserted this time of morning. If he made love to her on the grass, hidden in the trees, no one would be there to stop him. After all, Lady Alameda had given him permission. He ached to do it. But, in his heart, he knew he wouldn't. Couldn't. His conscience wouldn't let him ruin Fiona. Why did he even speculate about such a thing? He was a heartless cad, that's why. Must be the reason. He'd known her since she was a baby. She was an innocent. Wasn't she? Of course, she was.

Yet, how could she be, living at Alison Hall with her depraved aunt and that cur Alameda? He glanced back at her and caught her staring at him. Her cheeks turned pink, and she looked away.

Tyrell frowned. He thought of the way she aroused such brutal passions in his body. Could a true innocent do that, he wondered. She seemed to possess some mystical skill, or womanly arts that made him incoherent with desire. Perhaps, while he was away fighting Napoleon, she had already exchanged her innocence for pleasure.

He nodded, agreeing with his own conclusions. A blaze of enlightenment awakened him to the obvious. Yes, she was far too adept at seducing him to be an innocent. That would explain Honore's willingness to offer him Fiona's virtue without a second thought. There was no real virtue left. Then why should he not take advantage of such an offer? He ached for her and he would have her. Damn the consequences!

He lied to himself all the way to Hyde Park. Perseus trotted eagerly through the gate while Tyrell continued to weave a glorious tapestry of convenient self-deception.

Why should he not make her his mistress? *Her family knows she's no longer an innocent, hence they didn't invite her to their own ball. They wouldn't want a tainted daughter spoiling Emeline's come-out. That explains why she doesn't even know they're in town. They don't want her. Well, I want her. I'll take her and set her up as my mistress. When I'm through with her, I'll give her a handsome diamond bracelet, or emeralds, or anything else she wants. That's how it's done. I'll leave her when I tire of her. Pay her off—no responsibilities.*

He grinned, quite pleased with himself, and patted Perseus's neck. *It's ideal. No responsibilities. No obligations. No expectations. I'd be a simpleton to pass up such an opportunity. The woman drives me mad with want, so why not satisfy myself with her—it might take a year or two, but what does it matter. She's a likable enough female, enjoyable to be with. What does it matter, if it takes three years, or four, before I get my fill of her?*

A niggling voice in the back of his head begged a question. *Suppose she gets with child? A child of mine?* Tyrell sucked in his breath. The image of Fiona naked and swollen, filled with his child, increased the unbearable pressure in his groin.

Perseus snorted and reared slightly, urging his master to a faster pace just as Fiona and the roan shot past him. Tyrell shook his head. The fog of his irreverent imaginings slowly lifted. Fiona galloped wildly across the field in front of him. It took him a moment to realize that her horse was running out of control. The mare swerved left then right, and kicked up her hind legs, tearing across the turf as if jackals were after her. Fiona held her seat, but only just. When the mare bucked again and threw her head down, it was all over with. Fiona catapulted out of the saddle.

Tyrell spurred Perseus into a gallop. He saw Fiona's body bounce like an India rubber ball and tumble to a stop. She lay unmoving on the grass. Tyrell heard a deafening shriek. Was it hers? No, it had bellowed from his own throat.

He felt as if he were trapped in a thick soup, unable to move fast enough. An eternity passed before he reached her fallen body. At last, he reined in and leapt down to kneel beside her.

Her hat was gone. Her hair fluttered about her face, blowing like the autumn leaves. Her eyes were closed. Mud flecked her pale cheeks. Silent and still, she lay. Too still. A low keening moan came from his throat, unbidden. He lifted her shoulders onto his lap and bent over her, smoothing her hair, rocking back and forth. His mind returned to the battlefield, he was holding Fiona, but the bloodied faces of his soldiers flashed before his eyes, young men dying, his men.

"No!" he cried. It was a command. It was a plea.

"No." He rocked and clasped her to his chest. "Not her. *Not her!* Fiona, wake up!" He ordered. He begged. "God, listen to me—not her. Make her open her eyes. Don't let her die. You can't let her die—I love her."

The truth didn't startle Tyrell. It made him groan. "God forgive me. I've been a fool. I've always loved her. Always. Just bring her back to me." He hugged her to him.

His lamentation was so deep, he didn't hear Fiona stirring until she whispered, "You're hurting me."

He squinted at her, unbelieving, as if she were a ghost. Then his face crumpled into tears and he clutched her to his chest again.

"Stop. You really must stop," she moaned.

Tyrell came to his senses. He looked down at her and saw for the first time that her right arm was lying across her lap, twisted awkwardly. From the elbow down it appeared to be screwed on backward. He tried to focus through his watery eyes. Finally, his sight and his mind collected enough information to draw a conclusion. "Your arm is broken. Don't move. I'll get you to a doctor as quickly as I can."

He unwound his cravat from his neck and yanked off the long white cloth. "We can bind your arm to your body so that it won't move about. Can you sit up just a little?"

"I think so." She leaned up, but the movement cost her

considerable pain. He didn't miss her tightly clamped lips, and the involuntary flinches, as he wound the cloth around her shoulder and anchored her arm to her chest. "How is that?"

"Better." She nodded, but he was unconvinced.

"Fiona, listen to me. Lifting you up onto Perseus's back— there's bound to be pain. I'm sorry for it, Fiona, but there's no other way. I've got to get you to a doctor."

She nodded. When Tyrell hefted her up onto his horse, she shuddered and turned white. Afraid she might faint, he quickly climbed up behind her.

"There's a surgery near here," she said, pain warping the sound of her voice. "Dr. Meredith."

Tyrell clicked his tongue and urged Perseus into a gentle walk. With one arm he held Fiona firmly against his chest. Grimly, he followed her directions, until they stopped in front of a two-story town house. He tied Perseus to a link and carefully lifted Fiona down. She looked alarmingly pale. He held her shoulders as they walked to the door.

"What about my mount?" she asked.

"Ran off. Doesn't matter. If I ever see the blasted beast again I'll put a bullet in her ignorant head." He rapped the knocker loudly.

"You needn't be cross with her. It was my fault. I don't ride at all well in a lady's saddle. I'll be all right once Dr. Meredith comes. Leave me with him, and go search for your horse."

"Don't spout nonsense."

"But—" The color washed out of her face, and her eyes opened wide. "Oh dear—" Fiona slid like a corpse down his side into a dead faint. He caught her, scooping her up into his arms.

The door opened. Dr. Meredith stood without a coat, his sleeves rolled up, squinting at Tyrell holding Fiona in his arms. "She looks familiar. Is that Miss Hawthornham?"

Tyrell glared at the doctor as if the fellow had biscuits for brains. "Hawthorn. It's Miss Hawthorn, and she's had a riding accident. Don't just stand there, man. Help me get her into your house."

When Fiona awoke, the sleeve of her riding dress had been cut open up to the shoulder, and the two men were standing beside her, arguing.

"I tell you—it's not broken. It's only dislocated."

"How can you be certain."

"Gad, man. I'm a doctor. I am supposed to be able to tell. I felt the bones. They're all intact. The radius has slipped out of the elbow joint. Simply put: Her forearm is upside down."

"What do you intend to do?"

"Well, if you will get out of my way, I plan to move the arm into position and snap it back in place."

Tyrell rubbed his brow. "No. There must be another way. That's going to hurt her terribly."

"Of course it will. But while we stand here arguing, the muscles and ligaments are stretching and getting weaker. Her recovery pain increases with every minute you delay me."

Tyrell exhaled through gritted teeth. "You're certain there's no other way? Something less painful?"

"No. I would have already done it if there was. Now, you must move so that I may attend to her."

Tyrell sighed, sounding like misery itself, and stepped aside. "Very well."

Dr. Meredith smiled down at Fiona. "So, you heard?"

She nodded.

"Then we'll begin." When he grasped her arm and yanked it into place, Fiona sank back into the gray oblivion from which she had just emerged.

Chapter 18
To Catch a Murderer

It was well into the afternoon by the time Tyrell walked with Fiona into her aunt's home. She sported a sling over her arm, and Tyrell held her other a bit more possessively than normal, but other than that she looked rather cheerful for an invalid.

She smiled up at him. "At least this time the Duchess of Disaster wounded herself. I can sympathize with my former victims."

Tyrell raked a hand through his disorderly curls and looked into her face. "Reserve some of your sympathy for me, Fiona. It is exceptionally hard to stand by, helplessly, while someone you care about suffers so abominably. I believe I have aged ten years in one morning."

Warmth flooded her cheeks. *He cares*. And in the hazy memories of the morning she recalled him shouting at God that he loved her. She tried not to betray her elation and decided the best disguise would be a jibe. "Now that you mention it, you do look older. Oh dear, now, Lady Haversburg *can* call you an old grouch."

"Just so."

As they walked across the foyer toward the sitting room, his boots reported crisply against the marble, and the noise echoed around the circular room. Out of the corner of his eye, he caught a flash of white descending on them. It didn't belong in the air above their heads. Before he could comprehend what was hurtling toward them, his instincts, honed on the battlefield, made him react.

He grabbed Fiona and dove against the wall. He hunched over her, sheltering her beneath his chest. A deafening crash followed, and chunks of flying debris pelted his back.

The moment the splattering stopped, Tyrell turned to stare at the foyer floor. One of the large Grecian urns from the balcony above their heads lay shattered at their feet. They looked at each other. Tyrell still clutched her shoulders.

Her voice choked, shook, and came out barely above a whisper. "That's twice today you've rescued me, my lord. But this time . . . this time we both might have been killed."

"Are you all right?" He held her tightly and waited for her nod, before helping her to her feet. Bending over the debris, Tyrell picked up a piece of the urn's base and studied it. Across the foyer, Honore stood in a doorway, also surveying the scene.

Mattie exploded into the vestibule, huffing and puffing. Trailing behind her were a number of maids, two footmen, and the butler. "I heard a great noise. What happened? What's this? What's this?" Mattie bellowed, coming to a halt in front of the broken heap of marble.

Honore walked casually forward. "This, my dear Mattie, is a dreadful tangle."

Tyrell stared at Honore. He thought her choice of words rather peculiar for the situation.

"Mattie, our Fiona has had something of a harrowing experience, and judging by the note I received earlier, this is her second such upset. She needs a restorative cup of tea and a rest. See to it, will you? And, Mattie, tell Lorraine to sit with Fiona for the rest of the night."

"That is unnecessary, Aunt Honore. Truly, I feel fine."

"Nonsense. I insist. Mattie see to it."

Mattie walked over to Fiona and put her arm around her.

"Come along, me dear. We must get ye to bed and see about that arm of yours."

Before Mattie could whisk her away, Fiona reached out for Tyrell. He took her hand in his, and she smiled warmly. "*Thank you* sounds rather feeble on the face of things. Nevertheless, I am deeply grateful to you, my lord. More than you know."

He said nothing, but lifted her hand to his lips and kissed it.

Honore issued a sharp command. "Lord Wesmont, a word with you in my study."

Mattie ushered Fiona away, and reluctantly Tyrell turned to follow Lady Alameda. Honore shut the study door after he entered and leaned against it. She wore a ferretlike expression.

He wearily drawled, "I suppose you want to hear what my decision is?"

"Don't be ridiculous," Honore snapped. "I've got more important matters to discuss with you. Aside from that, I knew what your answer would be when I first laid eyes on you, probably before."

"You flatter yourself, Lady Alameda. You could not have known, nor can you yet know, what I have decided. I only came to a conclusion this very morning."

She took a deep breath and rolled her eyes. "Oh, very well. Shall we see how far from the mark I fell? You discovered this morning that you're hopelessly in love with Fiona. She stirs your blood and engages your heart in a way no other woman can and you won't be truly happy unless you wed her. Well, Wesmont, did I get it right?"

His countenance turned dark and hard, like a man who thinks he has been cheated at cards.

Honore smiled up at him, the corners of her mouth playing dangerously into a smirk. "Good grief man, I saw the symptoms the first day I met you. You're not such a dolt that you actually believed I'd offer my niece to you *carte blanche?* A virgin on a platter?" She laughed at him and shook her head.

Tyrell's jaw flexed, and his glower deepened. Honore

stopped laughing abruptly, and anger flashed across her face, matching his. "Don't be a fool, she's my flesh and blood."

"Obviously, I am a fool. For I not only believed you—I nearly took you up on your false offer."

"Fiddle-faddle. You are sadly ignorant of your own character, my lord."

"Perhaps you played too deep this time, Lady Alameda. You misjudged me, at the risk of your niece's maidenhood."

"Fa! I never misjudge." Honore waved her hand at him. But her face suddenly altered, and it looked as if she might crumple. "Or at least, I usually don't." She pursed her lips and studied the shelves of books lining the wall behind him until she regained control of herself. "Come, Wesmont. I didn't ask you in here to bicker with you."

She waved him to a chair, which he refused, and seated herself behind the desk. Studying his face, Honore absently scratched at the felt ink blotter.

"Then pray tell me, Lady Alameda, why *did* you call me here? To gloat?"

"Hardly. No. I need your help."

"Ha! That's difficult to believe—after you've just explained to me how you manipulated me as if I were nothing more than a pawn on your chessboard."

"Fustian! I didn't manipulate you. I merely put you in a position to examine your own feelings. Was it so terrifying to discover that you loved my niece? Are you unhappy? Do you wish to call me out for my part in it?"

"Yes!" He slapped his hands on her desk. "It was terrifying. You have no idea." He dropped his head and lowered his voice. "But no, I don't want to call you out. Ring your neck, perhaps, but no, I'm not unhappy."

"Good. Then perhaps you won't mind helping me. We have a somewhat bigger problem to deal with. You see, I think Fiona's life may be in a rather precarious position."

Honore picked up a quill and pinched the feathers as she pulled it through her fingers. "I seriously doubt whether she is safe here at Alison Hall any longer. Maybe she never was. I don't know. I miscalculated. It seems impossible to me—but there it is. One can't deny the facts that one sees with one's own eyes. It must be true. I misjudged someone, wagered incorrectly, and now, I fear, Fiona's life hangs in the balance." She looked speculatively up at him.

"What are you saying?" Tyrell squinted and tried to make sense of her ramblings. "Someone is trying to hurt Fiona? Kill her?"

"Yes, I believe so."

Honore merely stared at Tyrell while his mind ticked through the short list of possibilities.

"Alameda! You saw him didn't you? He unbolted the urn and pushed it down on Fiona, didn't he?" Tyrell gripped the edge of the desk as if it were Lady Alameda's shoulders and he might squeeze her until he got an answer. She looked down at the blotter and slowly back up to him. The answer was obvious.

"I'll kill the bastard." He turned to go.

Honore jumped up and ran to the door, blocking his way. "If Marcus *were* a bastard," she said calmly, "I would hand you the pistol and count the paces myself. But Marcus is Francisco's only heir. You must allow me to handle this in my own way."

Tyrell stared down at Honore through the smoke and flames of his anger. "Step aside, my lady."

She rested both her hands on his chest. "Believe me," she said soothingly, "we will make him suffer far more under my ministrations, than if you were to simply run a blade through his heart. That's far too easy, too quick. There's no beauty in it—no science."

Tyrell's eyes narrowed skeptically. He didn't care about beauty or science; he just wanted to protect the woman he loved.

"Think carefully, Wesmont. Do you really want to be forced

into exile just so you can shoot a hole through Marcus's sadly confused head? Are you willing to let his greed ruin your life?"

"I'll do whatever I must, to protect Fiona."

"Noble of you, but Fiona is safe for the nonce. Tomorrow— well, that's why I need your help. Let me explain . . ."

He hesitated, and then listened as Honore unfolded her plan. They bent their heads together, conspired and argued, bickered and compromised, until Tyrell went away satisfied.

Chapter 19
Stranger in a Pomegranate Face

The next morning dawned with a sienna sun. It flickered on the eastern horizon like a great candle trying to burn a hole through the murky brown vapors covering London. Servants padded quietly through the hallways of Mayfair, silently preparing for the magic hour when the aristocracy would arise from their beds.

Marcus stumbled out of a hack and staggered up the stairs into Alison Hall. After clambering loudly through the house and shouting for the servants, he finally undressed and collapsed on his bed. His cheek sank blissfully into the deep softness of his starched white pillow, but his slumber was interrupted by the sound of a shrill scream.

A second scream shattered the morning calm entirely. A third scream split through Marcus's head like a hatchet. His eyes popped open.

The sound of feet clattering through the hallway roused Marcus to action. He flung open his door and hung on to the woodwork as he shouted at the servants. "What in God's name—"

His words were cut short. All the way from the west wing he could hear Honore screeching. A young maid scurried past, gasping when she saw Lord Alameda leaning out of his doorway. Marcus looked down and remembered he was naked. He went back to his room, fished a dressing gown out of his wardrobe, and followed the throng headed for the east wing.

In between screaming at the top of her lungs, Honore yelled, "It's her fault! This is all because of that accursed child. Fetch her to me! Fiona! Fionaaa!"

She was already running to her aunt's bedroom, her bare feet pounding against the wooden floorboards, her white night rail billowing around her, and her hair flying wildly about. She stopped in the doorway. Her hands flew up to her mouth.

Her aunt's dark eyes stared back at Fiona from a face so red and swollen it was nearly unrecognizable. Mounds of bright red hives bulged, one on top of the other; her taut skin looked as if it were stretched to the bursting point. Honore viciously scratched at one hand, and Fiona noticed the puffy fingers and realized that Honore's entire body must be covered with swollen red patches.

She hurried to her aunt's bedside. "What is this? What has happened to you?"

"What's happened?" Honore looked at her incredulously. "You dare ask? I'll tell you what happened. You! You are what happened. Are you blind? It's your curse."

The doorway filled with spectators from the household. Among them stood Marcus, hair askance and his dressing gown hanging loosely around him. Fiona searched their faces, hoping someone had a better explanation, but they were obviously as shocked and clueless as she.

"Surely this can't be—" She bit her lip as a wave of hopelessness washed over her. Numb, her stunned mind failed to form any more words.

Honore's swollen mouth began to move again. Fiona heard her aunt speaking, but it sounded as if it came from a long way off. A tunnel stretched between the two of them, a tunnel that dulled the words and slowed the movements. Honore's red puffy hand waved imperiously through the air and directed a bloated finger at Fiona. "This is all your fault! How dare you bring that curse of yours against me."

Plump pink fingers grasped Fiona's chin and pulled it closer to the lumpy mass of hives set with livid black eyes. "Look at me! I look like an overripe pomegranate. Your fault. You and that wretched curse. Well, I won't have it. I won't, I tell you."

Honore started screaming again. "Get out. Get her away from me. I don't want you in my house. Do you hear me! Out! Out!"

From the end of the thick echoing tunnel Fiona heard her aunt's final decree. She backed away from the bed, and stumbled. Someone took her shoulders and guided her out of the room.

An hour later, Fiona found herself seated on a trunk in front of Alison Hall. Several bandboxes were stacked beside her. She couldn't clearly recall the servants' hushed movements as they packed for her, nor did she remember walking down the winding staircase out of Alison Hall. It all happened so quickly. She'd watched the activity from a great foggy distance, like a rabbit knocked over the head, sitting stunned in the killing shed, awaiting the cook's ax.

Very slowly, the distance between herself and reality began to shrink. She could feel the hard metal ribbing of her steamer trunk beneath her bottom. She considered the heap of luggage and realized she was in something of a predicament. The front door opened and closed. The soles of Lorraine's half boots pattered down the stairs toward her, and she set another bandbox on top of the pile.

"That's it then, miss." Lorraine fiddled with the fabric of her apron. "I'm that sorry, I am. It weren't like her ladyship to take after you the way she did. It were probably that awful swelling in her head what did it. You'll see. She'll come to herself in a day or two. An' don't you go blaming yourself for my lady swelling up like that. No, miss, it were probably somethin' she ate. Why, once I seen her swell up an' turn red as a beet on account of eatin' mollusk soup. It weren't nothing but a harmless little bowl of soup, mind you. Ooo, but she was fit to be tied, she was, what with all that itchin' and scratchin' and swelling up like a great red cauliflower."

Fiona stared at Lorraine and blinked, trying to comprehend the waterfall of words pouring over her. Behind them the door opened, and the butler stood, rigid as a post, signaling the maid back into the house.

"Miss, I got to go." Tears started down Lorraine's cheeks. "Oooh look at me—turning into a waterin' pot. I can't stand to be parted with you—what with you saving me from drownin' an' all. You know I'll be grateful till my last breath." With that, the older woman planted a kiss on Fiona's cheek and fled up the stairs. The butler closed the door, and Fiona sat alone.

From an upstairs window, Honore and Mattie peered down at Fiona sitting on her trunks. "I think that went rather well, don't you?" Honore's garishly swollen face actually puckered into what resembled a half smile.

Mattie patted Honore's shoulder. "Aye, me girl. Ye played it to perfection, that ye did. Mind you the girl took it hard."

"She'll recover. Did you keep an eye on Marcus?"

"O' course I did. He was convinced sure enough."

"Good. Gagging down that oyster was not easy—I can tell you that."

Mattie laughed. "The wee slimy creature did its part, too. Ye are a sorry sight, Honore, red as the hair on me old head."

"Yes, well now let us hope Wesmont does his part."

"Oh aye, I wager he'll not disappoint ye. See, here comes his rig now."

"Good. He's right on time. How very punctual."

"He'll be takin' our Fiona to that dreadful dull Lady Hawthorn, won't he."

"Yes. It really is too bad. If only he were a less conventional man, he might run off with her and set the society hens cackling for weeks. That would be jolly fun, wouldn't it?"

"Aye, but would the lass do such a thing?"

"Maybe, Mattie, she has more bottom than I gave her credit for. Gets it from me, no doubt."

"Aye, she's a good girl, that one. Ye'll miss her."

Honore turned away from the window and scratched at her puffy red arms. "Gad! I itch like all the bees from hell are swarming on me. I want a bath, Mattie, and I want it now."

Mattie stooped to test the water temperature in the copper tub. "All will be well, Honore. We'll find ye another bairn to love, ye'll see."

Honore didn't look at her old nanny. She spoke as if she hadn't heard the comment. "Mattie, put that powder in the water. Let's hope it eases this confounded itching."

Tyrell sat in the back of his barouche. From this vantage point he saw Fiona perched atop her luggage long before his coachman pulled up. He tipped his hat to her, but she didn't seem to notice. Kip hopped down from the back of the carriage and opened the small panel door. Tyrell stepped out, donning his most pleasant attitude. "Good morning, Fiona. I've come to see if you would care to take a ride this morning? The day is so fine and—"

She turned her face up to him. Her blank expression caused him to stop midsentence, then he noticed her white pallor and stricken features. His insides wrenched with guilt. Honore's wretched plan was costing Fiona far more than they'd bargained for. He immediately dropped his pretense and put his hand on her shoulder. "Come. I'll take you to your family."

When Fiona did not stand up, he bent down and made her

look at him face-to-face. "Fiona, listen to me. You can't sit here in the street, now can you?"

She shook her head.

"No, of course you can't. Will you let me help you?"

A moment passed before she nodded. Her answer came out hoarse and small. "Yes. Thank you."

The sound of her own voice seemed to break through her stunned silence. It freed her tears. They washed down her cheeks in two streams. She didn't sob or shake, the tears just silently flowed down. Tyrell handed her a handkerchief and guided her up the step into the barouche.

Kip strapped on her trunks and slung her bandboxes into the opposite seat of the carriage.

Fiona wiped self-consciously at her eyes. "I don't suppose you would believe me, my lord, if I told you that under normal circumstances I rarely cry."

"Quite the contrary, my dear, I believe you to be an extraordinarily brave woman."

She looked at him doubtfully through watery eyes.

"No, I'm not flattering you, Fiona," he answered, reading her mind. "I've admired your intrepid spirit since you were a little girl. You were never afraid of anything. I used to hold my breath when you went flying over some of the obstacles on the hunt. It was difficult to comprehend your father allowing such recklessness."

"Oh, I see. I have just slipped in your esteem from fearless to reckless."

He chuckled, glad to see her spark returning. "Well, mustn't fan your vanity into too great a flame. Imagine how my friends and I felt, watching a mere slip of a girl leap without hesitation over the very hedges and streams we had all just mutually decided we would go around. Poor Freddie Boxstrom cracked his ankle when he flew off his horse trying to jump a hedgerow you had just sailed over. He swore he would never hunt with me again if you were allowed on the field. He called you the impertinent daughter of an overindulgent father."

"I'm charmed."

"Yes, well, he was humbled by your fearless nature."

"I'm hardly fearless. You have only to stand me in a roomful of people and I will quake in my slippers."

"Ah. So, there is a chink in your armor."

The carriage lurched as it rolled over a fault in the pavement. Fiona swayed back against the seat and into the protective circle of Tyrell's arm. It was dangerously comfortable. Fiona looked up uncertainly.

"It's much easier," she said, "to deal with animals and nature, than it is to manage the society of human beings. No matter how hard I try, I continually upset the people around me."

"Sadly, all of us upset the ones we love now and again. Yes, Fiona, people are deuced difficult to deal with, but they also give us joy and all manner of pleasant sensations." Tyrell looked meaningfully at her.

He saw the heat rise in her neck and flood up her cheeks. Tyrell pulled his arm out from around her shoulders. This time he wasn't pulling away from her because he was afraid of his feelings. He was doing it because he knew the time was not right. She would need her wits about her when they stopped in front of Lady Hawthorn's town house. Nevertheless, he couldn't help stroking her reddened cheek as he took away his arm. She was so inviting. He wished it were another time and another place.

He cleared his throat and addressed her in his lecture voice. "Promise me you'll approach the people around you with the same fearlessness with which you used to take your horse over the hedgerows. You may need that courage in a few minutes when I present you to your family."

"Oh, but surely it will be days before—"

"You are unaware that your stepmother and Emeline are in town?"

"In town?"

"Yes. Here." The carriage rolled to a stop in front of a town house.

"No, you must be mistaken."

This was proving to be a day full of startling episodes. The door of the rented town house opened, and Fiona recognized the face of her family servant. The butler led them into the hall. "A moment, Miss Hawthorn. I'm afraid we're all at sixes and sevens at the moment—what with Miss Emeline's ball to-morrow evening. Just one moment, please." He dashed away, leaving Fiona and Tyrell standing in the entrance.

"I didn't know Em was having a ball," she whispered. "They didn't tell me that they were in town. Not so much as a note to Aunt Honore, nor an invitation. Heavens, Tyrell, they can't want me here."

He shook his head, denying her supposition, even though he inwardly concurred. He didn't like to see her distressed. "There must have been a mix-up in the post."

"No. No, it's me, me and my dratted curse. They don't want me to spoil things for Em. Take me away, Tyrell. Oh please, take me away. I'll put up in a hotel. I—I'll take a mail coach back to Thorncourt in the morning."

She started for the door, but he clasped her arm. "Wait! At least, speak to your family. Surely they ought to be advised of your situation. If they aren't pleased to see you I'll drive you back to Thorncourt myself."

Just then Lady Hawthorn's voice cut through the air. "No. No. No!" she shouted, running after a footman who was lug-ging a tall potted palm. "I told you before, put it in the dining room. The card room is already full of plants."

The footman stopped in his tracks, and crisply murmured, "Very good, my lady," and then he turned around and headed back to the room he had just exited.

"Stop right there." Emeline's sharp command halted the foot-man once more. She entered from the other direction. Followed by the butler who appeared to be seeking an opportunity to announce their guests.

"Have you forgotten, Mama? I moved all those plants from the card room into the ballroom. The ballroom was much too bare. We don't want it looking as stark as Almack's, now do we? I'm certain the guests will prefer the larger, thicker greenery in the ballroom. These palms are so thin and scrawny—he may put them in the card room."

"Stark? Bare? How can you say the ballroom is bare? I spent a small fortune on flowers—-entire hedges of them."

"Oh yes, Mama. The flowers are gorgeous. They smell divine. Heavenly. But you must admit they don't provide near enough privacy."

"Privacy? Privacy, is that what you are after? Listen carefully, Emeline, I am not going to turn my house into Covent Garden, with couples doing heaven-knows-what behind the shrubbery. Good gracious—"

Tyrell cleared his throat, loudly. The wrangling women looked over and saw the Earl of Wesmont standing in their hallway. Then they saw Fiona with one arm in a sling and the other arm tucked proprietarily in his embrace.

Lady Hawthorn choked. She converted it into a polite cough and straightened up her gown. Emeline put a hand up to check her hair. The footman set the potted palm on the floor and sighed with relief.

"My dear Lord Wesmont and Fiona, how good to see you." Lady Hawthorn walked forward, her hand extended, a smile plastered on her face. Emeline followed in her mama's footsteps. Tyrell did not release Fiona's arm to take Lady Hawthorn's hand. He feared Fiona might bolt for the door. Indeed, her continued struggle convinced him she would, in fact, run away if given half a chance. He pulled her closer to his side and bowed his head to the ladies.

Fiona glared at him momentarily and turned to face her stepmother. "I am sorry. I see that I, that is, *we,* have come at an inopportune time. We will leave." Fiona tried to turn and go.

Tyrell held her in place. "Unfortunately, Lady Hawthorn, we have come under rather distressing circumstances. Lady Alameda has contracted a strange malady and she feels it would be safer for Fiona if she left Alison Hall. Her luggage is in my barouche."

Fiona stared at Tyrell. He was twisting the facts and forcing her on her family. Well, he wouldn't get away with it. "It is of no import. I will find other accommodations until I can return to Thorncourt. I assure you, my lady. I did not know you were planning a ball for Emeline. We would not have come, had we known."

Emeline tittered. "Why, Fiona—what must Lord Wesmont think—of course, you knew. I'm certain Mama wrote you weeks ago and told you all about it, didn't you, Mama?" She fluttered her eyelashes at Tyrell.

Lady Hawthorn frowned. Obviously, Emeline meant to pin the indiscretion on her. Her eyes compressed into thin lines, but her lips remained smiling, and her voice sounded placid and sweet. "Why, Em darling, I'm certain I told *you* to write to your sister."

"Oh, how silly of me. Here I thought you were going to do it." Emeline curved one hand artfully in the air next to her golden curls. "You must think us all dreadfully scatter-brained." She simpered at him with a slight pout on her cherry-shaped lips. "Our only defense for this absurd mix-up is that we have been frightfully busy with the move to town. The preparations for the ball have been exhausting. Oh but it is going to be such a grand affair. I dare to hope that it will be one of the sensations of the Season."

Hurt and confusion were plain on Fiona's face when she faced her sister. "I didn't know you were coming to town for the Little Season, Em. You never said a word."

"Oh bother." Emeline stamped her foot. "Well, that is not my fault, for I did write you before we left. The letter must have gotten mixed up in the mails. That is the only possible explanation."

"Yes, I suppose." Fiona chewed her lower lip. "Still, I should not trouble you on so busy a day. Lord Wesmont will see me to an inn, won't you, my lord?"

Lady Hawthorn, who evidently was not made entirely of stone, patted Fiona on the shoulder, and for just a moment donned a motherly expression. "Nonsense, my dear. You will stay with us. Anything else is unthinkable."

She urged Fiona closer and called over her shoulder to the footman standing beside the potted palm. "You there, bring Miss Fiona's trunks in from Lord Wesmont's carriage."

The beleaguered footman headed out the door.

Lady Hawthorn dropped her hands from the brief intimate contact with her stepdaughter and turned to Tyrell. "Lord Wesmont, you must allow me to thank you for bringing Fiona to us. We're most grateful. May we expect to see you tomorrow night?"

He bowed handsomely to her and managed a smile at Emeline. "I wouldn't miss such a grand affair."

Then he turned to Fiona and grasped her hand, pulling it to his lips, and kissed her fingers. When he released her hand, he smiled at her, wishing he could smooth away all of her concerns. "You must promise me the first waltz."

"Thank you, my lord, but no. I am afraid I must keep to my rooms. You see my—my arm is not healed well enough for dancing."

"Surely the waltz is not too strenuous an exercise for your arm."

"I cannot," Fiona insisted and tried to appeal to her stepmother. "Surely, my lady, you can see the reason. If I come down to the ball, there will be the inevitable catastrophe. Someone may get hurt, and all will be spoiled."

"Perhaps . . ." Her stepmother tapped the side of her cheek. "However, my dear, according to the latest gossip you have become quite an attraction. Is it not so? Have you not received dozens of invitations? It must be true, because several ladies have applied to me. Of course, I sent them your aunt's direction.

I'm thinking that your notoriety might benefit Emeline—and if a small mishap occurs, well, it will merely create the sensation Em is hoping for." She clapped her hands together. "Yes, Fiona, you must come down. I insist upon it. And by all means, dance the first waltz with our dear Lord Wesmont."

Lady Hawthorn beamed at them both, quite satisfied with her logic. Emeline squinted at her mother, obviously not nearly as pleased.

Tyrell grinned at Fiona. She was caught. She spoke softly, more for his ears than anyone else's. "Then let us pray no one is seriously injured. Lately, I have been causing rather more damage than normal." Clearly, the memory of a Grecian urn smashing at their feet was going through her mind. Fiona lifted her troubled eyes up to his.

Tyrell wanted nothing more than to hold her and kiss away her fears, and to reassure her, but he had given Honore his word that he would not tell her of her cousin's treachery until the matter had been dealt with.

"Come, smile. All will be well. You must trust me." His tone was deep and comforting. It pleased him when she responded by bravely trying to force the corners of her mouth to turn up.

"Regrettably, I must leave you. I have some pressing business matters to attend to. However, I will return tomorrow night to collect the waltz you promised me."

He left the Hawthorns' town house. In his mind he began composing a note to Lady Alameda. She had better hold up her end of the bargain. Otherwise, Tyrell planned to find out if Marcus de Alameda was as good a shot as the rumor mill claimed. One way or another, that reprobate was never going to bother Fiona again.

Chapter 20
Crime and Punishment

The next morning Countess Alameda lounged in her bed. She sipped her morning chocolate and casually scanned the newspaper. The swelling and redness had nearly abated. Marcus shuffled into her room, wearing his dressing gown and massaging his temples. Honore glanced up from her paper and smiled. How endearing he looked, with his tousled black hair and sleepy eyes.

"You summoned me?"

"Yes, my dear. Sit down. Here you are, Mattie sent up a tray for you as well. I thought we might have breakfast together and discuss a few business matters. She made you one of her excellent omelets."

Marcus rubbed the bridge of his nose and looked reluctantly at the tray of food. "I never take breakfast before noon."

"Yes, well, I just heard the clock strike eleven. It is close enough. I daresay you will be uncommonly interested in the matters I would like to discuss. However, I refuse to discuss business on an empty stomach."

Marcus's eyes flashed momentarily. He ambled over to the chair and dropped into it. "I rather thought you had called me here to listen to your dying words."

"That's silly. I would hardly make my last confession to you. Besides, only *good* people die young, and I am certainly not *good*."

"You certainly aren't young," he muttered.

"What was that?"

"Nothing. I just said you certainly look recovered."

"Yes, that's what I thought you said." She lifted a mouthful of omelet to her lips. "Eat your eggs before they get cold."

Marcus sipped his coffee and set the cup down. He picked up his fork and jabbed at the eggs, withdrew it, and poked at them again.

"Marcus, must you dawdle? I want to get an early start today. I've done nothing but lie in bed and take baths since yesterday. I'm bored senseless, and I have a dozen things to do before the Hawthorns' ball this evening."

He looked up, startled. "You don't plan to go to that, do you? You just booted the chit out. You can't show up at their ball." He shoved a forkful of omelet into his mouth. The textures rolled across his tongue. He discerned mushrooms in a rich creamy wine sauce and leaned forward to take another bite.

Honore shook her fork in the air at Marcus. "Of course, I can. I can do whatever I please. I don't recall an invitation—but it hardly matters. They can't very well turn me away, can they? I'm family."

He swallowed more eggs and asked, "Why the devil would you want to go? Have you forgotten so quickly what Fiona did to you?"

Marcus scraped some mushrooms and cream sauce out of the center of his omelet and scooped them into his mouth.

Honore picked up a piece of toast and crunched down on it. "Oh, you mean because I puffed up like a toad and turned red."

"Yes. Her fault. Said so yourself—her curse and all. Excellent omelet. Mattie outdid herself."

"I'll tell her you said so." Honore watched her stepson

shove more eggs into his mouth and smiled. Then she laughed. "Oh Marcus, Marcus, my dear boy, you don't really believe that twaddle about a curse, do you? It's bad enough Fiona and her witless stepmother believe in such drivel. Never say *you* believe in curses?"

"Well"—he considered her carefully while chewing another bite—"perhaps, not in the ordinary sense. But in Fiona's case things *did* happen."

"Oh yes. Things did happen." Honore nodded and took a vicious nip at her toast. "I wonder, Marcus dear, how many of those *things* were your doing?"

Marcus sputtered, choked momentarily, and finally swallowed. After composing himself, he asked her, in the most innocent of voices, "What can you possibly mean?"

"You're a clever man. You tell me. How many failed attempts on Fiona's life were there? Let me see. My maid's plunge into the ocean—did the wrong woman fall off the pier? Was Fiona's riding accident really an accident? Or did you help it along with a burr under the saddle. What about tripping the Prince Regent—"

"Hold!" Marcus jumped to his feet. "Tripping the Prince Regent? I had nothing to do with that. Your niece managed that without any help from me."

"I see." Honore sipped her chocolate and set the cup down. Indeed, she did see. His calumny was crystal clear. "What was it, Marcus? Did you think I wouldn't leave you my money?"

He raked his hand through his hair. The color drained from his face. He looked uncomfortably around the room. "What did you expect me to do? What did you think I would live on when you're gone? You were planning on giving it all to her, weren't you? I couldn't have a whey-faced little chit running off with what was rightfully mine." He looked earnestly at Honore.

Her eyes were on her plate. She pushed the yellow eggs around with her fork.

"Well?" he demanded. "You were going to give her every-thing, weren't you?"

She looked up at him. "No. There was no need. I knew from the start Fiona would marry Wesmont."

He stared at her, stunned. He shook his head and pointed his finger at her. "No. No, you're lying! I know you are. You thought of changing your will in her favor. You as much as said so the night of your soirée."

"Oh yes, that was the night you tried to shoot a hole through my head. Was it not?" She arched one eyebrow.

He licked at his lips, which suddenly felt very dry.

"No, Marcus. I never intended to make Fiona my heir. I was teasing you, amusing myself at your expense. I'm well aware that you pant heavily after my money. It's great sport to watch you squirm when I pretend to give it away to someone else. Besides, I hoped you'd stop counting on your inheritance from me, and start taking better care of what you already have. Tell me. Do you actually know who benefits from my will at the moment?"

His eyes narrowed into two slits. He felt a sweat breaking out on his forehead and his innards cramp. Pushing his hand against his belly to assuage the pain, he answered, "Very well, Honore, I'll play your game. Who is your beneficiary?"

"Hmm. I wonder if I should tell you? I've had to go to such extremes to protect Fiona. I saw you push the urn, you know. I must confess, theses hives were all a ruse, a most uncom-fortable ruse—I might add, to lull you into a false sense of security." Honore tapped her cheek and scrutinized her step-son. "No. I'm not at all sure I should tell you who my beneficiary is."

He clutched at his cramping stomach and dropped back into the chair. "It doesn't matter. Obviously, *I* am not."

"Now, *that* would have been foolish of me in the extreme. You inherited almost all of your father's wealth and man-aged to go through it in a matter of months. Granted, he was not as rich as crocuses, but—"

"Gad, Honore. When will you get it right? Crocuses are flowers. *Croesus,* as rich as Croesus, the king—not *crocuses.*" Marcus swiped at the perspiration dripping from his forehead.

"No matter." Honore tapped her fingernail against her tea tray. "Flowers, kings—you went through it all. My Francisco left you a sizable fortune and a vast estate in Portugal. Yet, directly after quarter day your pockets are for let."

Honore shook her head and clucked her tongue. Marcus rubbed his temples and licked at his lips again. They were drier than before, and a foul-tasting gas mounted up from his stomach.

"You play too deep, Marcus. My money would evaporate like water running through your fingers."

He moaned. "Must you mix your metaphors? I'm not in a mood to sort through them."

She ignored him. "No. I shall leave my fortune where it can be of some real value. Oh, that is not to say I won't leave you something. I'm really quite fond of you, Marcus. You're just a trifle spoiled. Spoiled children can be such nuisances. But did you know that I had five brothers? Five married brothers, and each of them had several children. Altogether, I have sixteen nephews and nieces. I regret to inform you, Marcus, you must murder all sixteen of them before you stand to inherit everything. Oh, and you must also do away with several of my business partners, including Lord Kinnard of the London Bank. All told, I have twenty-two beneficiaries."

He moaned.

She laughed. "A messy business, that. Nineteen murders, just so you can throw my money away on whores and gambling."

"Twenty-one." He corrected and sat forward with his head in his hands. He rocked slightly. His stomach felt like the fires of hell were burning in it. Slowly, he dragged his face up from his hands, elongating his features. He squinted at Honore. "Can we discuss this later? Right now I feel like the very devil."

"I imagine you do, dear. However, we must finish this now because you're embarking on a rather long trip. Did you enjoy your omelet, Marcus? Mattie made it especially for you. She used a particularly rare type of mushroom."

His eyes flew open wide. "Good God!" His voice rose to a high frenzied pitch. "You poisoned me!"

"Tich." Honore glanced at her fingernails. "Really, Marcus, *poisoned* is such a strong word. Didn't I just say I was fond of you? No, dearest, I haven't poisoned you. *I have sickened you.* That is a much better way to phrase it. 'Poisoned' sounds so very final. You won't die. At least, I don't think you will, not if you get to Portugal in time. You see, I've sent a man on ahead with the antidote. He'll be waiting for you at your estates." She set the tea tray aside and threw back the covers.

"We must hurry, dear. My coachman is prepared to drive you as swiftly as he can to the wharf, where I've chartered your passage to Aveiro on the fastest ship available. You should get there in two or three days if the weather holds. When you get there, drink up the entire bottle—you'll be right as rain—in a few days—or weeks—I can't remember which. Never mind."

He stared at her. She was completely mad.

Honore motioned to him. "Francisco's steward, Rodrigo, has agreed to nurse you back to health, and then he'll help you get your estates into repair. He's most eager to assist you. Perhaps you remember him? He loves the people and continually complains to me of how they are suffering because of your neglect—"

Marcus stood up and stumbled toward her bed. *He would kill her. Strangle her—squeeze her scrawny neck until her eyes bulged out.* If only the room would stop spinning and his legs would not wobble so. He lurched forward and collapsed across her legs.

He cried out, an anguished, wordless cry, and then he simply lay there groaning.

Honore felt a strange sensation. Pity. A small unusual seed of compassion twisted and grew inside of her. She tentatively placed her hand on his black curls. Her fingers combed gently through his dark tousles. "Oh my darling," she murmured. "Don't you see? I couldn't let them bring you up on charges. You might have been hanged, or worse yet—thrown in a dark smelly prison. And Wesmont—he wanted to put a bullet in your 'diseased brain.' Those were his exact words. I couldn't let him do that, now could I?"

Marcus merely moaned.

"No. You'll see. This is the best way. You'll feel better about it in a few months. You must promise to stay at your estates for at least a year. Otherwise, I will have to do something truly unpleasant. I expect regular reports of your diligence and industry from my friends in Portugal and from Senior Rodrigo."

She stroked his hair back from his face. "Try to make a go of it, Marcus, my darling boy. Prove that you are something besides a spoiled man with a beautiful face."

Marcus began to shiver uncontrollably.

Honore leaned back and yanked on the bell cord.

Chapter 21
Custard Shackles

Lady Hawthorn fluttered her fan and assessed her step-daughter's ball gown. It was most definitely not white, and there were no ruffles or flounces or bows. The simple lines revealed far too much of her figure. In her opinion, the gown did not suit a young woman. It was a roguish color of blue silk, too. It would not commit to one shade, for it was shot with dark green and purple, so that it shifted under the light.

"Must you wear that color, my dear? It is so—so unsuitable."

Fiona looked down at the gown. She quite liked the color. It played nicely against her eyes. "Unsuitable?"

"Yes. It is a color better worn by a mature woman, not a young girl."

"I'm hardly a young girl, my lady. I'm very nearly on the shelf. I considered wearing a turban, but I didn't have one to match this gown."

"A turban? Good gracious! Well, thank heaven you didn't do that. Never mind then, that dress will have to do. Where is Emeline? Our guests will be arriving shortly. Do go and see what's keeping her."

Fiona climbed the stairs to the third floor and found Emeline still standing at her mirror, smiling at her reflection. She turned and swirled out her skirts. "Well? What do you think?"

Fiona smiled at her sister. "You look perfectly adorable."

"I know that, silly. I mean, should I wear the pearls or Mama's diamonds?"

Emeline was gowned in white embroidered voile, with a silk underskirt and a Brussels lace ruffle stood up around her low neckline. A pink silk ribbon was tied under her bosom, and matching pink silk roses trimmed the top of each flounce. She held up a string of graduated pearls and then traded them for an elegant diamond collar.

Fiona stood with a finger to her cheek considering the choices. "I think perhaps you should wear the pearls, they don't detract from the lace on your dress."

"Hmm." Emeline turned back to the mirror. "No. The diamonds are more impressive. I shall choose them." Emeline's abigail scurried up to fasten the diamonds in place.

"As you please, Em, but hurry. Mama is asking for you. The guests will be arriving soon."

"Fiona, I have a request." She addressed her sister while examining the effect of the layer of diamonds at her throat.

"Yes?"

"I wish that you will remember that this is *my* ball. I would not like you to draw attention to yourself or monopolize the guests."

"I have no intention of doing such a thing. I prefer, as I always have, not to draw attention to myself. And you know it."

"Never mind that. I don't want you to monopolize a *certain guest's* time, Lord Wesmont for example."

Fiona's mouth dropped open, then it slammed shut. That did it. Her patience with her stepsister ran out. Her voice came out with a decidedly sharp edge to it. "So, that's what this is about. You are hanging out for Wesmont? Well, let me assure you, Emeline, his lordship is not a docile plaything you can lead around on a ribbon. And it would be nigh impossible to *monopolize* him unless he chose to be. Quite the contrary, I have it on good authority, that he has no intention of getting leg-shackled to you, or anyone else."

Fiona slapped her fan against her thigh. "Furthermore, if he chooses to spend time with me, then so be it."

She turned on her heel and headed out of the room. At the door she stopped and spun around. "And one more thing." Fiona lifted her chin. "His tastes don't run to arrogant debutantes, who look like overly decorated wedding cakes." She silently thanked her aunt Honore for lending her exactly the right words as she walked away down the hall.

Emeline stamped her foot and turned back to the mirror. Fiona would pay for those insults. Her sister would not have Wesmont, not if she could help it. Emeline smoothed away the frown marring her brow and assured herself she was not overly decorated. Then her fingers caressed the diamond collar.

"Take the diamonds away," she ordered her maid. "I will wear the pearls."

No one was more astonished than Fiona, when later that evening Honore came down the receiving line. Although the *décolletage* was daring, her aunt wore an otherwise fairly respectable ball gown. Although Fiona thought the color of the dress boded ill. It was a purple so dark that it was nearly black. Jet black stones of onyx glittered at her throat. Her hair was a perfect shade of auburn. She looked magnificent, but somehow threatening. When she approached, Fiona was not sure what to expect. Would thunder and lightning suddenly shatter the ballroom?

Honore took Fiona's hand and smiled genuinely. "Fiona dear, we miss you at Alison Hall. It's so very dreary without you. Your cousin Marcus has taken himself off to Portugal. I am bereft. The house is a veritable tomb. You must come back immediately. Now, look who I have brought with me. Here is Lady Haversburg and Maria."

She leaned very close and whispered conspiratorially. "You may notice Maria has an escort, a physician, a Dr. Meredith. Lovely man, but then I believe you know him."

She winked mischievously at her niece before moving down the line to greet Lady Hawthorn, whose jaw had dropped to her necklace. "Do shut your mouth, Evelyn. You're letting flies in. Yes, I am here. I was quite certain my lack of an invitation was an oversight on your part. Don't fret, dear. I forgive you. And see here, I've brought you some of my friends."

Honore placed one finger under Emeline's chin. "And what is this? Our pert little Emeline? You look divine, my dear. Just like something out of the bake shop window." With a smug little chuckle Honore walked away.

Maria Haversburg greeted Fiona with her hand looped over Dr. Meredith's sleeve. "I hope you don't mind our coming to your party. Lady Alameda insisted. She said you were terribly sad without her, and that we must come and cheer you up."

Fiona was pleased to note the absence of any noxious gases coming from Maria's mouth, and felt a sense of triumph. "I'm delighted to see you." She grimaced at the doctor, remembering how she had lied to him.

Maria guessed at her discomfit. "Oh it's all right, Fiona. I've explained everything to him. He forgives us completely for our little deception. Mother sent for him herself, the day after she saw what he had done for me. She thinks he is a genius. She's in complete alt. Can't wait to show him off to everyone. Yes, and she plans to make sure he gets that knighthood you spoke of."

Dr. Meredith bowed his head. "A pleasure to see you again. How is the arm?"

Maria leaned forward. "Oh yes. We heard all about your dreadful riding accident. We were that relieved, when Dr. Meredith assured us he was able to fix you up right as rain. And, Fiona, I never told Mama that you were the one that took me to see him. You see, Mama was so amazed that I had the backbone to take matters into my own hands that I rose several notches in her esteem. You don't mind do you? It's terribly jolly how it all worked out."

Fiona beamed her approval.

Dr. Meredith nodded and smiled. "You might have told me the truth, Miss Hawthorn. I would not have refused treatment. Indeed, after I laid eyes on Miss Haversburg I could not have refused her anything."

Maria giggled. "Isn't he marvelous?" she asked without the least degree of self-consciousness. The twosome floated down the receiving line. Fiona smiled after them, and turned to greet the next guest.

An hour after the receiving line broke up, the third dancing set was forming. Fiona sat behind a bank of hothouse flowers snapping open her fan and shutting it again. Tyrell had not come. Her aunt played in the card room. Emeline was holding court for several young men. Maria Haversburg and Dr. Meredith walked toward the balcony exchanging mooncalf gazes at one another. And she sat alone. Snap. Fiona shut her fan.

She found little solace in the fact that her *dreaded curse* had not injured anyone yet this evening. Even a mishap was preferable to the emptiness she felt. Why hadn't he come? She knew the desolation she felt was her own fault. She had allowed herself to hope. Hope was dangerous. Hope could be painful. She told herself that just seeing his face would be enough. Aspiring for more than that was pure foolishness, and she knew it. Yet, tonight she would be denied even seeing him. Why hadn't he come?

Fiona peeked around the bank of flowers to examine the doorway once more. This time she saw Tyrell framed in it. She blinked and opened her eyes wider, wondering if she was hallucinating. His name rang convincingly through the air as the butler announced him. Throughout the room, female faces turned to take stock of the eligible earl.

He came. She felt like cheering. But then she noticed that she was not the only happy female. Fiona glared at the roomful of matrons and their charges. They looked like a pack of hounds that had just got scent of a fox.

Tyrell walked in, searching the bevy of female faces for the one that meant something important to him. After some dilige nce, he spotted a pair of sea nymph eyes peeking around a hedge of flowers. Ah, that was the face he looked for. Chuckling to himself, he tilted his head to mimic her odd pose.

Fiona quickly pulled back behind the flowers, her heart thumping rapidly in her chest. *I mustn't wear my heart on my sleeve*, she told herself. But, it was too late. Her cheeks were hot. She pressed her hand over her unruly heart and tried to moderate her breathing by concentrating on the view of the ballroom in front of her.

But then she noticed the matchmaking mamas and their offspring mentally penciling the hither-to inaccessible Lord Wesmont onto their lists. Skirts fluttered in his direction. They weren't precisely like flies headed for a carcass, thought Fiona. No. They looked more like a flock of turtledoves cooing and mincing toward a morsel of bread. Well, if it was a fight they wanted, it was a fight they would get.

Fiona stood up, shook out her skirt, and lifted her chin into the air. She stepped forward, ready to march out into the fray, but a hand clasped her forearm and restrained her. "So, you mean to come out of hiding do you?"

"Aunt Honore, I thought you were in the card room."

"And so I was. One can only fleece these bumpkins for so long before one gets bored. Now, didn't I just hear Wesmont's title called out?"

"Yes." Fiona frowned at the fleet of white skirts setting sail in Tyrell's direction.

Honore laughed. "Let him come to you, my dear."

Fiona looked at her aunt, doubt written clearly in her eyes.

"Honestly, child, haven't you learned anything from me?" Honore fluttered her fingers at the people in the room, as if trying to flick something from the back of her hand. "For pity sake, these ladies are all wasting their time, Wesmont is the independent sort, he won't tolerate being run to ground. If they are able to get near him at all, he'll brush them off like so much vermin. Calm yourself. Obviously, the man is mad for you. He'll come to you. Now, shall we discuss more important matters?"

Fiona's bottom lip fell victim between her teeth. At the moment there was nothing more important to her than Tyrell.

"I do wish you would stop biting your bottom lip every time something vexes you. A most annoying habit, my dear, bound to disfigure your mouth."

Fiona released her lip and snapped open her fan.

Honore smiled a quirky half smile. "Much better. Let us discuss your return to Alison Hall; tomorrow suits me admirably."

"Do you think that would be wise?" Fiona fanned herself. "You were rather unhappy with me, last time we spoke. If I remember correctly, you accused me of nearly causing the collapse of your entire house, not to mention, being responsible for your personal disfigurement."

"Oh that." Honore waved through the air as if dismissing a mere butterfly. "A simple case of hives. I was better by the next morning. Your cousin, however, is not at all well. Poor fellow is retching his way across the Bay of Biscay, as we speak."

"I suppose *that* is the fault of my curse as well." Fiona fanned herself briskly.

"Fiddlesticks! You know I don't give a fig for that ludicrous curse of yours. No such thing as curses, never has been, never will be. It's all a bunch of Hottentot nonsense."

"But you said—"

"Twaddle! Forget that. It was a ruse. Had to do it. Now, as I said, I want you to move back to Alison Hall, and that's an end to the matter. Tomorrow, I'll send Lorraine with the coach."

Fiona and Honore stood face-to-face, oblivious of the ball going on around them. Fiona pushed her nose slightly closer to Honore's. "No, thank you. I don't believe I will."

"No? But, I insist. This is absurd. You can't stay here with *her*. The woman is a thick-witted ninny, dull as a post. Even your father stays away. Where the devil is he, anyway?"

"You know perfectly well, he's in Spain, on the King's business. You're intentionally changing the subject. I most certainly can, and I will, stay here, dull or not."

"Fiona, *think* what you are saying. How can you tolerate, day after day, those two peahens pecking away at you? And just look at the company they keep. Have you ever seen any room in London filled with more humdrum provincials than this?" Honore swung her arm around, indicating the entire assembly.

Her arm collided with the midsection of a gentleman wearing a black coat. She glanced up at the owner. "Ah, Wesmont. There you are. Tell her. Tell Fiona she must come back to Alison Hall with me. I refuse to let her molder away with these—these brainless twits. She belongs with me."

"No." He squared his shoulders, like a captain issuing orders. "She cannot, will not, return to Alison Hall. I forbid it."

"What?" both women asked in unison. Fiona looked at him, astonished. It was one thing to be devastatingly handsome, and quite the most wonderful person on the face of the earth, but it was quite another, to assume he could run her life without permission.

"You heard me well enough. I said Fiona will not return to your house."

"I say, she will." Honore smiled thinly and spoke in a low dictatorial tone.

"No, Lady Alameda. She won't. I think you will find that the greater authority resides with me."

"That is impossible. This is outside of enough! I'm her aunt, her benefactress, her mentor, the closest thing to a mother she has." Honore folded her arms across her chest. "She belongs with me, at Alison Hall."

"Be that as it may," he responded in clipped tones. "I have spent the entire afternoon and into the evening procuring a special license." He pulled a folded document from inside his coat. "When next Fiona moves, it will be into *my* house, not yours." Tyrell cocked his eyebrow and grinned triumphantly. "Checkmate, Countess."

Fiona stamped her foot. It was a slight sound because silk slippers simply do not make near enough noise on a wooden floor. It was, however, enough. Wesmont and Honore both looked her way. Fiona's hands hung at her side. Her fan dangled from her wrist. Her face was flushed, her eyes—round with hurt. Then, those eyes flashed dark, and Tyrell knew the sea had turned stormy.

"You will both kindly *listen to me* for a moment. I am not a puppet, to be moved here or there at your leisure, Lord Wesmont, nor for your entertainment, Lady Alameda." Fiona rapped her fan angrily against her thigh and glared at each of them in turn. "How dare you, Tyrell, presume to decide my future without so much as a by-your-leave."

"If I was presumptuous, I beg your pardon." He reached for her hand, but she refused him. "I thought you felt as I did. In the absence of your father—" He didn't get to finish his defense because she turned and fled the room.

Tyrell frowned at Honore as if the whole incident were her fault.

"Oh dear." Honore shrugged her shoulders.

She watched Wesmont stride off, rushing after her niece. "Hmm, well, that will undoubtedly clinch the deal." Honore sighed wistfully and headed back to the card room.

Tyrell found Fiona, but it was not easy. She had retreated to a small service gallery off the dining room. He pushed open a door disguised in the paneling, and in the dim light he saw her leaning against the wall. A table, laden with silver platters and bowls of food, took up one side of the narrow room. Obviously, the small room served as a convenience for the servants bearing courses up from the kitchen.

Tyrell walked quietly in, hoping that Fiona would not bolt out of the far door. She glanced over at him and stepped away from the wall, but didn't run.

"Hear me out," he said.

Fiona merely lifted one eyebrow as she considered him. She had cooled since stomping out of the ballroom. After all, Tyrell had gone to the trouble of getting a special license, and while it was heavy-handed, ill-mannered, arrogant, and yes, presumptuous, it meant he wanted to marry her. If he truly loved her, nothing in the world could please her more.

She would hear him out, Fiona told herself. She tried to clamp a firm hand on the eagerness and hope dancing inside her. Be still, she told these children of her heart. But they would not obey.

Tyrell came nearer, trying to form the right words to woo her with, but they wouldn't come. He approached her, groping for words, but finding none, stumbling over a morass of emotion. He held out open hands, and looked at her, completely lost. Feelings were so blasted difficult to sort through, but he knew what he wanted. He wanted her.

He moved closer and looked down into her irresistible eyes, waiting for the words to materialize. When they didn't come, he started without them. "Fiona, I . . ."

But one doesn't say, *I want you,* as if another person is a biscuit to be eaten, or a horse to purchase. Tyrell's mind failed him. His mouth froze halfway open. No clever sounds mixed together to become speech, so he put it to better use. He bent his head down and kissed her. His lips fell on her soft mouth, and together they spoke a far more eloquent language than ears can hear.

Fiona and Tyrell were thus communicating when the service door to the dining room cracked open. The crack was wide enough for an interloper to peer into the dim room. What the trespasser spied enraged her, and made her golden curls shake with frustration. Emeline could barely keep from screeching with envy, but that would not suit her purpose. It was a good thing she had followed Lord Wesmont out of the ballroom. One more minute of this disgusting behavior and the man might propose to her sister. She had to do something quickly.

At that moment, a footman climbed up the stair from the kitchen and entered by the far door. Fiona and Tyrell pulled apart and shifted uneasily. Tyrell cleared his throat.

In a broken whisper, Fiona asked Tyrell, "You said you wished to speak to me? Well, my lord, I am ready to listen."

Tyrell chuckled.

The footman, a well-trained fellow, did not take notice of anyone in the room. He carefully averted his eyes from their direction and walked hastily to the buffet. He picked up a bowl of custard. Cook had chastised him for bringing it out prematurely. Clearly the old chef was daft. Up and back, up and back, take this, no, bring it down again.

The preoccupied footman stepped in front of the door concealing Emeline. It was too perfect. Emeline saw it as a sign from God. She shoved the door forward, slamming it into the servant. It clipped him in the heel. Indeed, the entire back half of his shiny buckled shoe wedged underneath the door.

The footman, his momentum suddenly curtailed, flopped forward, out of his shoe, and fell onto his knees in an attitude of accidental prayer. He fumbled. He reached. He stretched to catch it. But it was too late. The custard continued its journey without him. It arced gracefully up and then, obeying the laws of gravity, began its descent, where it connected predictably with the floor, and bounced up again, making a series of smaller spinning somersaults.

Remarkable, that an egg custard in a silver dish should bounce so well. With each clatter the occupants of the room were showered with plops of yellow custard. The bowl gyrated across the floor and, with a whirling metallic clank, came to a halt at Tyrell's feet.

In the silence that followed, a triumphant giggle resonated from out of the dining room.

The footman pried his heel out from under the door and inspected his marred shoe. Then he stood up, looked over the splattered room, and groaned. "Cook will have my head."

"Not before I catch the culprit who rammed that door open, and hang her by her vicious little thumbs." Tyrell started after Emeline. He grabbed Fiona's hand and pulled her with him.

Fiona called back to the footman as Tyrell tugged her through the door. "Tell Cook it was my fault—you know—blame it on the curse."

She trailed behind Tyrell as he rushed through the dining room, set on vengeance. In the brightly flickering candlelight, Fiona immediately perceived the error in their hasty pursuit. "Wait!"

She tugged on his arm. "Tyrell wait! We can't storm into the ballroom looking like this."

He turned around and stared at her. Custard dribbled down her forehead, and dappled her cheeks. Her blue silk gown was speckled with yellow blobs. Tyrell considered her for a moment. She looked deliciously comical. A grin burst across his face.

Fiona smiled back. "Don't laugh at me, my lord. You will find that you are quite as custard-covered as I am."

"Ah, so I am." He chuckled as he glanced down at his splattered attire. Just then, the soothing strains of three violins penetrated the dining room. They were beginning a waltz. The rest of the orchestra swelled behind the violins, an inviting flowing melody that compelled him to listen.

He exhaled and all of his annoyance at Emeline vanished. "Do you hear it? It's a waltz. My waltz, I believe." He held out his hand.

She lifted an eyebrow. "You would risk such a thing?"

"I would." Tyrell opened his arms. "Here will do nicely."

She stepped into his embrace and he held her close as they waltzed beside the dining table laid out with glistening silver, radiant crystal, and bouquets of aromatic roses.

"Do you truly wish to marry me?" Fiona asked. "After all, I cannot promise you freedom from the wretched accidents that seem to follow me wherever I go."

Tyrell smiled at her. "Life would be inordinately dull without a few surprises now and again." Abruptly, he leaned down and licked a drop of custard from her cheek.

Fiona shivered in response.

He laughed softly. "I would not have it any other way." Tyrell kissed away a little dollop from her forehead and then lightly touched his tongue to a small portion near her mouth. He murmured. "I love you, Fiona. I'm afraid, my dear, that tranquility and solitude have entirely lost their appeal. I don't think I could bear life without you. Marry me."

She answered him eloquently, with a tirade of kisses.

HISTORICAL NOTE

Dear Readers,

It may interest you to know that the Prince Regent actually had a ballroom mishap with a young miss not unlike the one described in *Lady Fiasco*. However, the real incident was so bizarre that if I had included all the elements the reader would have shaken her head in disbelief. Prinny was a true eccentric. I enjoy hearing from readers. If you would like to write to me, you may reach me via my website at: www.kathleenbaldwin.com